STORM
ON THE HORIZON
A Megan Hernandez adventure by
C.C.Chamberlane

ISBN Print: 978-1-7753732-6-1

ISBN Ebook: 978-1-7753732-5-4

Copyright 2023 by C. C. Chamberlane

Published 2023 by C.C.Chamberlane

Dedication

I first heard about the Humber School for Writers from Globe & Mail staff writer, Ian Brown. He was the one who gave me the initial push, encouraging me to apply for acceptance to the Creative Writing Graduate Certificate program at Humber College. When the Humber School for Writers accepted me, I had no idea the impact their decision would have. It truly has been one of the best educational experiences of my life.

I cannot thank the inimitable Donna Morrissey, my mentor in the program, enough for her support, encouragement, and willingness to teach me so much about the craft in which she excels. I appreciate how much her commitment to teach and pass along her vast storehouse of knowledge improved my skills and created a place for this book to blossom into something in which I take immense pride. Writing is said to be a solitary pursuit, but this experience felt anything but that, reminding me of a quote from one of Donna's favorites, Carl Jung.

> *"One looks back with appreciation to the brilliant teachers, but with gratitude to those who touched our human feelings. The curriculum is so much necessary raw material, but warmth is the vital element for the growing plant and for the soul of the child."*

My heartfelt thanks to Donna Morrissey, writer extraordinaire, and Alissa York the program lead at the Humber School for Writers.

Last, and definitely most important, I want to thank my wife Jennifer for her love, support, understanding, and willingness to let me pursue my pipedream of being a writer, or at least trying to become a writer.

Without Jennifer, my life would be immeasurably darker and nowhere near as interesting and enjoyable!

Other Books from C.C.Chamberlane

Abbadon
Samaela
The First Female Navy SEAL
Saving Ukraine
Let Them Breathe

Prologue

Megan Hernandez had done it all, at least in her professional life, including becoming the first female to successfully complete training, and be deployed as, a US Navy SEAL. Since then, she has worked tirelessly to right many wrongs, sometimes on the right side of the law, other times straying far over that line. Whether it was avenging the planned execution of her friend's wife, the retribution she unleashed on the drug cartel responsible, or protecting women from men they had once loved, Megan has been about helping others. She had always tried to do things legally but as she got involved in increasingly risky situations, that was not always possible. It's likely that, given her highly specialized training in all forms of combat and defense, and her expertise in executing those skills, she is quite simply someone you would never want to go up against.

Thanks to smart investments under the guidance of two of her closest friends, Jonathon, and Luke, and a multi-million-dollar estate left to her by a generous aunt, Megan really has no reason to work, at least no financial reason. But a life of leisure wasn't in her wheelhouse at the moment. Nor was it her traditional line of work that was occupying her thoughts. It was a completely different kind of concern. That concern, if one can call it a concern, Michael Morrissey.

Like Megan, Michael had served his country. He had been a member of the highly respected Canadian Special Forces division known as Joint Task Force 2. JTF2 was the equal of the Navy SEALS, Army Rangers, Green Berets, you name it. In typical Canadian fashion they were lesser known, a humble bunch, preferring to operate as close as one could get to anonymously.

It sometimes seemed just a little odd that he had simply *popped up* in her life. Shown up out of nowhere really, but who was she to question fate.

Chapter 1 – Bon Voyage

Michael and I were the first to arrive at Kathy and Jonathon's beach house. I secretly smiled at his boyish look of wonder as he let out a quiet, "Wow," when he caught his first glimpse of the opulence, and that was just in the foyer.

"Yeah, it's definitely NOT your average beach house, is it?"

"It most certainly is not!" he replied emphatically.

Michael was awestruck as we entered the architectural masterpiece.

He had lived the first seventeen years of his life with his parents and his only brother in a tiny suburban tract house. They never went hungry but burgers on the BBQ far outnumbered steaks. They always had clothes, although none with "big" labels like other kids. He had seen houses like this, just never been inside one, and it was much more than he had imagined. It was a huge concrete and glass monolithic structure designed by a famous architect, so well done that the state requirements to be earthquake-proof were barely noticeable. In California at least, money did seem able to facilitate happiness.

I knew the door was unlocked so I opened it, stuck my head in and announced loudly to nobody in particular, "Hey guys, we're here."

"Woah," Michael whispered as he scanned the interior and began to take it all in.

Soaring light blue ceilings perched atop towering concrete walls covered in expensive art made it feel more gallery than house, museum-like even. The furniture was straight out of Rodeo Drive, and there was glimmering marble tile as far as the eye could see. As he was trying to observe without gawking, the fresh Pacific ocean air breezed through the house, caressing our faces. The whole back of the house consisted of glass doors that disappeared into the walls allowing unobstructed access to the private beach with its white sand that had been gently sculpted into tiny ripples by the wind and last remnants of dying waves settling onto the shore.

Kathy strode confidently toward us looking every bit the wealthy Californian trophy wife with her bleached blonde hair hanging like strands of gold framing her sun-kissed face, but she was so much more than that. I noted Michael admiring her just as I had when I first met her at the gym. I recalled how even sweaty gym wear did little to disguise her elegance and beauty. I envied the way she looked; so much womanlier than I had ever felt. As she led us both toward the huge kitchen, I remembered my surprise when I first met her husband, Jonathon, years ago. I was embarrassed for assuming he would be a rich, old, bald guy. Angela and her husband Luke, his best buddy and business partner, were waiting for us along with Jonathon.

As I introduced Michael and everyone shook hands, I couldn't help but think they were clone-like in their similarities and Luke's wife, Angela, could have been Kathy's sister. I was as wrong about Jonathon and Luke as I had been in my initial, unflattering assessment of their wives.

Turned out the only correct assumption I had made about them was their wealth, and they had plenty of that. They were young, handsome, in-shape guys who loved to surf and were just tons of fun. I learned early on that neither was a braggard nor flashy about their almost obscene wealth. They had definitely worked hard but still seemed incredibly young to have so much and not be the typical dot-com millionaires found roaming those beaches. Kathy and Angela were both driven, business-owners themselves, anything but the vapid, shallow, trophy wives typical for the area. Work hard play hard was an overused phrase these days, but it was exactly how they all lived, and I admired that quality in each of them.

Kathy grabbed six crystal champagne flutes from the bar area and emptied a chilled bottle of prosecco into them, sliding two over for Michael and me. The four of them raised their glasses as one and Jonathon said, "Welcome to the group Michael, we're really happy to meet you."

Michael smiled, a little uncomfortably it seemed, "Thank you very much for the invite, you have a beautiful home."

I was amused watching Jonathon and Luke resisting asking the questions I knew they wanted to ask. Jonathon made googly eyes at me when Michael looked away, followed by a kissing motion while flexing his own muscles. Luke just smiled at me and gave an almost imperceptible nod of approval. I looked at them both and gave them my strange face so they would understand it was nothing like that. This guy was no Bobby! At the moment I didn't think there would ever be someone special in my life anyway.

I supposed the closest anyone might get would be Sonny, but that was before I met Michael. Sonny and I were like two ships that didn't simply pass in the night but tied up together in the foggy harbour for a few months at a time, bobbing through the highs and lows of the tides, never quite connected but never really apart either. Afterward, each patrolling a different ocean with a different purpose until coming together once more in the future.

When I was with Michael it was more like we were on the same ship. He had a confidence and personality that virtually forced people to like him. It sounds corny, but his smile really did light up a room and when you were around Michael you were generally just happier, at least I was.

More people began to filter into the house to help celebrate the Southern California Lifestyle and the noise level ramped up.

Curiously, my stomach started feeling queasy and my palms grew sweaty as more friends arrived. I was not often nervous, especially not around Colin or Norie or anyone else here. Colin was in his usual Hawaiian shirt and shorts, making his best attempt to not look like an FBI agent but failing miserably in that charade. Norie was looking professional as always but still with a certain lightness to her attitude. As the second female District Attorney for the county of Los Angeles she carried many burdens kept secret from the world. That didn't apply to me, Norie and I had no secrets, there was nothing one did not know about the other. Arlo and Sage, dressed like the sixties hippies they truly were, always just there. Content and happy to be together, wherever.

My nervousness made no sense to me. Even during extremely risky operations I was always calm, detached, doing my job, scanning the area like an eagle searching for prey, ears perked up for the familiar, metallic click of a rifle bolt that would, within seconds, turn me from quarry into hunter. I was always on a hair trigger it seemed, and I often worried those feelings might never go away, like a nagging, earworm of a song of which you cannot seem to rid yourself.

"What's everyone drinking?" Jonathon enquired, jolting me out of my thoughts. "The usual I expect?" hinting at margaritas for all, he loved that machine of his. I grasped Michael's arm, introducing him to each new arrival coming towards us with wide white smiles and perfectly aligned teeth decorating bronze tanned faces.

I chuckled to myself as I thought California must have more orthodontists per capita than anywhere, I've never seen so many perfectly aligned, brilliantly white, teeth in my life. Jonathon flitted around filling emptied glasses with his frozen concoction made by his special machine that groaned and hummed as it crushed ice, juiced fresh limes, added tequila and triple sec, and produced pitcher after pitcher of ice-cold perfect margaritas. He had designed it himself and paid a mechanical engineer he knew to draw it and have it built. That machine was his pride and joy. Boys and their toys.

I wondered how I would make the announcement that Michael was going with me on this sailing vacation *as a friend* only. I didn't want them to worry unnecessarily about my being alone on a sailboat I had only recently purchased, and with scarcely a few hours worth of sailing lessons under my belt. Undoubtedly, there would be innuendo and comments that would come with the announcement, perhaps that's why the greasy palms and queasy stomach had surfaced? They hadn't seen me *with* anyone since Bobby. Was it their imagined response or my own feelings about the whole trip causing me to feel this way? I, who had chased down villains, subdued Somali pirates, and killed more people than I care to remember was actually standing here amongst a roomful of friends, apprehensive about announcing a new friend would accompany me on my trip.

Maybe these feelings were being reinforced by the way Sonny reacted when I told him about Michael and this trip?

When we chatted on the telephone and I first mentioned Michael, I could tell something was up with Sonny. He seemed skeptical of someone he had never even met yet. I had not yet adjusted to the thought myself; I think that was what caused my queasiness. I watched as Michael moved around the room, spending a few moments with each group, glancing my way with a furtive smile every now and then. He was a commanding presence, even when contrasted against a couple of very fit guys like Jonathon and Luke. Those two were in great shape but, even concealed by a shirt, Michael was clearly a force. Jonathon and Luke's muscles had been built in a gym, pretty to look at but not wholly practical. They had worked at building their bodies the same way they built their business, commitment and dedication to an end-result. Michael's powerful build had been forged in fire and honed like a stainless-steel sword to keep himself, and others, alive in the most dangerous of situations. I had much more in common with Michael than anyone here. I gave in to the fact that I did find him attractive, his strength, confidence, and personality only bolstering his good looks and aura.

I completely understood that. I recalled when I first met him in Avalon, and how he stopped three guys from harassing a fellow who was gay. He stepped in without hesitation, ready to take all three down, but completely disarmed them when he took the scared fellow's hand and asked where he had been hiding all day, as if he was his boyfriend. As a JTF2 operator I was well aware what he could have done to those three jerks, but he found a simpler and safer method. I felt in that moment that maybe I could learn a few things from this guy. I was predisposed to just grab those three and pound them senseless, I knew I had to start thinking differently. There had been no sign of anything happening between us, but I'm wise enough to never say never. After all, I had been in love before, it simply didn't end well, for me or Bobby.

I reminded myself I had only broached the subject to Michael about sailing to the Cayman Islands just a few days earlier, trying to justify my nervousness. I had never been and had heard wonderful things about Georgetown and Grand Cayman. I was surprised when he pounced all over the idea. I explained that I had really been working on my sailing, studying like one of those wild-haired, Einstein-like mad professors, incapable of finding a comfortable place to pause. I recalled sometimes being like that when preparing for a mission. I would be unable to sleep, holding on to the last words on a page, my eyelids getting heavier and heavier, concentration waning as I struggled to remain lucid. Too often, I would awake to the bright light of a new day, papers scattered around my pillow, my eyes more tired than before I had attempted sleep. I thought those days of intense studying and learning were long behind me. But my boat was now my passion. She was originally named *Seal Paradise,* but I had recently renamed her, eschewing any reference to my former life that might draw unwanted attention. I felt no need to advertise so brashly what I was, but I knew I wanted something ocean or water related. I have always loved to hear the backstories of non-traditional boat names, if there can be such a thing, and I wanted that. I had been a fan of Greek mythology since I was young, so the choice quickly became obvious.

I renamed her *Amphitrite,* who was known as the female personification of the sea. Although, unlike me, she was a wife to the Greek God Poseidon, there was always creativity in naming a boat. I was fairly certain I would never be a wife to anyone at this point in my life, but I suppose that you never really know, until you know. Now here we were, settled into the party at Jonathon's, appreciating being with the gang. The brilliant sun reflecting off the surfboards and the water, so bright it almost stung your eyes, even behind the reflective, expensive, surfer-specific sunglasses most of us wore.

"Let's grab some boards and get out there, the waves are a wastin," Jonathon yelled out to everyone.

"It's been a minute since I've been on a board," I sheepishly replied. Nevertheless, the water looked perfect and the urge to do something was too strong for me to resist. I wasn't a follower and had never been driven by peer pressure, I just really wanted to surf again.

I ran along with a few others, grabbing boards and heading to the water, partly in hopes of working up an appetite before Jonathon began grilling. I left Michael with the rest of the crowd, grabbed my favorite board and we began to make our way through the cool, frothy waves. As we headed out, keeping our eyes on the horizon while ducking under wave after wave, I was reminded of how much I enjoyed surfing. I kicked and paddled with the same cadence my surf teacher, Dukie, taught me, heeding his words that positioning is everything.

I quickly caught the excitement of the others as we took turns slipping beneath the waves and popping up beyond them, saltwater streaming down our faces, the sun gleaming off our wet hair, we were like a pod of frolicking dolphins. Finally, after paddling and struggling through thousands of gallons of seawater we were sitting calmly on our boards, waiting for the waves to make us feel like we were flying. I envied the others looking so relaxed, feet moving lazily in the cool water as we watched for incoming waves. I usually enjoyed this time, alone with my thoughts, the feeling of the sun warming my back, legs dangling almost weightless on either side of my board, bobbing gently up and down in almost silence. That was not the case today. I was weighed down and distracted by something in my head that I couldn't quite put my finger on and there was still that feeling deep in the pit of my stomach.

Finally, some rollers began languidly making their way toward us, each of us trying to anticipate their path to position ourselves and catch the best ride. I looked over and saw Jonathon paddling furiously, water splashing up all around him as his hands slapped through the surface, feet thrashing powerfully as he caught a good one. He effortlessly brought his feet up under his chest in one smooth motion, gained his balance, and was standing on top of his board. He yelled out a *yahoo* as he began to work the wave, up and down the face, cutting back and forth, his legs straining, feet constantly adjusting minutely to keep his balance. My own body tensed as if I were the one on the board as I watched him work the wave, muscles fighting to maintain control.

I flashed back to my last great ride, which had been immediately followed by my last great crash. That was one thing I hated about surfing, or at least crashing. The sandy, sometimes rocky bottom, tearing and ripping at your skin like a wild animal as the wave treated you like a wayward piece of garbage. I glanced toward shore and saw everyone on Kathy and Jonathon's patio looking our way, so I knew he had a good ride going. Each time he reappeared at the crest of the wave, I could see every muscle in his body straining to keep him on his board and not tumbling and crashing along the unforgiving ocean floor. My body was mimicking the movements he was making on its own, as if I were the one on the board, on that wave. That should have been a sign.

I spotted a good wave and paddled hard, grabbed the edges of my board, and got my feet under me just in time, the sticky surf wax holding them in place. I dropped in and swooped down the face of it, loving that familiar feeling of being almost weightless once again, but something just didn't feel right, I think I was a little rusty for a wave this big. I accelerated towards the foaming trough at the base of the wave, spray soaking my face, tasting the salty ocean on my lips. I cut back up toward the crest where I aimed to execute a perfect turn.

I spun out completely as my legs were snatched from under me as if Poseidon himself had reached up and grabbed them. The invisible god, tossing me into the churning seas. The wave crashed over forcing me under the water, driving me headfirst into the sand and bouncing me along the ocean floor like a loose pebble, filling my nose with a gritty mixture of sand and seawater. When I finally stopped tumbling, I opened my eyes and pushed up towards the light. I popped out of the water, my lungs straining to fill with air and waved my hand high to signal I was all good. I tugged my board back to me and just held on to it as I floated on the surface, taking a few moments to breathe and get centred, just like I had been taught. Once I was calmer, I hopped back on and paddled out to where the boys were waiting, knowing I would have to endure their playful ribbing.

"Hey, where'd you learn how to surf, Drowning School," Jonathon called out. I knew more shots were on the way.

"What's wrong, board not waxed to your liking?" he added.

"Wow, you looked great, right up until you tried to drink half the ocean," chipped in Luke.

I took it all in wholesome fun until Luke's observation. I shot him a nasty look on that one, and just turned and paddled away, his comments unearthing some harsh memories. I recalled when I had almost drowned on a mission, coming conscious flat on my back, lungs searing, as I gasped for a breath that wouldn't come. I could almost feel the pounding of a hand on my chest as someone exhorted me to *breathe, c'mon breathe dammit.*

I knew the ribbing was all good, clean fun and there was no malicious intent in any of their words, how could any of them have known?

That was one of the many things even my closest friends did not know about me – the hidden scars. Those events that affect your psyche are often far more dangerous than the visible ones. That was what pissed me off more than anything, not that I had almost died or almost been killed multiple times, but the fact that, even with all my physical training and psych training, I could not simply erase or ignore the shame I felt for such failure. It wasn't even so much that the failure might result in my own death, which was an accepted risk, but what such a failure would mean to my parents, my brothers, my team.

I would do better next time! I had never really been able to remove competitiveness from anything I did, from combat to board games, I just wanted to win! Surfing was no different. I wasn't sure whether that was a good character trait or a bad one, but it had definitely kept me alive more than once, even if it sometimes made me a little difficult to deal with.

Soon after, we all glided slowly back to shore, the wave generator called the Pacific Ocean taking a break, all of us just laying lazily on our boards and steering towards Jonathon's section of the beach. I stepped onto the shore, the water-hardened sand giving way to silky soft, hot white sand where each footstep sunk in, and walking took a little more effort. One by one we sprayed off the boards and placed them back into the racking and then everyone gathered on the deck.

We were soon engulfed in the aromas from Jonathon's grill, the slightly sweet smell of apple wood chips infusing the beef he was stewarding toward perfection. We all settled into seats around the large outdoor table as Jonathon and Kathy delivered bowl after bowl of food, I was salivating like a wild animal as the delicious smells hit my nose. I have always known and embraced the fact I am a serious *meatatarian*, about as far away from Vegan as one could get.

As we sat around the table enjoying the food and drink, I decided to just tear off the Band-Aid, so I took a gulp of wine and boldly announced, "I'm sailing to the Cayman Islands."

There was nothing but silence, raised eyebrows, and confused looks from almost everyone. I quickly added, "Don't worry, I'm not going alone, Michael is an expert sailor and he's coming with me."

As expected, everyone's attention swung to Michael, then back to me, with looks of worry or surprise and one smile. I felt myself flush, which doesn't happen often, and mercifully Michael came to the rescue.

"I understand your friend here," he added, making a toast towards me, "Likes to lead the way, so we'll see how that goes. I imagine we'll either become great friends or strangle each other during this adventure."

"Ohh, she's the worst," Angela said. "If it gets out of hand just pour her a glass of excellent wine or an ice-cold beer – that always distracts her." Blissfully, after a few jibes about my temper and love of wine, Kathy, the only one who knew almost the full story of my abusive ex-boyfriend Bobby, and why he would never bother me again, deflected the conversation back to a safer topic.

Kathy pursed her lips and with furrowed brow added, "You know she has four big brothers, Michael. If she ends up in the ocean, you'll have all of them looking for you."

"*Four* big brothers," Michael turned to me with raised eyebrows as he leaned back in his chair and responded, "No wonder you're so feisty."

I grinned at his comment, "Was like having my own full-time life-coaches, tough ones at that. They were always challenging me and roughing me up. Testing me as if I were one of them. They helped make me the Division 1 basketball player that I became." I thought how there was slim chance I would have become a SEAL either without those four, and my parents, influence. Now, if I could just extricate myself from this tricky dinner party without more attention falling onto me, Michael, and our upcoming trip.

Surprisingly, it was Michael who veered the conversation into a new direction, one for which I was not prepared.

He raised his glass to Jonathon's cooking, thanked the hosts again, then asked unexpectedly, "Has anyone heard about the verdict in the Derek Chauvin trial?" I wasn't sure if he was just trying to change the subject and take the spotlight off of our trip or if there was something more to it.

Colin Sharpe, my FBI Special Agent friend, quickly replied, "Every cop involved should have been jailed for life." I knew that Colin had no tolerance for such reckless disregard for human life, even if they were criminals, which of course George Floyd was not.

"Life in prison is nowhere near a harsh enough penalty for taking the life of an innocent man," replied Michael. "George Floyd was suspected of trying to pass a counterfeit twenty-dollar-bill. The man was killed over a measly twenty bucks. He had the life slowly squeezed out of him by a cop, while six others stood by and did nothing. They all heard him gasping, *I Can't Breathe, I can't breathe*, and did nothing! I say an eye for an eye."

Colin shot me a sideways glance, as did others, when Michael started becoming increasingly agitated as he spoke of the inordinate number of black people dying in police custody. The agreement of everyone around the table that the situation was horrifying did little to settle him down. I knocked his leg under the table and raised my eyebrows in hopes he would back off. I had never seen him angry like this and it concerned me. Yes, he was a black man who had certainly experienced racism but there seemed to be something even more behind his words, if that's possible.

Of course, I knew where he was coming from. As a partly Hispanic woman, I had endured my share of racism, misogyny, and other BS, but I could never, nor would I ever, claim to fully understand the challenges of being black in America. My military father, Esai Hernandez, was a decorated Navy man who looked every bit of his Hispanic heritage, but he never had to endure the typical taunts, thanks to his commanding stature and occupation. Nobody would EVER have the guts to call my father a beaner or a wetback, pejorative terms for Mexicans, or any other slur. My Mother, a successful LA detective, was lily white but never shied away from discussing the reality of privilege. She knew what was happening and tried to change it. I was brought up to value all lives, taught that all people need to be treated equally. I personally dealt more with issues caused by my gender rather than my ethnicity but there were always one or two who chose to view me as something other than white, something less in their narrow, bigoted, opinion.

As the party carried on and I considered what had transpired, Michael's comments kept creeping back into my thoughts. Even though Sonny didn't appear to be a huge fan of Michael I knew he thought the same on this topic. SEALs didn't see color, or religion, and most didn't see gender either, at least around me. We were all family and we all depended on each other to succeed, often to stay alive.

Chapter 2 – Planning

As people began to drift out Michael and I left too, agreeing to reconvene at the boat this weekend to get started planning. The ferry we took over from Catalina Island had now stopped running so we crashed back at my house in Newport. The ferry schedule was a bit of a hassle, but I loved living on my boat for most of the summer. The town of Avalon was always so welcoming, and the view of the Pacific and California coast seemed endless from that vantage point. I enjoyed my boat, but I also loved my home in Newport, my Aunt's gift to me.

We drove leisurely down the Pacific Coast Highway, windows wide open so we could enjoy the fresh smell of the ocean filling the night air. The dark sky was illuminated by thousands of stars with the blackness of the ocean broken up only by a few lights from the odd ship. Michael didn't seem himself; he was unusually quiet and mostly gazing out his window at the sea. I wondered if he regretted his outburst back at the dinner table or if something more was going on. Not knowing him very well yet, I too slipped into a silence, keeping my eyes focussed on the road ahead. I turned on the radio in hopes of making the quiet less awkward.

Finally, we got to Balboa and as we drove down my street, I marvelled at the way people in my neighborhood left all their lights on and window coverings wide open, allowing passersby an unobstructed view into their homes, into their lives.

That was one of the reasons I loved walking around my neighborhood after sunset, I could sneak peaks into the worlds of the not-well-enough-known neighbors that surrounded me. Everyone was cordial and pleasant, there were always waves, smiles and hellos during walks but in most cases it ended there. I didn't see what I was doing as snooping, I was just trying to know them a little better. If they didn't want people to do that then perhaps, they should close their blinds. I spotted couples sitting in front of TV's so large they covered a complete wall, young families playing with their kids before bedtime, some houses you could see clear through to their back yards where people often sipped large goblets of wine. This was not the Southern California you often saw splashed all over the newscasts, there was no evidence here of the crime ridden city, its murderous gangs operating with what seemed like impunity. There was just fresh, ocean air, clear skies, and friendly neighbors. It was easy to imagine my aunt taking this exact walk before she passed and left me such a wonderful legacy. Much like Michael's aunt, she had always tried to help people, to be a *good* person, and leave the world a better place. She was the smiling, happy neighbor who always had a good word on the way past and noticed the tiny things that people take pride in around their yards. She made everyone feel like they mattered.

We rolled up to my house and I tucked the car into my small garage. We walked through the house, and I grabbed wine and glasses as I followed Michael up to the deck to unwind and contemplate what we were about to attempt. We each grabbed a chair and adjusted them for the best view of the harbor. Michael just stared blankly out at the water, giving no clue to what he was thinking, as I filled our glasses.

I looked at him, "I can't believe I am finally going to traverse the Panama Canal."

He replied with a grin, "WE! We are going to navigate the Panama Canal."

"Yes, yes, I know, team above all," I acknowledged with a grin.

I knew I needed to confront him about his reaction at the party, but the time didn't seem right, although I wondered if it ever would. I tried to engage him in some general chit chat about our trip and the harbor laid out in front of us like a massive mural but didn't have much luck.

I was extremely excited to experience the Panama canal and hang out in Georgetown for a while. So many of the larger yachts and sailing yachts I had seen moored in the various Southern California marinas were flagged in Georgetown, Cayman Islands. When I saw those massive, opulent yachts, I always wondered who owned them. Were they idle millionaires? Were they professional sailors? Sports stars? Dot-com kids? What were they really like? This was California after all, so they could be just about anyone. Southern California was not only a melting pot of ethnicities, but it was also a melting pot of wealth and lifestyles.

The super-rich in their ridiculously expensive sports cars idling past those not knowing where the next payment on their almost invisible, cookie-cutter sedan was coming from. The stark contrast between the groups seemed almost painful at times. I wondered if they even noticed me when I sailed past them.

You would often see those yachts leaving the harbor and I noticed two distinct types. One boat would be brimming with too well-dressed, perfectly coiffed people, that I imagined were new money, who even from a distance looked pretentious. The second type filled with more comfortably attired, but still very wealthy looking old money folks, casually sipping their drinks, oblivious to both the beautiful surroundings and the multi-million-dollar yachts on which they were partying. Like the disparity in wealth and social status, there were clear caste lines in the boating world too. After the yachties there were the true sailors, the elite group of adventurers, able to go wherever they wished with only the winds to power them. That was the group I aspired to join. We finished off the bottle of wine after minimal conversation and I was ready to sleep.

I stood and looked at Michael, who made no motion to get up, "I'm heading to bed, you know where your room is and don't stay up too late, we have a LOT of planning to do."

Without even looking up at me he replied, "See you in the morning," his gaze still focussed on the harbor.

I slept fitfully that evening, wondering what was *really* on Michael's mind and how much it might affect us over the next month or two.

Next day, I was awakened by the sun streaming through the cracks in the blinds like fingers of light reaching out for what the morning might bring. I rolled out of my bed, pulled on my robe, and descended the stairs, inhaling deeply the mouth-watering aroma of frying bacon. I smiled broadly as I stepped into the kitchen where Michael was busy preparing breakfast.

The knife rapidly slicing mushrooms, and the chop, chop, chop against the wooden cutting board he looked like a real chef, or at least a decent sous chef.

He asked cheerily, without even a hint that anything was up, "How about a Denver omelette?"

"I'd love one, as soon as I have some OJ, I need my juice," I shouldn't have had to say.

I was thankful I kept meeting people who knew their way around a kitchen, it really injected some variety into my usual, boring but healthy fare. I caught the earthy smell of freshly brewed coffee, grabbed a mug, and filled it to go with my glass of OJ.

"You'd make a great first mate," I said, doing my best to match his cheerfulness.

"I was thinking more like co-captain," he replied, as he stood tall and official, holding the knife like a sword.

Without hesitation I grabbed a butter knife, placed it first on his left shoulder, then on his right and as I rested it on top of his head said, "You are now officially co-captain of the *Amphitrite*, goddess of the seas."

His smiled broadly as he graciously accepted the ersatz commission.

As we savored our breakfast, I told Michael that I had already printed off nautical charts and had them waiting at the boat. In addition to all the electronics onboard including plotters, radios, and beacons, I wanted to make sure we had paper backup. No matter what the situation, one could always resort to consulting the detailed work of a cartographer.

I had also loaded up a couple of websites that supplied ocean and shore data, including GPS coordinates, using only a smartphone. As much as Michael and I could take care of ourselves, I had no desire to risk our lives on a vacation and not preparing as well as possible would be reckless. Our hunger sated for the time being we headed to the dock, eager to board the Fast Cat ferry back to Catalina.

I was in my head a bit as we walked, wondering about the two very different Michael's I had now seen. How many more were there to discover? We all have different sides to our personality and behaviour, and I had only seen a couple of his thus far. It was only about an hour's ride, and he took the opportunity to ask me about the people at the party. I gave him the full background on Jonathon, Luke, Kathy, and Angela and then he asked about Norie.

"I recall reading about your friend Norie in the papers, she seems like quite the DA," he said in an admiring tone.

"She's the real deal for sure, there is nothing I wouldn't trust her with, and Colin is the same. I suppose everyone there fits that bill too though," I said, feeling the contentment of having such a group of friends I could trust.

Michael casually added, "She's pretty easy on the eyes too. Where was her partner last night?" He caught me a bit by surprise asking such an obvious question about one of my closest friends.

"She's great looking, plus smart, and surprisingly strong, but I'd keep focussed on our trip if I were you."

I really didn't know what I was feeling in the moment or where my words came from. I always felt protective of Norie although I had no idea why I felt that way, I knew she was more than capable of taking care of herself. Michael came back with, "Arlo and Sage seem to be quite the couple!" "Yeah, they are a real blast and exactly what you see. Two aging hippies who remain as completely in love with each other as the first time they met." I smiled and continued, "I recall the first time we were all at a party there and Arlo watching Sage strip down for a skinny dip in the ocean. She was clearly extremely comfortable in her own skin and Arlo stood admiring her as if they were both still 18-year-old kids."

Michael looked like he was somewhere else as he replied, "It would be nice to find that some day."

We walked along the beachfront from the ferry, the soft, white sand flowing around our shoes with each step. Michael stopped to line up at my favorite coffee wagon, Java The Hut. The line was long, so he told me to go on ahead. As I strolled toward the marina the Amphitrite came into view and I soaked it all in.

She was completely equipped for any type of sailing, and she was a real beauty. Two sleek hulls able to cut through the heaviest seas while being propelled forward by ultramodern sails, her only limits being those of her captain and crew, their knowledge, experience, adaptability, and confidence. I sometimes thought I was in over my head and the comment from the seller that *she sails herself* may have been a bit of an overstatement, but I was improving every day. She included multiple methods of keeping in touch with the mainland including VHF radio, sat phone and satellite uplink.

It was not like the two of us would have any worries about robbery or piracy on the high seas anyway, but safety was paramount, and communication is the most important aspect of that.

I decided to go up top while I waited for Michael and the coffees. I watched from my perch on the sundeck as Michael strode through the marina, and noticed his strong wide shoulders as he made his way towards me, the deft manner in which he held himself amongst those trying to get his attention. He certainly had a presence. I felt that his sailing experience, combined with what I was learning from my coach, sailing my cat to the Cayman's would become reality. Michael handed me my coffee and sat next to me. I took a sip right away and promptly burnt my lip, oops. I decided I had to know what the deal was with him at the party sooner rather than later. It was clearly a real trigger for him, so I knew I needed to tread lightly.

"So, will your restaurant be in good hands with you away for an extended time like this," I asked, trying to be nothing more than conversational.

He smiled at me, "I have 100% confidence in all my staff at The Heavenly Pie. My Aunt always did her best to help people and I kept the bulk of her staff, especially those who might not be alive if she had not stepped in, so they are very loyal. They're all like family and I have zero concerns."

"I have a concern or two, one about last night Michael. I've never seen you react so strongly to something as when you spoke about George Floyd and Derek Chauvin," knowing my statement might cause an issue, but I had to dig.

A stern look washed over his face as he slowly began to say, "Look, I know it was a bit over the top but there's something you don't know. The reason my aunt left me her restaurant and I moved here was because of my brother."

"Michael, I didn't even know you had a brother," I replied, still trying to be casual.

His stern look quickly melted away as his eyes welled up, "I do, I mean did, have a brother but he was killed."

"Oh my God, was he one of us?" I asked, assuming that military service became a *family business* for him just as it had for me.

"He was, but that had nothing to do with his murder. He was killed during a traffic stop. A goddamn traffic stop, and my only brother was gone!" Just like that his look reverted to grave and sombre as he went on.

I looked on incredulously as he spoke in measured, sombre tones, clearly trying to remain calm, "Two white cops pulled him out of the car, one claimed he saw a gun. They hit him with tasers multiple times, provided no medical help after he went down, and that was it. One more black man dead in the streets at the hands of the police. My brother didn't even own a gun and, like you and me, had little need for one, at least in most cases."

We had both experienced loss in our job, but I had no idea how to respond other than, "Michael, I'm so sorry that happened to your family." I knew now was not the time to talk about the work I had done with my friend Norie on that same issue, although I very much wanted to. As the Los Angeles County District Attorney, Norie was a real fireball and only when she met Bobby, did I find out about her many other skills in addition to being a kickass lawyer. I supposed I had my own share of secrets and struggled with why I couldn't let Michael keep some of his own. We just sat there for a few more moments in silence until I turned to him, "Let's go down to the salon and have a look at what we've got." He nodded his agreement with a forced smile.

We descended the stairs and Michael stopped short at the entrance to the salon and looked at me, his usual demeanour back, "Good God, we might not make it if you're THIS messy all the time."

"Hey, I've never even seen your place. Maybe you're a slob and I just don't know it yet. And, no, I am not like this all the time," but I got where he was coming from. Charts and other papers were strewn about like leaves blown from a tree, completely covering the large table in the salon, and spilling onto the surrounding surfaces. My sailing buddy and coach, Mark Mulrooney had stressed to me the importance of paper charts but in that moment, I thought I may have gotten a little carried away. After all, we did not have to rely solely on wind power. One of the other benefits of a multihull boat the size of the Amphitrite was that it had two powerful engines, not just one. One or both could quickly propel us to safety in case of a storm, or just help us stay on schedule when the wind was light. A small backup engine was a necessity, having two matched powerplants was a luxury for which I was willing to pay. That was one of the reasons I really liked the catamaran style over a monohull. If one's good two's better, I like to say.

I stressed to Michael that, even with multiple backup systems, we really needed all the data I had compiled, and he readily agreed. We began to build our list of provisions. One page became two and two became three as we tried to cover all the bases. My boat has a sizable wet well where fish we caught could be kept for extended periods without taking up room in the fridge or coolers. The *Amphitrite* even had a water purifier that could desalinate the sea water and make it drinkable. It always struck me that although you were surrounded by billions of gallons of water, you could still die of thirst out on the open ocean.

Once we addressed all those items, we turned to creating an actual itinerary and that was where the whole trip became more real! It is one thing to discuss going "here and there" in general terms but quite another to create a real plan. A plan where you start to actually map out and calculate sailing times considering tides, currents, prevailing winds, and other weather conditions.

Of paramount interest to us both at the moment was navigating the Panama Canal. We were both eager to experience that engineering wonder from a new perspective. Our stops would likely include Huatulco and/or Cabo Mexico, San Juan Del Sur in Nicaragua, Puntarenas Costa Rica, and Panama City before entering the Canal. We planned to be anchored at Georgetown about thirty-six days after leaving Catalina and set our departure for two weeks. We went about gathering our supplies and provisions, including picking up a spare motor for our tender as well as an ocean capable inflatable life raft complete with cover. We packed a couple of disaster bags that included bottled water, freeze dried food, medical kit, a tiny stove with fuel, and more items that could possibly save our lives if the situation arose.

There was so much to do and so many things to get, it felt like we were preparing to set sail on the Ark itself, soon to be alone in the open ocean with only our thoughts, as we sailed our course.

Due to the fact we would be out there alone we also stashed a few weapons. We did not expect a need for guns, but decided to hide pistols and ammo where nobody but us could find them. The Coast Guards and various navy and police vessels along the way often checked yachts like this for contraband of one sort or another, so we needed to be cautious. We used special hermetically sealed containers to effectively hide the scent of gunpowder from any search dogs and stashed them away.

We began scheduling in earnest keeping our target departure day in focus. The paper got messy quickly with scratch outs and erased patches dotting the pages like a freshman's first term paper as we scribbled, discussed, and adjusted. Another hour or so and we had what we thought was a workable draft of a schedule and began to mark in key tasks to complete each day. Fresh provisions would be secured a day or two prior to our planned departure while we could pick up all the medicines, water, dried food, and the like any time before. By the end of this exercise, I felt quite confident in our plan and our itinerary but still had those nagging concerns about Michael. After all, how well did I really know him?

At least I knew his training matched very well with my own. Although I'm not completely sure that *training* is an appropriate word for what I had endured. Training belied the true nature of what it was I had not only survived but conquered.

I recalled how it often seemed closer to torture, even approaching brainwashing at times. The searing pain in your lungs as you struggled to take a breath while the icy cold ocean washed over your face and splashed up your nostrils, the drill Sergeant barking at you, "Don't be a PUSSY, don't be like little Megan *boy*, hold that head up *high*." I had no choice but to disguise the contempt I felt at his words as, even though he was a SEAL, I knew I could kick his ass if I wanted to, but that was not what this was about. This was about executing orders without question or concern for anything other than the order itself. Besides, I knew that sergeant was dead wrong, "little" Megan was going to be top of class and his words didn't bother me at all, they actually levelled the playing field in my mind, giving me additional motivation.

He had six months to make me *ring the bell* and it never happened. Ringing the bell, three times, was how you quit SEAL training. No warm fuzzy talks, no exit interview, no interaction with anyone, simply ring the bell three times, remove your helmet, set it on the ground next to the bell and walk away. The Navy was not in the business of handing out participation ribbons or pats on the back for failure! Failure often meant death so only the best of the best would make the grade. I spent every minute of every hour working hard to succeed, not to prove that ignoramus wrong but to prove myself right.

I fought through it all.

I battled past the aching muscles as you struggled to hold my head out of the water while keeping a massive log high above with your teammates as your arms shuddered with exertion. I ignored the intense pain that radiated through every fibre of my body and destroyed the willingness of many to continue. The agony, verbal abuse, and physical challenges left many with no choice but to ring that damn bell! I knew Michael had endured something similar but, if I'm being honest, I didn't think it was equal to what I had been through. Teams like the SEALs may not see color, but I can assure you they see gender. I was always aware of that fact, but I also knew that once I bested a few of the guys the smart ones would prefer to have me at their side when lives were in jeopardy. In that way the Navy SEALs were the ultimate meritocracy, no politics or anything else could get you through that program. I find it interesting that the originator of the term meritocracy, sociologist Michael Young, used the word in a pejorative sense in his treatise on the subject, The Rise of the Meritocracy. I, like the masses, see a meritocracy as one of the best philosophies, nothing dystopian about it.

Michael's voice got me out of my head as he said, "We're really making headway here. Stay focussed."

I knew he was right, and I was perturbed that he had already developed a way to read me. I had to remember that all the training and torture was behind me now, I was going to be a real sailor! The tests and challenges in this arena would be more manageable and much less painful, as far as I was currently aware.

Chapter 3 – Departure Day

I had been watching all the marine charting sites and weather data very closely. My sailing coach always stressed planning but in the very next breath would add that flexibility was the ultimate key to success. Based on the expected weather and sea conditions for the next six weeks, we could spend two nights in each port if we wished. That wasn't our current plan, but it was nice to have options. We both needed to work on making this an experience by enjoying the journey and not just another mission to be completed. Those missions were typically life threatening and often large groups of people would rely on our small teams being successful. That was a lot of weight to carry around, the burden a constant pressure like massive bags of stone sitting on your shoulders trying to slow you down, make you stumble, or even fall to defeat. The knowledge that there were many others incapable of bearing such a burden motivated people like us to take it all on. This trip was meant to be as far from life-threatening as we could get and nothing like one of those missions.

Michael grabbed his bag, reached inside, and pulled out a beautifully made wooden sign that he held up like a trophy. It looked like a long-removed piece of a weather-beaten barn, the edges rough and scalloped, and the whole thing a light grey.

The letters were both carved into the wood and colored with bright paints stating quite succinctly, "It's ALL about the journey, so enjoy."

"Where'd you buy that?" I asked.

"Why would you assume I bought it? I made it," he answered matter-of-factly.

"Really? I can't picture you to be an artist."

I hadn't intended my comment to sound derogatory, but he looked a little hurt when he replied, "You've got quite a mean streak, don't you?"

"No, sorry. I only meant, you surprise me, that's all," I countered, still wondering what else I didn't know about him. He gave a serious kind of smile, looking around for a spot to mount his work of art. I was discovering more about Michael each day, but I just couldn't shake my concern that there was something more going on and it was eating away at me constantly. It took another day and half of preparing, then all too suddenly, the eve of our departure arrived. Planning to leave early the next morning we crashed on the boat, and I got one of my best sleeps of the last year.

We were already up on deck when the sun began to rise the next day, both of us eager to get this adventure started.

"Look at that sunrise, I never get tired of watching it," I said as the brilliantly glowing star eased its way leisurely out of the ocean, slowly ascending towards its lofty perch for the day. I drank in the fresh morning air, the unique smell of the sea, enjoying the slight chill just as much as the saltiness. This was one of my favorite things about staying on the boat, the mornings. Each one unique, but comfortably similar. The dawn of a new day was always like a rebirth for me. Everything new again, not knowing what was yet to come, what experiences I would have. A chance to start over. Even when I was deployed, I did my best to begin every day happy. We got everything stowed, released the mooring lines, and began to slip out into the brilliant blue Pacific. The gentle current moving South would help us reach our destination.

Michael flashed a huge smile as we left the cozy confines of Catalina Island and announced to the world, "Cabo San Lucas, here we come."

The temperatures quickly climbed into the high seventies, and I was thankful to be blessed with such a day, another gift. Just after we passed the edge of the marina, we felt a nice tailwind. The sails flapped briefly as we rolled them out and seconds later, they were fully filled, and we began to pick up speed. I enjoyed the sounds of sailing, the silence interspersed with splashing, sails flapping, the raw power of the wind driving us forward. Soon, the massive mainsail was fully deployed, the boom angled to take best advantage of the prevailing wind. Having all of the controls in the cockpit was one of the reasons I really liked this boat. It made her a real pleasure to sail and gave you the flexibility to adapt quickly to changing conditions, without risking life and limb scrambling around on the deck. I recalled how confused I was when I first began to sail, there was so much to learn, and everything seemed to have a different name than was obvious. I mean, who would think to call a rope attached to a sail a *sheet*?

As we sailed South with the warm salt air misting our faces, a pod of dolphins leaped out of the water to the side of us. We watched as their super sleek, smooth grey bodies sailed effortlessly up and down, in and out of the water, their innocent looking faces seemingly smiling up at you as they glanced toward the boat.

I called over at Michael, "Are you catching this? Aren't they amazing, so beautiful, calm, and playful. They have no idea what we are doing to their environment though, it's easy to misplace trust for any mammal I suppose."

"Geez, that's a bit of a dark view, isn't it?" Michael asked, and he wasn't being rhetorical.

"I just mean that at least we are not the ones polluting their environment. I think they somehow know they can trust people like you and me," I said as if they were sentient beings, wishing them to be that aware and present.

"I'm not sure that anyone can be trusted after what I've seen," Michael replied. He seemed to have a faraway look after that comment, so I just left it alone for now. Having put the boat on auto pilot, Michael joined me up front on the trampoline, as I pointed toward a pod of orcas.

"It's just stunning, isn't it?" I asked.

"I suppose it is," he said.

I noticed that boyish look of wonder on his face as we watched the orcas and dolphins splashing around though, frolicking in the wakes created by the hulls. They used the gentle waves like a wakeboarder would, sliding up and down on the smooth waves then disappearing beneath the surface before repeating the ride.

The Scripps Oceanographic Institute could be seen with binoculars on the coast in La Jolla, just North of San Diego proper, obviously the ideal location for such a place. I sometimes wondered about a graduate degree from there when I left the SEALs, but life kept getting in the way. Watching the marine life living in this environment really put me at ease. SEALs spent so much of our lives in the ocean that you began to feel like you truly were a part of it, even though we were only visitors. I had not done very much pleasure diving, but each time I did I felt as if I were as free as they were, if only for a few brief moments. The ocean silence broken only by the scuba gear sending a trail of bubbles snaking up to the surface.

We saw more great sights along the way but otherwise, it had been an uneventful sailing day. In the sailing world those times were always gratefully accepted, at least by sailors like us. In contrast to competition sailors, we enjoyed skimming across the surface of the ocean quietly and effortlessly as the winds propelled us forward with little for us to do but enjoy. Handling overly rough seas and hasty sail changes due to wind conditions were never the high points of a recreational sailor's day, at least not this sailor. I will admit there is a sense of accomplishment when one is able to adapt to challenging conditions and still make way, but these easy times were to be savoured for the respite they provided. Time flew, and I glanced at my watch as we turned Eastward and began to round the point then turned into the inlet towards the Cabo marina.

Michael excitedly proclaimed, "That was an excellent first day."

"I agree, let's hope they're all like this one," knowing that's never the case. We slipped past Pelican Rock towards the entrance of the harbor as we returned the mainsail slowly to its home. We watched the gennakers furl tightly around their drums and then I hit two switches and the engines roared to life.

Cabo San Lucas is an extremely popular spot for three main reasons. An abundance of beautiful white sandy beaches bordering turquoise hued warm waters, lots of fun water-based activities, and plenty of bars and restaurants that make for a great night life. Cabo sits at the Southernmost tip of Baja California in Mexico. Its popularity skyrocketed in the seventies when Hollywood's glitterati began to travel there. Their lithe, tanned, oiled up bodies littering the beach like sunbathing seals.

It had been a seedy area for quite a long time before, but the gentrification happened quickly due to the boatloads of cash the stars and other rich folks had to spend. As usual, when rich folks gather, hangers-on show up to profit from their wealth. As high-end resorts continued to open, the restaurant and bar scene grew right along with them, all wanting to reach deep into the pockets of the wealthy Americans and secure their own futures. Cabo seemed to have seedy characters on almost every corner reeking of the hopeless desperation of caged animals as they stalk their fences, seeking an escape from that which can control their body but not their soul.

The only difference being when you looked into the dark, lonely eyes of these people no soul was revealed, just a lack of light, lack of hope. We knew that darkness and I sometimes worried about my own soul, stained by the things I had done. People like Michael and me had seen too much, done too much, we knew well what floated just beneath the surface. Now I wanted my thoughts focussed on boats.

There was a wide variety of boats gently lolling on their moorings, bobbing slowly up and down. Smaller monohulls, power yachts, and other cats were crammed into the inner berths like tract houses, so close you could hear the guy next door snoring. The much larger outer spots were filled with 150-to-200-foot luxury yachts and all manner of larger sailing craft. The place oozed wealth and they were the representation of that. I spotted a large wooden boat that stood out from the rest of the costly cookie-cutter toys. It had three masts that looked like an old Spanish Galleon, we could see the pristine condition it was in. Once tied up, we decided to take a walk around and get the lay of the land and we met the Captain of that ship, the Kawaloon, an older gentleman named Harley. His flowing grey hair and full grey beard along with his crusty countenance made you feel as if you were speaking to a sailor from the 1800's. He had deep set, dark eyes that conveyed the likelihood he had forgotten more about sailing than I would ever be able to learn. His gnarled, thick fingers told me he was no lawyer or doctor, he was a man who loved sailing, probably lived for it at this point in his life.

I knew one would need a great deal of skill and knowledge to sail a vessel like that and I admired him for that. The three substantial wooden masts stuck out of the deck like perfectly skinned, deadly straight trees, polished to a shine, sails hanging from each by rings of similarly polished wood. Harley gave us a full tour and with obvious pride pointed out the many things he had done to improve the craft from her launch day more than eighty years prior. When Harley mentioned he was Canadian, Michael went wild, as if he were meeting a long-lost family member.

"No kidding, me too," said Michael excitedly.

Harley asked, "Where ya from bud."

I picked up little of the exchange that followed except for a bunch of ehs, buds, and other typically Eastern Canadian phrases and words. Harley and his two companions had sailed down from a small seaside town called Chester in Nova Scotia, known for its sailing and boat races. His boat had been there for many years surrounded on buoys at the marina by all types of motor craft and sailboats. They were owned by "real" sailors like him but people like me too, and of course the doctors and lawyers who usually owned much more boat than their skills could handle. Harley cracked a few good-natured jokes about those folks, but you could tell he had some sort of admiration for them.

We thanked Harley for the tour and continued on our walkabout.

There was a section in the marina where some of the serious ocean-going race type boats were moored, their Captains and crew eagerly anticipating the next challenge. Long glossy hulls powered by 1,500 or 3,000 HP worth of engines hidden beneath the rear deck. Two, sometimes three engines, which sounded like jets when they were opened up. I was startled when one roared to life, as ear-splittingly loud as a race car with straight pipes, and my brain took me back to my fight with the drug cartels not far from here. Those cartel boys loved their boats. I recalled the RPG's I shot into two similar boats and the massive explosions when they hit, the aviation fuel used to power them going up like a roman candle, launching a massive orange fireball into the bright blue sky.

It seemed I not only had PTSD from being a SEAL, but also from my subsequent *adventures*. It was the same for so many vets. The knife wounds, bullet holes, torture, and other physical damage needed only time to heal, the mental scars were a completely different story, many never healing no matter how much help you got. The scars in your head festered forever like an open wound, a constant pain, the only difference being that your body was rotting from the inside.

"Hey, where are you at right now," Michael said, jolting me back to the present.

"Nowhere really, just thinking," I replied, not wishing to share with anyone what those thoughts were. Sometimes, even comrades and brothers weren't ready to hear they had company thinking the same gloomy, depressing things they were.

"Why don't we go for a run and wake ourselves up," he asked.

"Great plan," I answered, as I'm always up for a good run. "Good to get the blood flowing, clear the brain, work up an appetite."

We went back to the boat, changed, and then took a look at the marina map. There was a pathway all around the marina that was about two and a half miles with an uphill trail that led to a resort high on the hill. That's where we headed. We were both running in a typical trance-like state when we saw the hill ahead.

"Game on," we both yelled out at virtually the same time as we began an all-out sprint to the top. We crested the ridge where it flattened out into a grassy area, faces dripping sweat. We cooled down a bit under a large tree while we stretched and taunted each other, finally agreeing it was a tie.

We decided to do a little noncontact sparring just to stay sharp, delivering glancing blows and attempted holds at about one quarter of maximum. It was about five minutes in when I got a sense we were being watched, but I saw nothing out of the ordinary as I scanned the area. When we started walking back to the boat Michael said he had the same feeling when we were sparring. We agreed it was probably just our nature, always on edge, always feeling like we were "at work." It is a tough way to live, always wondering if your next breath might be your last. Some never got used to potential death being around every corner or delivered by the least likely person or object.

A mother carrying a baby wrapped tightly on her back, the wrap concealing not a baby but an improvised explosive device. A child on the roadside asking for help for his dog, the innocent animal already dead and concealing a lethal IED. There was often no way to be certain. When operating in those countries it felt like you were constantly knocking on death's door and coming back home was an exceedingly difficult adjustment. I guess that's why charities like the Wounded Warrior project exist. That was why, when I began to acquire more wealth, I always donated to them.

We planned a night out on the town to really kick off our big adventure. We decided we wanted Italian and made a reservation at Luna Italiana, one of the highest rated spots in the area. We caught a ride over from the marina and were shown to our table. The smell of the food made my mouth water as our server led us toward large double doors and stepped aside to wave us ahead, knowing we would be struck by the amazing, panoramic view.

The whole marina and harbor laid out in front of us like a massive painting. We really enjoyed our dinners and wine and, most especially, the never-ending view.

After dinner we decided to head back down towards the marina and find somewhere to grab a night cap along the way. We stopped into a quaint little spot called La Pintada and ordered a couple of spicy margaritas.

The place was just as you would expect in the area. There were small tables scattered around in no particular pattern and large colorful umbrellas mixed in with palm palapas. There were couples and groups of four huddled around the tables, many drinking from a coconut or a glass with a tiny umbrella sticking up. Those were expensive tourist cocktails likely built with the cheapest ingredients, but what did tourists know anyway.

As night began to slowly descend upon us, we decided we should head back. We walked down a well-kept gravelled path towards the marina, enjoying the view of the night sky. No wind and almost no noise, I was already looking forward to being gently rocked to sleep in my berth. Michael stopped and put out his arm in front of me as he put his finger to his lips and then tapped his ear while pointing to the bushes. We both listened as we scanned the area around us, trying desperately to see through the leafy growth that defined the path.

"I thought I caught movement at your ten o'clock," he whispered.

Chapter 4 – History Lesson

Just as we looked left, a small group of birds took flight out of the bushes. We both jumped a bit.

"Jeezus," Michael yelled out. "Damn birds."

"Better birds than anything else," I said with a chuckle.

Just as I relaxed, six men burst out in front of us, their heavy military style boots crunching noisily onto the gravel. I saw no guns or knives but then one of them flashed a shiny badge. Michael asked in a cool voice what they wanted and added that we had just landed and were tourists from the US. As the man with the badge began to speak, I noticed one of the other men off to the side. Although it was getting dark, there was still enough light to see that he had a severely scarred face. I made eye contact with him, and as I did, we were abruptly looking down the barrels of six pistols.

"Whoa, whoa, we don't want trouble," I said, as the man with the scars stepped forward.

"If you didn't want trouble, *Puta*, you would never have messed with Mochismo," he growled back.

"Do I look like a prostitute to you?" I asked in a tightly controlled voice, trying to disguise my shock. "What is a Mochismo anyway?"

I quickly added, "Look, I think you must be mistaken, my husband and me are just on a vacation."

"You can call it whatever you want bitch, it's going to be your last," he growled at me through his long-ignored, sparse teeth, the lack of dental hygiene made me feel like puking.

I could smell the disgusting stench of stale cigarettes radiating from him as he moved closer, his scraggly knotted grey hair hanging around his wrinkly sunburnt face like the strings on one of those old art deco lampshades. He gritted what few were left of his brown teeth as he reached forward and lifted my chin with the barrel of his gun. I felt the rage building inside me, the pent-up power in my fists like a tightly wound steel spring ready to lash out and destroy him. I knew as close as he was, I could easily disarm him and get his weapon, but I caught a look from Michael cautioning me it would not be a clever idea to tussle with six men right now.

Michael mimicked me as I slowly raised my hands, "Okay, let's try to get this straightened out then. This is the first time we have even been to Mexico. Do you want money?"

The two goons in front of us laughed as the four behind shoved us forward, I winced when I felt the gun barrel grating against my spine. We soon emerged in a parking lot where none of them even bothered to hide their weapons. As we stood waiting to get into the back of the vehicle, they roughly zip tied our hands behind our backs and warned that any funny business and we would both be shot.

They pushed us inside the large SUV, four of us jammed into the middle seat, one goon on either side of us blocking the doors. I knew they would be rewarded whether I was dead or alive, although alive was the preferred method of delivery. The cartel would want to inflict painful revenge on me. I looked at Michael with a *sorry about this* shrug and started to evaluate the situation. If they were successful getting us to the desired destination, I knew we were both going to die, not quickly either. The "cop" was hopefully a fake, but I knew going to the police would never be an option anyway, even if we escaped. There was always an assumption of guilt when it came to Americans in Mexico so I was certain involving the police would only add a brief time to our lives. I used my eyes to communicate to Michael that I could get out of my ties, he almost imperceptibly nodded in agreement. Like me, he would have flexed his wrists in a way that would not be noticed when we were restrained but would allow us to slip out later. We sat and waited. I used my eyes to signal him to take out the front two and I would do the two behind us.

"Hey, I need to pee, or you'll have a big bill to clean out your boss's car," I announced to the driver.

"Perras estupidas," (stupid bitch) he said as he jammed on the brakes. I laughed internally as I thought how much I would enjoy some one-on-one time with this dolt.

As the car slowed, Michael and I head butted the men on each side and grabbed their pistols.

In seconds, after four precise shots, we had dispatched the other four, and the vehicle drifted slowly into a tree. We sat there with two men unconscious and four others dead or soon to be dead.

I shrugged my shoulders at Michael, "In for a dime in for a dollar," as I jammed the pistol into my guys' ribs and blew him wide open, his blood and guts painting the door a grisly red. Michael did the same to his guy and we climbed over them and got out, confirming all were deceased.

Michael said, "We really need to cover this up, you got any ideas?"

"Staging a fire would be easy, but would certainly draw even more attention," I replied.

Michael said, "What if we left everything and everyone as is and let the authorities assume another cartel did the damage? I mean, this mess certainly *looks* like the result of a drug war."

"I like that idea. You Canadians can be really sneaky," unable to hide the admiration in my voice as I smiled at him.

Michael chuckled back, "Not sneaky so much as practical, I prefer to think."

The cartel clash made a lot of sense, Mexico was still Mexico and there was no way to tell who was corrupt and who was not, but there was one constant here, there was no cooperation between cartels. We cleaned ourselves up as best we could and began to walk quickly back down to the marina.

Michael raised his eyebrows, smiled sarcastically, and commented, "Well, that was an interesting little sidebar. Anything you'd like to tell me?"

Reluctantly I began, "All right then. It was an operation in Mexico when I came across the Mochismo cartel. Like most cartels, they are a deadly bunch."

"Yes, I can see they are," Michael said with not a hint of humor.

"I inflicted massive damage on them when I blew up two of their boats with a bunch of their people on them, including three of the top guys. I think maybe that guy with the scars may have actually been on one of those boats," although I didn't see how he could have been.

"Well, he was obviously pissed about something. If you were the cause of him looking that nasty, I can understand why."

"It's a much longer story involving Colin Sharpe and a case he was working on. I'll tell you the whole thing when we get out of here alive." I kept the information about Colin's wife private for now as it would not have improved anything. We got to the hill above the marina and did some recon for about a half hour to see if anyone was on the *Amphitrite* or if she was being watched. It was a clear night, and the Marina was well lit which made it easier. The main concern now was whether or not our kidnappers had contacted anyone between the time they first saw us and their gruesome demise, and we had no way to know that.

"I'm sure you know that cartels like these always have leaders-in-waiting," I offered.

Michael glared at me, "Of course I know that. I'm Canadian, not an idiot."

"Okay, so you know that tracking down a former boss's killer is a big feather in the hat of whomever takes over."

"I get it, let's just focus on what we need to do to get out of here," he said very calmly and business-like.

I was apprehensive about going near the boat tonight, but I had to retrieve some gear. I had stashed a bag in the tender that contained some surveillance equipment, including small binoculars, along with supplies to make a garrotte, an international cellular phone, and a few other key items.

"Keep an eye on me and the boat, I'm going to swim over to it and grab some things," I said.

"Really? You want me to just sit here and wait," he responded, looking like I had somehow just insulted him.

I tried my best not to sound condescending, answering, "I'm the SEAL here, let me do what I do." I moved to where there were trees close to the path and little light. I left my shoes and clothes beneath a tree, walked the ten or so paces to the rocky edge, and slipped silently into the dark water.

Even though nobody had been spotted, I spent most of the time underwater as I swam toward the boat. After a couple of minutes, I surfaced against the inside face of the harborside hull. I knew there was no lighting under there so I would be out of sight of any prying eyes. I had hoped I might be able to pull myself up and peek inside a porthole, but there was nothing to grab, the slick surface being made even more slippery thanks to greasy ocean scum.

I slid along the hull and pulled myself up onto the rigging at the stern so I could reach inside the tender. I held myself in position with one hand while the other searched the small inflatable boat, reaching under the edges and even checking beneath the seat. It took longer than expected to find the bag, but thanks to my SEAL days, I had good tolerance for the surprisingly chilly water.

I finally found the bag, grabbed it, and slipped quietly back down into the water. I lashed the bag around my waist and sunk under the calm, cool waters of the inner harbour once more. I slipped silently through the water until I reached the edge, pulled myself up, and made my way over to the tree where I left my clothes. I wiped the water off me with my hand before pulling my clothes back on and went back to where Michael was waiting.

"All good?" he asked.

I simply nodded in the affirmative, although not certain it was all good.

"No sign of anything," he said, "Perhaps let's wait it out a bit."

We took turns watching throughout the night. I trusted that the egos within cartels were still massive so our attempted captors would have passed nothing along, they would want to return home like warriors with their spoils. If that were the case, we could simply get back onto the boat and sail away in the morning, hopefully putting all of this behind us. I knew that would still be our best chance at survival.

Sure, there was a possibility we could die the same death their bosses did, but at least we would never know what hit us, annihilated by an unseen projectile just like they had been. We maintained our vigil through the night and neither of us saw anyone on or close to the *Amphitrite*.

At first rays of the sun, we packed everything back into the bag and walked casually back to the boat. We were both in full recon mode as we warily approached the dock. It appeared nobody was on the *Amphitrite*. I reviewed the security footage and was able to confirm that no one had boarded her in our absence. I scrubbed through it quickly, as all cameras were motion sensor activated, and the only things that activated them last night were birds and fish. I also had a scanner that would pick up anything electronic or bomb-like, and that came up empty too after I combed every inch of my boat as an extra precaution.

The glorious morning sun supplied welcome warmth as we took in all our mooring lines, stowed the fenders, and got underway.

I looked at Michael apologetically as we motored out into the gulf and set course for Puerto Vallarta, "Look, I'm really sorry that my past came back to haunt us."

"I know, I know, people like you and me carry considerable baggage," he replied in a consoling tone.

"Isn't that the truth. I can't get out of here soon enough so let's get moving."

We released all the lines, loaded the fenders, and began to leave. As I piloted the boat Michael scanned around us continuously with the powerful binoculars. We thought that if we were attacked from a distance, we might have enough time to dive deeply before the boat was vaporized. Fortunately, all he spotted was a pod of killer whales and a few large sailfish as they exploded out of the water only to crash back in whilst seeking a meal. We had to cross the Gulf Of California waters to get to Puerto Vallarta and it was about 260 nautical miles, so I was relieved the winds were again in our favor.

We hoisted the massive main sail, let out both Gennakers and were soon ripping along at close to 28 knots. If we could maintain that speed, we should be in Puerto Vallarta in a little over nine hours. While not the fastest cat on the water, the *Amphitrite* was a smooth and fast boat, the morning silence broken only by the wind occasionally buffeting our sails, the sleek mirror smooth hulls slicing through the water like airplane wings cutting through clouds. I finally settled down after a couple of hours and began to enjoy the pure serenity of sailing. While never completely out of mind, the immediate danger from the cartels had diminished. The sounds of the wind and the boat moving easily through the water often lulled me into a dreamlike state, similar to those long runs where the mechanics of the activity happened without thought, becoming an almost involuntary action like breathing. While we were traversing the Gulf, I gave Michael more detail about what had happened with the cartels.

"Sorry about the whole cartel thing," I said, trying to sound casual about it.

Michael seemed to force a smile, when he replied, "Would have been good to know in advance, I suppose."

"I'm a little worried now about tying up in Puerto Vallarta though. It's even closer to the Jalisco Cartel's home base," I explained with another apologetic look.

I was surprised when he chuckled back, "With what you did to the Mochismo Cartel, I would think the Jalisco boys might give you a trophy." As unlikely as such a fete would be, I had done so much damage to their competition, if this was the biker world, I'd probably be an honorary member by now. The cartels were an opportunistic bunch and didn't much care how or who eliminated any of their competition so long as their valuable territory was protected.

My skin felt as if it were shrinking as the wind, sun, and salt air attacked us, sucking the moisture from any exposed area. Dehydration was always the biggest danger if you found yourself adrift in a life raft in the open ocean. Even if you had enough food and water, if you were unable to protect yourself from the ravages of the environment you would surely die, shrivelled up like those dried-out apple head dolls you see at state fairs. I was grateful the next few hours of sailing were smooth and uneventful, just makin' miles and taking in the sights.

I scanned the area and took the binoculars away from my eyes smiling at Michael, "There's Paradise Village, on the left."

"Thank God for that, my Canadian skin isn't used to this much sun," he said with a laugh.

We searched for an open berth as we motored slowly along, the bow bobbing up and down gently. I manoeuvred into one without incident as Michael hopped off the bow, taking the main line with him. In a few minutes we were completely tied off and ready to relax. We had already decided to eat on the boat, forget the sightseeing, and get a good night's sleep. We knew that our next stop would likely be Acapulco as we continued to work our way down the coast so we could enjoy ourselves a bit more there. It was almost 600 nautical miles between Puerto Vallarta and Acapulco so, even at twenty knots average, would still be about 28 hours. We had agreed that with a good night sleep, and provided the wind conditions favored our route, we would make our best effort to sail/motor straight through, which would require sailing at night. We planned to take turns sleeping during the daylight so that we could both be awake throughout the evening. Solo sailing at night was a somewhat reckless thing to attempt, and we needed to be ready.

We rustled up a tasty dinner of fresh fish, no liquor or wine, and took our time enjoying the meal, savouring each bite. As we sat digesting, the gentle evening breeze began to cool things down, night beginning to slowly exert its influence over the day.

We were both racked out not long after sunset, thanks to a long, sweltering day on the water. We slept in the anonymous safety of all the similar boats around us, more or less hiding in plain sight. I enjoyed being gently rocked to sleep by the subtle motion of a boat, as if in your mother's arms, ever so slowly rocking back and forth. Michael's cabin was in the other hull and that was one of the things I liked most about this layout. You basically had a master stateroom, with its own head, on each side of the boat. It gave us privacy but also might help get us out of a jam. I put some music on at low volume and set it to shut off after an hour. I hoped I would be asleep quickly. I had a few cartel thoughts but then drifted off to a well-deserved deep sleep.

We were both up early, eager to get going, scurrying around the deck in the morning twilight. While it would be a long day, after checking the weather and ocean charts, it was potentially going to be shorter than originally expected. Based on the current wind direction and speed as well as the forecast for the day I felt we should still be able to maintain a speed of close to twenty-eight knots, if not faster. If we were able to do that it would mean a total of thirty hours under sail. We were soon ready to cast off our lines and set out just after the sun awoke from its own slumber. We had gotten everything ready and were enjoying a morning coffee when we both felt the wind on our faces. Even though it was only just now morning, we were already preparing ourselves mentally ready for the blackness of the night as we stowed everything and got underway.

I was in my head, considering what we were about to undertake and the challenges the night might present. I glanced over at Michael and could tell by the serious look on his face he was having the same thoughts, at least I hope that's what was causing the look.

Chapter 5 – Acapulco Bound

We sailed down the coast all day, taking turns at the helm while the other slept, so we would be fully ready for night sailing. I took my naps on the trampoline as, except for the odd light splash, it felt like a giant hammock, air circulating all around you and the springy mesh cradling you like a big feather bed. On smooth days, it was like riding on a cloud, gentle movements lifting you along and often rocking you to sleep.

For the first twelve hours we were awake together on deck at the same time for only about sixty minutes as we reconfirmed our course using the paper charts, our planned path laid out with a purple highlighter, stops circled in yellow. Night began to envelope the bright day in a dark shroud, catching me a little by surprise even though this is exactly what we had both prepared for. Sailing becomes an almost surreal experience as your eyes adjust to the darkness, the distance gradually fading into nothingness until your pupils expand enough. On a clear night, as you slip through the water with the moon and stars glinting off the tiny peaks of the swells, it can feel like you are actually IN the stars, the horizon where earth and sky meet melding into one. We watched the sun settle lower as we skimmed over the ocean smoothly, like a glider in the sky, the winds gently guiding us this way and that. Soon, all our instruments were glowing dimly as we continued our journey, the darkness now completely engulfing us.

We switched all our lights off and left only our nav lights on so we could enjoy the starry night for a bit, feeling as if we were a star ourselves. The nav lights were critical to any boat on the water after dark and shutting them off was contrary to maritime law. Often, there were clouds that would obscure the night sky but that was not the case tonight. The sky and everything in it were fully revealed to us, stars sparkling and shimmering like so many diamonds under a bright light.

"I find the stars fascinating," I said, trying to get Michael talking again.

"They sure are, always an amazing sight," he answered matter of factly.

"I like the way things are always changing, but for navigation the consistency of the stars can still guide us," I said.

When he offered nothing more, I chose to just let it lie, but I knew I had to find out what was really happening with him at some point.

As we sailed through the darkness of the night it felt like we were the only people on the planet, until a shrill alarm pierced the peace. I scanned all the gauges and noted it was coming from the radar equipment. I grabbed the powerful searchlight on board and shone it forward as Michael took the helm and checked the electronics. I slowly scanned back and forth, seeing nothing, but whatever it was showed clearly on the radar. We charted our course to keep the mass on our port side and give it plenty of clearance. Michael said, "It doesn't appear to be moving. Maybe it's just a new island or uncharted rocks."

"Let's not take any chances out here and keep our distance," I said. As we approached the mass I added, "I'll get us a better look."

Michael recognized it first and yelled out, "Jeezus, it's a yacht. A big one."

"I wonder what they're doing there with no nav lights and no other lights on?" I asked rhetorically.

Michael answered, "Maybe they have a death wish, or they are just idiots."

"Don't be too hasty, maybe they're in real trouble," I offered.

Law dictates that boaters are obligated to stop and check on the health of the people and the vessel in cases like this. The yacht did not appear to be in distress, other than being captained by what we assumed was a moron, but appearance alone does not subjugate maritime law.

"I know it's not kosher, but I think we should just try to sneak past," discretion definitely being the better part of valor in this case.

"After our last encounter, I agree," Michael quickly responded.

I went to the console, "I'll kill all the lights and hopefully we can just slip by."

We eased past them leaving our lights off for another two nautical miles before turning everything back on.

Just as our lights powered up, Michael pointed out the stern, "I think I hear something."

I cupped my hands around my ears, "I can hear it too. Sounds like an outboard."

As we watched, Michael said, "Maybe they were in trouble after all."

The words were barely out of his mouth when we both heard a loud bang and saw the muzzle flash of some sort of gun.

"Dammit, they're firing at us. Kill the lights. Let's get the sails dropped."

"Great idea," I said, "You stay here, I'll grab the guns," and I scrambled below.

It took a little longer than I expected to get the guns and load them, before I could get topside, I heard the hatch slam shut. I ran to the front but heard that one latch too just as I got there. I knew there was no way out of here at the moment, but I still scrambled around searching. When I heard the discharge of a weapon, my heart sank. I kept quiet hoping they would think he was alone. I could hear a lot of bumping and thumping coming from the deck and hoped everything was okay. I decided I could not wait so I went to the hatch and shot the locking mechanism open.

As I kicked open the hatch Michael yelled out, "It's okay, everything's all right. It's just me."

"Good to know," I sneered up at him as he stood there looking defiant.

He smiled as he held one of the men by the head, adding "well, I was just a wee bit busy to be chatting."

Then with one twist, he snapped the neck of the wannabe pirate, killing him instantly. He dragged the lifeless body to the edge and tossed him overboard, "Shark food now."

"How many were there?" I asked.

"There were only three of them, I had them outgunned," he said with a sly grin.

I was calmer by now and cracked back, "That's the trouble with people, you just never know who you're picking a fight with."

"Ain't that the truth. Took a little longer than I thought though, maybe I'm a bit rusty," as he shrugged his shoulders and held up his hands. There were always goons on the water trying to take advantage of tourists who were ignorant of the dangers out here, these ones just picked the wrong people to mess with. I hoped that was all it was. The rest of the night was uneventful although the winds did die for a while, so I started the motors and eased the throttles ahead. We were only under power for about an hour when the hands on the clock slipped past 4:00 AM and the winds picked up again, we were able to reset our sails and kill the engines. We looked at the charts and the local marinas and I suggested we simply get close to the island of La Roqueta and drop anchor. We didn't need any provisions of any sort, still had plenty of fuel, propane, and water, so there was no reason to actually be in a marina. The marine forecast all around the region was for calm waters and I thought a bit of a break would be a good plan. Michael agreed, so we charted our way to the inlet where Playa Las Palmitas was.

There were a couple of nice resorts on the island, the googled pictures showed pristine semi-circular beaches cradling blue-green waters. In most of the photos the waters were teeming with tourists all splashing about.

It was close to ten AM when we finally did set our anchor just inside the beginning of the inlet to the beach. We discussed taking the tender, or the kayaks as it was only a couple of miles, but minutes later hopped into the crystal-clear bay and splashed around a bit, happy to be in the water.

We swam around the boat and then towards the shore before circling back, marvelling at all the colored fish easily visible just beneath the surface. The water was so clear, you could see right to the bottom, where there was even more sea life and a rainbow of colors. We were about a half mile away from the boat when Michael said, "I'm getting a bit hungry already, how about you?"

As if on cue, I felt my stomach rumble its agreement, "Yeah, I could definitely eat a little something." I launched into an all-out sprint. I was in full compete mode as my powerful kicking worked in concert with a stroke that had not weakened since my university days. In short order I reached out and grabbed the lowest rung of the ladder as if I was stretching to touch the wall after a 200-metre sprint, in my mind I was breaking a world record, the crowd going crazy.

I glanced back at Michael with a broad victory smile as I pulled myself up onto the deck. We showered off the salt, changed and grabbed the fishing gear.

We were hoping to get some Dorado, also known as Mahi-mahi or dolphinfish. It got that moniker mostly because it has a bulbous rounded forehead area that makes it appear similar to a dolphin. They are a brightly colored fish and found all down through South America, especially in Costa Rica.

We had been casting and trolling our lines for only about fifteen minutes when Michael yelled out "Fish on."

I glanced over and saw him working the reel in hopes of tiring the fish. Dorado range from 6 to 20 pounds and the Hawaiians named it Mahi-mahi, meaning powerful in Hawaiian. We both had just enough fishing knowledge to cause some damage, but we were very well aware that to land a fish like this one needed patience. I reeled in my own line and set my rod down as I watched Michael battle with his prey. His muscles twitched and flexed as he worked the rod and I chuckled to myself thinking that poor fish has no idea who he is fighting.

Sooner than I expected, Michael told me to grab the long-handled net as he brought his line in, guiding the fish between the hulls. I laid down on the trampoline, leaned over and submerged the net. A minute or so later I was pulling what felt like a twelve or fifteen-pounder out of those clear waters. Michael snatched it from me and held it triumphantly over his head as he yelled out, "Dinner!" Quickly adding, "And lunch, and dinner!"

Indeed, it would be three to four meals of the tastiest fish in the area. It was rewarding to have to work a little bit to catch a fish like that. I watched as he grabbed the fish board and filleting knife and expertly cleaned the fish in record time so we could get it on ice.

When he was done, he triumphantly took a large fillet in each hand and said, "We're smokin' this baby." He had a huge grin on his face as he asked, "You DO have a way to smoke fish on this tub, don't you?"

I laughed back and answered, "I've got a wine cellar on this *tub,* do you really think I wouldn't have a smoker? Let's grab a couple of beers and head up to the salon."

Michael had a big smile, "It'll be good to get out of the sun for a bit too. You know, me being Canadian and all."

Everything cooled a bit as we moved under the protection of the fabric roof that helped to ward off the effects of the burning sun, the open sides allowing a soothing cooling breeze through. At some point, we both dozed off.

I stirred first and woke Michael up with, "How about another swim?"

As he stood and stretched, he replied, "Sounds good, let's go out the starboard side and avoid the touristy beach."

We had checked with the binoculars earlier and there was beach we could explore for a bit before swimming the mile and a half or so back to the boat. We both dove in and started swimming toward the shore, Michael kept trying to push the pace. Each time he would speed up a bit I would catch him and then move ahead a little. Apparently, our last *race* to the ladder was maybe a sore spot for him.

I was surprised at the speed at which we were now swimming. I know I could have overtaken him but figured it best to let him win this one. I was quite accustomed to managing the sometimes-fragile male ego and had no issue doing so to maintain the peace in this case.

We stood up on the sand at almost the same time and I looked at him and said, "Where exactly did you learn to swim like that in the great white North?"

He laughed at me, "There are lakes everywhere and even a couple of oceans you know."

I knew that, of course, thanks to my time in and around Halifax and other parts of the country. We wandered around the beach for a bit and then decided to race back to the boat. I had to push myself, but I was able to beat him by a few strokes. We high fived at the ladder.

"I'm starving, I sure hope you can actually smoke a fish," I chided him.

"Don't you worry about me. Remember, I'm the one who can cook," he answered with a laugh.

He was bang on with his assessment of his cooking prowess while I embraced my own lack of that skill. I can't honestly recall what he served with it, but it was some of the best fish I have ever tasted, and that says a lot. It was perfectly done and lightly smoked so that you could still taste the delicious flavor of the Dorado. Before we were even done eating, he said that provided we had the supplies, he would make us fish tacos for dinner tomorrow.

"You mean like Wahoo's fish tacos in Huntington Beach? Can you do their Baja fish taco sauce too," I asked with excitement, like a child begging for ice cream at the fair.

He raised his hands in front of him, his brow furrowing and eyes narrowing as he answered, "What do you think. Of course, I can make the sauce."

That kicked off a lengthy conversation about Huntington and that whole area of the west coast. As we chatted, we discovered that he enjoyed Huntington Beach just as much as I did. The same restaurants, lounging on the beach, surfing, and people watching from Duke's patio next to the sand. What I found even more humorous was when I mentioned my affinity for jumbo burritos from a place called Taco Lita in a small inland city called Arcadia. He knew exactly where I was talking about as he said how much he loved their hot sauce. I knew I was glad to have him as a friend and liked the fact that he was a lot like me, but for a moment, considered it odd that he was so well acquainted with two of my most favorite spots.

I mean, no surprise that he enjoyed Huntington Beach, but the burrito place was almost an hour inland and it was curious that he knew of it, even though he had never lived there. To my knowledge, it was one of those hangouts only the locals frequented.

That being said, Michael had an edge like Sonny but, other than wartimes, I felt I had much more in common with Michael. He had more diverse interests than Sonny and most would say Michael was more *worldly*. We had all travelled globally when we were operators, but Michael had clearly taken the time to be a tourist and explore, at least when we weren't fulfilling a usually deadly mission.

We lounged around and planned our next leg of the trip, most likely stopping at Huatulco which was 215 nautical miles away.

Chapter 6 – Let's Get Going

We both just laid around and did not much of anything. I glanced over a few times and saw his eyes drooping and head bobbing the same as mine.

"I suppose we should get some sleep so we're ready for tomorrow." It was more statement than question and we both stood at the same time and headed to our berths.

"See you in the morning," Michael said with a big yawn.

All I could muster was a "Yup," as I headed down the stairs on my side.

I crashed quickly and was in the middle of an excellent dream when I heard banging on the hull which caused me to shoot bolt upright. I quietly got out of my berth and was in full self-defence mode as I moved slowly out of my cabin, my eyes darting from spot to spot in case there was an intruder aboard. Michael was coming out of his room at the same time, and we made eye contact. I put my finger to my lips, pointing a V of two fingers at my eyes and then to the upper deck, the universal military, and police silent shorthand for *let's go take a look*. He nodded in agreement, and we moved silently up the gangway, our feet making no noise as we moved one step each at a time.

Michael scanned the stern while I looked toward the bow, he put his fingers to his eyes and then nodded his head no. We returned below and we heard the noise again and I recognized the haunting sounds of whales singing. We looked at each other and listened as I turned on the underwater microphones to bring the sounds to life. It was as if we were swimming alongside the very whales who were singing. They went from squeaking, high-pitched dolphin-like sounds to thunderous, deep growls and back to a clicking noise that seemed like sonar.

"That's amazing," I said to Michael, "There's no way those massive, majestic mammals are not actually talking to one another." I felt a kinship with them, the whole planet, and all the wonders of the sea, as their *talking* brought me a sense of calm, maybe even wonder.

Michael replied, "I love the way you try to see the good in everything," in a tone that seemed somewhere between admiration and sarcasm.

"Let's just listen a bit more," I pleaded.

"I'm going back to bed; I need my beauty sleep more than I need to hear whales, I think." He added a quick good night and disappeared back to his room leaving me again to wonder what he was keeping from me, the way he seemed to close himself off which told me there was something up.

The next morning began just like the ones before, the bright sun warming us quickly as it rose from its nocturnal hiding place. Being on my boat on mornings like these never ceased to bring me a feeling of contentment and anticipation for what such a beautiful day might bring. Michael boiled water and loaded the coffee press with freshly milled beans, soon after he delivered a perfect cup of coffee to complement our morning. We really were not in any particular rush to leave this spot.

We sipped our coffees slowly, taking time to savor it as the freshly crushed beans released their flavor along with the needed caffeine. We ended with a protein shake each and then felt the wind begin to move gently through the salon spreading that fantastic, fresh ocean smell. We prepared everything and then hauled anchor, the chain pulling the heavy sledge into its home and once again freeing us to the currents of the sea.

We continued on down the coast with stops offshore of Guatemala, Nicaragua, and a couple of days around Costa Rica. Finally, we were anchored at Panama City and making the various arrangements needed to traverse the canal, anxious to experience it. As we moved into the first of three locks that would lift us one portion of the ninety feet, it was daunting. We were guided into position and once we were tied off, a small container ship moved In behind us. As the massive steel gates slowly creaked closed, we could hear the pumps begin to inject hundreds of thousands of gallons of water into our chamber. We both looked up, our eyes travelling higher and higher up the smooth steel sides of the lock. They seemed to go on forever from this vantage point. The handlers actively worked the lines, as the water kept rushing into the lock from below, gradually raising us up to the level of entry of the next chamber. Once the water levels were equalized the massive front gates slowly swung open. The handlers eased us forward into the next lock, and everything was repeated once more.

As we finally exited the third lock, we were both amazed at the engineering and construction involved to connect these two oceans. We were thankful our agent had been able to book us a single day transit as when the final lock opened, we would be free to sail directly to Portobelo, Panama. The closest port is actually Colon but that is often home to many large ships that can cause traffic jams. Our agent also mentioned that there is a criminal element in Colon that preys on tourists and wealthy yachties. We were neither and were not in the least bit worried about criminals, but the possible aftermath of any skirmish concerned us. I had no idea how far South the cartels reached and there was nothing to be gained by taking chances. It was only about seventeen nautical miles from Colon to Portobelo, so it was no big deal anyway and would be an easy sail. We had scheduled to be in the Shelter Bay Marina, as I had heard it was the safest and best equipped marina in the area. I liked the idea of being in a completely protected marina, virtually isolated from the ocean. The seas could be rough around here, and I always opted for comfort and safety.

The next few days were somewhat anticlimactic for us, after experiencing the Panama Canal. It really was well worth the price of admission, one of the most amazing man-made things I have seen. It was obvious why it was designated as one of the Seven Wonders of the Modern World. Michael even said that the American Society of Civil Engineers had dubbed it a Monument of the Millenium.

Chapter 7 – Georgetown C I

Soon, we were easing our boat into the central marina in Georgetown on Grand Cayman, the capital of the Cayman Islands. Georgetown is the financial hub of the islands and gives the anonymity of the old Swiss Bank Account a real run for its money. I can't even imagine how much cash is stashed here, much of it legally hidden from the IRS's long tentacles.

Morning seemed to arrive early, and we were up and at it right along with the sun. I was already looking forward to the lively night life that made Georgetown so popular. We explored all over the main island and had a fun time wandering here and there. It seemed no matter the day or time there were always at least four or five cruise ships anchored in the serene Georgetown Harbor with a never-ending stream of cruisers pouring out of them like circus clowns emerging from Volkswagens.

We agreed that we needed a night out to sample the local food for which the area is known and had chosen the Caboose, a gourmet smokehouse. We had consumed a great deal of fish and both of us were excited to have some land food for a change, a nice thick steak perhaps. We left the boat, just as dark was beginning to fall, chatting about nothing in particular as we walked. We strolled around the harbor bathed in the golden light from the many restaurants and shops with the other tourists.

We closed in on the end of the waterfront area where we hailed a cab to the restaurant. We were both surprised when we entered the restaurant. It looked a bit like the wealthy Miami hot spots back in the fifties and sixties. Trendy, stainless-steel framed leather chairs and expensive, somewhat gaudy, fixtures that made it feel like an upscale restaurant one might find in Havana, New York, even Los Angeles. I suppose when you are catering to the wealthiest people in the world it was a benefit to give them a little something from home to make them comfortable. The place was packed with all kinds of people. Based on their dress I would say a mix of full timers, part timers, and others who simply go to visit their tax protected cash. The weather made the Caymans a desirable place to live full time if you had the means to do so and the need to stash your boatloads of cash safely out of reach of a greedy home government.

The waitress handed us each a beer menu. Michael thanked her and commented, "That is a LOT of beers. I take it Cayman Islands brewing is your main supplier?"

She shuffled her feet and grinned at us, "Gee, what makes you say that?" she laughed and added, "Actually they own the restaurant, so we really don't have a choice. But they are all really tasty."

We each ordered one and sipped on those frosty mugs as we perused the menu.

I spotted the photo and description of the smoked ribs and immediately began to salivate as if I hadn't eaten in days. Combined with the wafting, delicious smells coming from the smokehouse out back, I was more than ready to get messy. Michael ordered the same and in no time, we were both carving up racks of juicy ribs.

Almost in unison we said, "These are awesome ribs," as we each gnawed on our first, BBQ sauce dripping onto the plates.

"I'm surprised how much I missed meat," I added, as I savoured the smoky, BBQ flavor of the perfectly prepared ribs. We each ordered another beer as a group of four people were led past our table. The four guests walked like they owned the place, reeking of wealth and importance. They sat at a table close enough to us where we could overhear some of their discussions and, me being me, I couldn't help but tune in for a bit. I tilted my head and heard the man who appeared to be the leader say, "Well, that last outing was certainly promising for us. I think we have the boat and rigging to win big this season." The other three quickly agreed with nodding heads and *uh huh's* all round, cementing the fact that my guess was accurate.

I leaned over to Michael and whispered, "He is clearly an accomplished sailor, most likely racing yachts to fuel a massive ego."

I had used nothing but a few words and his appearance to pass judgement on the man. I considered my crass words, shook my head, and screwed up my face, "I need to stop making baseless assumptions about people. I hate that I do that."

Michael answered, "We all do that type of thing to some extent. In our business we often have to make those assumptions to stay alive."

I didn't like that part of me and decided I needed to work harder to change.

Our server dropped off our new beers as two men stormed into the restaurant, knocking a chair over as they went. They walked between our tables as they each pulled out a gun. I expected the weapons to be pointed at me, some sort of cartel retribution again, but they trained them on the people at the table next to us. I watched as the four of them slowly raised their hands, but the gunmen told everyone to put their hands on the table, "We're only interested in fat Tony here, the rest of you are just baggage."

He then reached into his jacket and pulled out three sets of handcuffs and tossed them on the table. He told the three to put them on, weaving their arms together to make it even more difficult for any of them to do anything. They told Tony to get to his feet and as they did Michael and I decided we were not going to sit idly by while a man was kidnapped or killed. We sprung into action simultaneously, knocking the guns out of their hands. They swung at us, hitting nothing but air. I chopped my guy hard in the throat before delivering another blow to the same spot and he crashed down to the floor, gasping for breath. In seconds, both men were face down on the floor, their guns kicked to the side, one bleeding profusely from his face, the other with his arm bent almost 90 degrees at the elbow, backwards. We found a handcuff key in one of their pockets and released the three left at their table, placing the handcuffs on the two criminals.

Tony turned and said, "Thank you, thank you. Who are you? Please let me reward you."

We smiled, "We don't need a reward, just happy to help," as if we had done something as simple as changing a flat tire for someone. He handed me a card and told us to get in contact as he would like us to be his guest for an evening.

We heard the screaming sirens and, before we even saw the police car pull up, we moved toward the back door. Many eyes in the restaurant were trying to appear nonchalant while stealing glimpses of us. Recognition was no good down here, so we did our best to hide our faces and get out of there. Once in the alley we moved quickly through the shadows to avoid any other confrontations.

"Well, I sure hope we didn't just save the life of a criminal mastermind," Michael said, trying to make light of the dangerous situation from which we had just escaped.

More seriously for us I added, "I just hope that nobody in the restaurant remembers what we look like. We don't need any extra eyes on us down here."

We made our way back to the marina using alleys and pathways, staying in the darkness as best we could. When we got back to the boat Michael said, "We should take him up on his offer, get an inside view of how the other half lives."

I chuckled and said, "We already know how the other half lives. You remember Jonathon, Luke, Kathy, and Angela, right?"

I needed to distract him, "Let's have a nightcap and think about it a bit," hoping he might forget by morning.

"Sounds good to me," Michael replied, as he grabbed us each a beer.

We really didn't discuss anything or make any decisions. We just sat, looked at the stars, and sipped our beers. We finished them and retired to the cabins for some sleep. As we lingered over our morning coffee, with some of the local cream liquor to spice it up, I finally gave in to Michael's pressure and dialed the number on the paper.

Surprisingly, it was answered, "You've got Tony, to whom am I speaking?"

"Hi, Tony, it's Megan here, from yesterday. You asked us to call."

He laughed as he replied, "Yes, yes, of course I know who it is. I don't often forget someone saving my life. I'm glad you called, are you two free for dinner this evening? If so, just let me now where you're staying, and I'll send a car."

I told him where we were moored and he laughed again, "You're right around the corner from my dock. I'll stroll over your way around six if that works for you both."

"Sounds like a great idea," I answered, trying to sound enthusiastic although feeling nothing of the sort. Situations like this always made me think there was an angle. What did this guy really want? Maybe the attempted kidnapping was faked by him? Geez, I really detested the way my mind worked sometimes, maybe he was just a nice guy wanting to thank us. I tried to focus on that point.

Shortly before six we heard a yell from the dock, "Permission to come aboard, Captain?"

I peered over the edge, gave him a big smile, and waved him up, "C'mon up sir, the bridge is open." I thought we would just grab Michael and leave but Tony was interested in having a closer look at the boat.

"I used to love sailing cats, great platform for blue water cruising. How long have you had her," he asked, genuinely interested.

"Only a couple of years, and it's the best investment I've ever made," not sure why I felt a need to use the word investment. I knew it was not an asset which would appreciate over time, but it was an investment to me. An investment in my own wellbeing and general state of mind. Like a service dog, a boat wouldn't cure PTSD, but I believed it could certainly help.

That led to a twenty-minute tour with Anthony making comment after comment that he was impressed. He kept insisting that we call him Tony, adding, "My friends call me fat Tony and, after saving my life, I certainly consider you friends."

I smiled as I chuckled about the moniker replying, "I'm sure there is some explanation why you are called fat Tony, that's obviously not the case."

The man looked close to anorexic he appeared so thin, although it was difficult to tell for certain because of how he was dressed. We finished the tour and he suggested we get to his boat so we can have an aperitif before dinner. We strolled side by side through the marina and as we rounded the corner, I saw it.

It had to be his, it was obviously a private dock and there was only the one boat there, one very impressive boat. As we walked towards the bow, I thought that it looked more like a state-of-the-art submarine than a sailing yacht. It looked to be at least two hundred feet in length and the gleaming, dark blue, ultra-smooth sides, raked slowly up from the rear towards a bow that had two headlights incorporated into her curves.

He smiled with obvious pride when he said, "There she is, that's my *Maasai*. 190 feet of fun I like to say." I was close in my two-hundred-foot estimate.

I immediately wondered about the name, "Where did you come up with that name?"

"I love Africa and I named her after the *Maasai* tribe in Kenya who are world renowned warriors."

"So, the *Maasai* is a warrior, is she?"

He smiled back at me, "We are both warriors."

We boarded her amidships, and ascended the gleaming, polished stainless-steel stairs, stepping onto the flawless teak decking that looked like it had just been polished. As I stepped onto the deck, I saw a bronze plaque stating it had been created by Dubois Naval Architects.

He saw me glance at the plaque, "Dubois Naval Architects are the Michelangelo of yacht designers," he said with a great deal of admiration in his voice.

Tony went on, "They built her exactly to my specifications enhanced by their own knowledge and engineering."

My eyes followed the main mast skyward as it reached higher and higher, seeming to almost touch the low-lying clouds. I had never seen a boat like this up close, much less boarded one. It had all the trappings of what I thought a fifty million dollar sailing yacht should have, including a crew that was easy on the eyes, both sexes.

A tall, blond, Slavic looking woman appeared carrying a tray filled with a reddish drink, the glasses dripping with condensation, "Ah, Ingrid, I see we have drinks for my new friends." She was a very striking woman, and I suddenly felt a bit like I was in a James Bond movie. I had long ago accepted my own body and was very comfortable in my skin but the old me would have been intimidated standing next to her, feeling like I was a little less. Not less as a human of course but less as a woman. I hated how those thoughts surfaced in my mind, my momentary lack of confidence throwing me for a loop. She asked if we would like a Negroni as she held out the tray, her muscle tone obvious as she steadied it easily with one hand.

Each of us took one and Tony saluted us as we all clinked glasses, "Thanks again to my newest friends for risking their lives to help me." Michael spoke for both of us, "It wasn't that big a deal, really."

Tony laughed, "Well, I certainly think it was a big deal. I might be dead if not for you two." He then directed us over to a teak dining table at the edge of the salon where the large, seamless curved glass panels had been opened to let in the evening. As I sank into the oversized, buttery soft leather chair and was enveloped in coziness, I thought maybe the *Amphitrite* could use a few minor upgrades after all.

"You must both have a great deal of training to remain so calm in such a situation." It did not seem rhetorical and felt more like a real question to me.

We just shrugged it off as I answered, "that was a prior life, long ago," hoping to prevent further enquiry, but he pressed on.

"Where are you two headed? Have you decided on a final destination, or just going where the winds might take you?"

I thought he was just making conversation.

"At the moment, we are thinking Halifax, Canada. I've been there a few times and have always wanted to return." I thought I was safe with that answer but was caught off guard when Tony responded anxiously.

"That's amazing, that is exactly where I am going," he said with a broad smile and high-pitched voice. He went on to explain that he was partners in a Canadian company, and he kept an office in Halifax to which he sailed two or three times a year.

"I love sailing across the Atlantic," quickly adding, "I could really use two companions like you on the journey, if you might be interested in joining me."

"Thanks very much for the offer but this is a vacation for us," I said with a look of polite apology.

Tony wrinkled up his face and his brow furrowed. His almost-glare told me he was quite used to getting precisely what he wanted, no matter what that was.

He pressed on, "I will pay you handsomely to make the trip. While my crew are not average, clearly you both are accomplished at keeping people safe, and that is precisely what I require."

I smiled back, "As I said, that was a past life for us."

Not giving up at all he added, "I'll pay you fifty thousand each."

Michael chimed in, "That's a lot of cash. What's your deal?"

"I've done things in my life of which I am not particularly proud and there are people who have taken umbrage to some of those things," he said that the way we handled ourselves we could replace his whole security team. He would be forever in our debt if we would agree to travel with him over and back.

"No promises, but Michael and I will talk about it later," although I really had no intention of seriously considering his offer.

I merely wanted to hold him off until we could come up with a solid reason to decline.

He responded, "No problem, I know it's a big ask, and thank you for even considering it."

We left not long after enjoying a perfectly prepared meal and started discussing as soon as we were out of earshot. Tony had offered a significant amount of money for each of us to take six weeks or so out of our vacation. When he explained his situation to us, he was a little shaky and not quite as confident as he had seemed earlier. It must be a serious situation, hence the bundle of cash.

I looked over at Michael, "Look, I don't want to sound like a total ass, but I really don't need any more money."

Michael replied, "I could really use that cash for a large renovation, and also to pay off a loan. That's a lot of money for me, life-changing really."

"Are we sure we want to do something like this, we have NO idea who this guy is." We didn't really know what he was about other than a couple of guys tried to kidnap him, and he was a wealthy guy who liked to sail. Not much to go on and certainly not enough to risk life and limb for a few shekels.

Michael smiled, "You had no idea who I really was and yet here we are sailing halfway round the world together."

I certainly did not want to disappoint Michael and if he was good with cutting into our supposed "non-working" vacation, then perhaps I could be.

When I began to think about it, I knew how much the Wounded Warrior project could use that much money. It could buy a lot of prosthetic limbs and give many veterans additional much-needed psychiatric support. I looked at it as a win-win with both my good friend Michael benefiting and being able to help out a lot of vets too. The average person has no idea what veterans go through when we eventually return home, we struggle to fit back in, fight against demons invisible to others. I decided I was in. We agreed to let Tony know first thing in the morning, but I would have a few more questions for him before we were all in.

When we got back to my boat, we packed up some bags, grabbed our weapons and a few other things and left them at the ready. I wasn`t sure what to do about the *Amphitrite* but was planning to go pay the marina the extra fees up front if we decided to go with him. We went for a run and stopped by the *Maasai* on the way. Tony spotted us rounding the corner and came down the gangplank to meet us.

"Well?" he asked, looking like an expectant child awaiting news on a trip to Disneyland.

"Maybe, but we have a few things that have been on our minds, Tony," I told him.

"And what might those things be," he asked, he seemed to be forcing it to sound casual.

I looked at him with a serious stare, "Who exactly were those people in the restaurant and what did they want?"

He tried, "Just some disgruntled ex-business partners who didn't like the way I work."

"We'll need a little more than that if we are going to accompany you on this trip, those guys were obviously serious, and they did not look like business partners." I was not about to risk my life just for money, whether Michael needed it or not.

A look of resignation crept over Tony's face, "Look, I've had some investment challenges and I think they were after something they thought I was going to sell."

"What are we talking here? Drugs? What?" as I banged my fist on the table.

Startled, Tony growled back condescendingly, "Do you really think I would be involved in buying or selling drugs?" He seemed genuinely upset that I had even suggested that.

"Well, we really have no idea what you're involved in other than what you have told us," Michael calmly replied adding, "I'm sure you can appreciate our concerns."

"Look, I need you two and I'm paying handsomely for your help. All I have with me is some papers and a couple of small cases of diamonds for my Halifax business. That is, it!"

"As long as we can take you at your word and you're not breaking any laws," I responded, doing nothing to disguise my concern.

He seemed to settle a bit and answered, "I can assure you everything is legitimate and legal. You'll see when we arrive in Halifax."

"Michael and I will need to discuss this in private first, if that's okay with you." I needed to find out where Michael's head was really at, how serious he was about this.

Tony quickly replied, "Of course it is, I know I'm asking a lot of you."

Michael and I went to the bow of the boat, away from prying ears, to discuss further.

Chapter 8 – Your Call

Michael and I stood at the bow, leaning on the rails, as we hashed through it all once again from start to finish.

I offered, "I'm good with whatever you want to do Michael. It will be nice for me to have more money to donate, but I don't need to do this."

Michael at first had a look of apology when he replied, "I kind of do, those loans are critical to me keeping the Heavenly Pie." There was a darkness in his eyes that briefly made me consider something else was going on, but I let it go figuring it was just me being me. The life I had led thus far caused me to have very genuine issues with trusting people.

I offered to just lend him the cash myself but was met with an emphatic, "That's not going to happen. I am not about to accept charity."

I shrugged my shoulders, "All right then, let's go tell him we're in." I still had some reservations, but I didn't want to disappoint Michael. We both walked back to the bridge where Tony was reviewing some charts.

"Okay, we'll do it," I said, and he burst into a huge smile before I added, "Any sniff of something dishonest and we leave immediately."

Tony nodded, "I understand what you're saying, and you have no worries."

Michael and I each shook his hand, "We're already all packed and our bags are back at the boat. We'll just go grab them. I'll have to pay the marina fees before we go."

"You will do no such thing. You can just move your boat to my slip," he said in an I'm-the-boss tone. "This dock is monitored 24/7 and two of my people are always nearby. Your boat will be very safe here."

"That's great" I answered.

"You can go finish up whatever you need to do and come over in the morning. We'll be anchored just offshore and can pick you up in the tender," he replied with another big grin.

"Thanks Tony, we'll bring the *Amphitrite* over in the morning then," I answered. I surprisingly got a good sleep that night and Michael was still out like a light when I began to move around the boat in the morning getting things ready.

When Michael finally surfaced, he apologized for sleeping in and I just chuckled, "I guess you needed your beauty sleep," quickly adding, "Although it sure didn't help much!" I hoped that I disguised my real thoughts well enough. Michael is a black Adonis, his dark skin accentuating how ripped he is. He looked like a cross between an NBA player, an NFL running back, and some sort of model. I noticed every time he moved around the deck those female crew members always kept a close eye on him.

We motored over in the still morning air, just a hint of color in the sky, and tied up at Tony's dock. All our fenders were deployed, everything was locked up tight, and we double tied both fore and aft.

I felt a bit like when I left her for the winter months back in Avalon, cover after cover to be put on to protect all the exposed seating and tables. Everything had to be either drained or topped up and I always wondered if I missed something, finding that feeling hard to shake. We grabbed our bags and tossed them onto the dock just as Tony pulled up in his tender. He greeted us with handshakes that seemed a little over the top to me, like one of those salesmen who is trying a little *too* hard to close the deal. We motored out to the *Maasai* and boarded, then watched one of the deckhands hooked the tender up to two crane lines. Each line was suspended from a beam, the tender moved slowly up out of the water and then the beams retracted, pulling the small craft into its spot inside the hull. Truly an impressive setup.

Tony joined us up on deck and took up his position at the starboard helm as the deckhands (tall, well sculpted men, boys really, who clearly knew their way around this boat) pulled in the heavy lines, laying them out meticulously on the deck. They wrapped them back and forth so they could be quickly re-deployed when required. Once the lines were stowed, they scurried around and pulled all the bumpers onto the deck. As we pulled away from the slip, Michael and I scanned the area all around us to ensure no other craft were following us. Force of habit, but it was never too soon to be aware of everything going on, especially after what we had witnessed at the restaurant. Soon, we were cutting through the waves easily as Tony brought the *Maasai* up to speed, one sail after another bellowed open and the winds propelled us forward.

It would take me a little time to get accustomed to being on a monohull again, they are considerably different than a multi-hull. I enjoyed the flat sailing of Catamarans, but these single hulls were always heeled over to one side or the other and you were often left clinging to the gunwales, or anything else solid to brace yourself. It was not a particularly comfortable feeling when you are not accustomed. When under sail, the ballast, which is the polar opposite to the top of the mast, was in a constant struggle with the large sails to maintain some semblance of equilibrium between the two forces. There was a lot of physics and math that went into the design of these to ensure they could remain stable even under the roughest conditions. As we caught a strong gust, I had to remind myself of that when the ship was suddenly heeled over even further, the gunwales lapping at the white-capped waves, while we held on tightly and braced ourselves against the movement.

I glanced over at Tony, his hands lazily resting on the large wheel, his gaze focussed far ahead, you couldn't even feel the minor adjustments that changed our direction slightly and produced more forward speed. He had an ear-to-ear grin as he looked at us and then back at the sails.

"She's a beautiful thing, isn't she, all the free power that nature can provide, one just needs to know how to best take advantage."

He was clearly in his element. I envied him that his only care in the world seemed to be navigating his craft. A feeling I aspired to experience myself but have yet to have.

2200 nautical miles ahead of us, Halifax seemed a distant dream but about ¼ of the distance less than crossing from Portsmouth, UK. We expected to be sailing for about nine days and would pass Turks & Caicos, New York, and Boston on our way to Halifax. Sailing the East Coast rewarded you with tremendous views, usually great weather this time of year, and excellent fishing, which made it quite popular a route with the nautical crowd.

After an hour, the sails weren't quite as full as they had been, sometimes flapping noisily, the trailing edge of the sails like bedsheets being blown about on a clothesline. I began to shed layers of clothing as the sun began to warm everything it touched. The deckhands removed their shirts and did their jobs only in shorts. They were powerful young men, strutting around like peacocks flexing their muscles. Not to be outdone, the female crew had changed into what looked like yoga gear. Their tight spandex shorts hugging every curve and muscle as if they had been painted on, cropped tops doing the same, the crew now appearing like a CrossFit convention. Not much later, Michael smiled at me and said, "When in Rome," as he pulled his own shirt over his head. The deckhands were all stealing sideways glances at him, a couple even exchanging looks, eyebrows raised while flexing their own muscles. Michael's dark skin contrasted against the backdrop of the stark white sail, his raw muscularity now on full display looking like a renaissance statue. That kind of definition comes only from a combination of serious training and needing to fight to stay alive under dangerous conditions. Gym muscles were for show, our bodies were both built and honed for survival, a much different type of power and much more practical. I recalled the first time I had seen Michael, the way he oozed quiet confidence as he strolled casually down the dock as if he owned it, not in a bad way, he was just assured. Tony doffed his shirt as well while standing at the helm, his eyes remained stoically fixed on the horizon as his powerful-looking arms steadied the large Captain's wheel.

Although more than twice the age of those deckhands, the 64-year-old Anthony Farnsworth was obviously in excellent shape. I watched him closely, admiring the ease with which he worked the helm to gently adjust the rudder. He was exceptionally lean with what I was certain was an almost too low body fat percentage. He looked powerful though, his sinewy muscles anchoring every move, twitching, and flexing as he applied pressure this way or that, exerting his control over the mighty craft. Tony's were neither gym muscles nor survival muscles, he was built the way he was for a different reason. His swimming background and all the sailing training had turned him into a very lean athletic machine. In a suit, one had absolutely no idea, he simply appeared to be a svelte businessman who had skipped too many meals. Rather than Arnold Schwarzenegger, he appeared more like Johnny Weissmuller, the original Tarzan, wiry with cat-like reflexes. Every muscle in his body had developed to help him excel at his chosen sports, it was quite obvious sailing was at the top of that list.

When I mentioned it later to him, he said, "When I was first racing, I started as a grinder." He certainly did not appear to have ever been a grinder. I wondered what else would be revealed about him during our trip.

With a look of surprise I replied, "Aren't grinders big, linebacker-type dudes?"

It was much easier to imagine Michael cranking the large winches that propelled the massive sails skyward, his much larger muscles and overall bulk easily handling the work.

Tony smiled back, "Sometimes it's more about technique than anything. One does not always need to be huge to be powerful." He didn't seem at all insulted and he kept his tone jovial, but I sensed something more. Just then I overheard one of the crew address him as Sir Tony. I had not heard him called that before.

"So, which is it - Fat Tony or Sir Tony? Is there anything else we need to know about Anthony Farnsworth?" I asked, as if we had been friends for years.

"Not much really, the whole knighthood thing is honorary, it's really not a big deal and somewhat embarrassing. Just as Sir Paul McCartney had been knighted for his music, I was knighted for sailing."

"Well, from my perspective, it's still quite an honor," I replied, as I recalled my own Trident ceremony when I became a SEAL, the sense of pride and accomplishment almost overwhelming at the time.

I wondered if he was being truthful about his own thoughts on the honor. He explained he had been a very accomplished international yacht racer and had raised quite a few trophies for his native England. He grinned as he told me about the pomp and circumstance of the actual ceremony of being knighted. He said watching the queen lift the broadsword and place it on each of his shoulders before resting it on his head, was a little bizarre.

"When I was in the ceremony, I imagined this being done in the medieval times of the late fifth century, the imposing King Arthur anointing me as a knight preparing for battle," he said, looking as if he could really see himself in those times. It seemed the knighthood business meant a little more to him than he originally let on.

"I can definitely see that Sir Tony," I said with a grin and an exaggerated bow of my head along with a half-hearted curtsy.

Of course, his battles were against the wind and the sea, which could be viewed in one moment as a battle, the next as a collaboration. This was nothing like the many life and death battles Sonny and I had faced, and Michael. Tony did speak fondly of that time in his life and grudgingly admitted what the knighthood really meant to him. Judging by the faraway look in his eyes and the respectful tone of his voice, I knew it meant a great deal more to him than he let on. That made complete sense, how could one be cavalier about receiving one of the highest honors from your country?

Over the coming days I would conclude that his relationship with the sleek, racing yacht we were currently enjoying was more symbiotic than anything, each entity anticipating the needs and wants of the other as they moved as one through the waves. He commented that he loved the way she responded to even his slightest touch as he feathered the controls, and the sails would adjust imperceptibly to extract a tiny bit more speed from the available winds. Tony always spoke of the *Maasai* in serious tones with a reverence usually reserved for deities or the love of one's life. I envied the connection he had to sailing, to his boat, made clear by his tone of admiration for her. This craft of his was not simply a very sleek and sexy amalgamation of fibreglass and titanium pushed along on massive gossamer wings, she was like a living entity, an extension of himself.

As we navigated our way Northward, I would come to learn a great deal more about, not only the *Maasai*, but also Sir Anthony Farnsworth.

"So," I asked, "What did you do before you had the means to just sail the world?"

He wistfully replied, "Well, in my younger days I was an underwater welder on North Sea oil rigs, one of the most dangerous jobs one can have on those rigs, or anywhere else for that matter, so it paid quite well, and I was able to save wisely."

I knew about underwater welders and how perilous their job could be.

Those folks were almost as unique as Navy SEALs, knowing the risks but doing the job anyway. I was surprised when Tony elaborated on his savings without being prompted.

"You asked how I acquired the means to sail and race and I'll tell you. I heard too many stories of rig workers in the ocean or the oilfields of Alberta or Saudi Arabia, who ended up almost penniless after squandering their earnings on frivolous possessions like trucks and boats. I invested almost every penny I made and in only a few years became the majority shareholder of a reasonably successful junior oil company."

I tilted my head and smiled at him, "How does one define a *reasonably successful junior oil company*?"

"Those shares are now valued at over nine hundred million USD, quite a chunk of change for an "ex-welder," wouldn't you say?" He wasn't bragging, his demeanor suggested he was simply stating a fact. I couldn't shake the feeling I got when he referred to himself in such a self-deprecating manner, it seemed completely at odds with who he appeared to be and how he sometimes behaved. He then leveraged that fortune into a partnership with a Canadian diamond producer and, right before that, an international security firm. When we found that out, I contemplated why he needed us, and I wondered what kind of trouble he was *really* in.

Our sixth day on the water began innocently enough, I hoped it would end in the same way.

Chapter 9 – Not Even Close

We sailed as the sun began to set for the sixth time, and I meandered down to my stateroom to shower and change. As I was pulling on my clothes, I heard a bit of a ruckus from the main deck. I peaked out the tiny porthole in my room and spotted one of those offshore boats bobbing up and down next to us.

"Shit! First the skiff from the stranded yacht, and now this," I mumbled to myself. My mind immediately went to the cartels, even though we were a long way from their base of operations. I grabbed my knife, and slipped it in the back of my shorts, as I prepared to go up on deck. I crept up the stairs at the bow as the bulk of the activity seemed to be stern and midships. I laid flat on the deck as I peaked around the corner and counted only two men, but noted each had an automatic weapon. Tony, Michael, and the crew were seated on one side of the cockpit, and I heard the man yelling, "Where is it. Tell me where it is, or I start shooting."

Tony replied, "We don't have anything on board. We're just on a trip to Canada. Please just let us go. You have the wrong people."

Tony appeared like he was having a casual conversation with friends in a bar, his look gave no clue to the danger we were in. He either had nerves of steel or there was much more to this than met the eye.

They did not look like typical cartel muscle so I assumed they might be just pirates. They didn't need to yell or scream, they looked menacing without saying a word, their faces wrinkled and mean, colored by too much time on the water. I became even more concerned when I observed what appeared to be a knowing glance from Tony towards one of the men. Was our new friend Tony involved with these guys, or was my imagination just a little too active? I crawled along the deck on the far side of the salon, slowly making my way toward the men. The boat was pitching side to side as the seas rolled so that would help me gain the upper hand. All I needed to do was give Michael a second or two, and I knew he could get to the one closest to him. I watched and waited as the back and forth continued between Tony and the gunman. Was I imagining the familiarity or was it real? I peeked around the corner and let Michael see me pointing to the one I would take. When the boat pitched, I jumped up and hit him hard on the side of his jaw with my forearm, knocking the gun out of his hands with my free arm. He didn't go down and took up a fighting stance as he turned towards me, staggering his legs for balance. I saw Michael deliver a kick to the head of the other guy while I went straight at mine. He went for my throat, but I was able to slip the punch and deliver a heavy blow down onto his forearm. I felt the crack, the man yelling out as the pain of his arm breaking registered in his tiny mind. I then spun beside him and hit him with a hard uppercut, and he was down and out.

Michael had already subdued his guy so we zip-tied them both, as Tony watched with a confused look. I had no idea why he would be confused; he had seen both of us in action in the restaurant.

Tony sent the crew below and in response to my questioning stare answered a little too quickly, "I have no idea what they're after."

He looked devious, like a child trying to avoid telling his parents the truth. I was certain he had not told us the whole story. His immediate response seeming rehearsed and disingenuous.

"Look Tony, we signed on to get you through this, get paid and then get out. I will ask again, have you got drugs on this boat?" I said, my whole body tensing as I stared at him.

"I definitely do not. As I already told you, why would I bother taking such a risk?" he asked, appearing genuinely insulted by the query.

As the three of us stood there, I said we had a few choices, "We can dump these clowns overboard, shoot them, or just set them adrift."

A look of concern mixed with fear crept over Tony's face as he added, "I don't think we should kill anyone. They only tried to rob us, not kill us."

I glared back, "All right, we'll do it the easy way then. Let's get them onto their boat, tied tightly, and put up the boater in distress flag."

Michael and I grabbed one, then the other, and dropped them onto their boat. Michael hopped onto their deck, and I watched as he ripped out their radio and tossed it overboard. He added more zip-ties to the two would-be crooks and scrambled back onto the *Maasai*. We unhooked the lines and set them adrift, then headed North. We both peppered Tony with questions before any of the crew came up top. Although we were not completely satisfied that he was being truthful we went along with him for now. We were still at least two days away from the port of Halifax, Tony rallied the crew and said we needed to get moving.

They scrambled around like robots performing various tasks, it was like seeing a well choreographed ballet as they each went about their duties while Tony manned the helm, barking out an order every now and then.

He looked over at us, "We're now at about the same parallel as Washington, DC, according to our instruments, so we should be able to get close to Boston today if the winds keep up."

Michael replied, "That would be great. I'm looking forward to getting to Halifax as soon as we can. How long are we expecting to be there?"

"Not more than four or five days, depending on the seas and winds," Tony replied, "and business needs of course."

That evening, as we sat around the teak table on the upper deck, we discussed all sorts of things, including security. I was now carrying my two Beretta pistols on me at all times. I was not about to bring a knife to a gunfight if it came to that.

Tony pointed at one and said, "You know you cannot have those in Canada, right. It's a felony if you get caught and you would be barred from entering."

I gave him a sarcastic smile as I replied, "Yes, I am aware of that. Don't worry, we'll stash them back where nobody will find them."

"What will Michael and me be doing while in port?" I asked him.

"Pretty basic, just keeping an eye on me and the boat," Tony answered.

"Is there anything else you want to share with us before we get there?" I asked, hoping there were no other curveballs. I was completely unsure what his concept of *pretty basic* meant.

He smiled as he said, "Nothing at all, I do this a few times a year and it should be routine."

He said he just wanted us with him as an extra precaution. Hmm, we were a very pricey *extra precaution* if that were indeed the case. We dropped anchor where we would have about a ten or twelve-hour sail into Halifax and everyone went down for the night, except for the crew member on anchor watch. Michael and I stayed up on deck a little longer, moving to the stern to get away from prying ears.

"Well, what do you think," I asked, "Are we in trouble here, or is this really just another operation as he claims?"

Michael replied with a concerned look, "I don't think we know the whole story yet, and I'm sure as hell not going to jail for this guy."

I lifted my foot onto the lower bar, leaned on the top one, staring out at the sea, "Not my goal either, big fella."

We went inside and reviewed the maps of where Tony's office was located in relation to where we would moor. We had detailed street maps and highlighted three different routes to travel the seven blocks from the mooring to his office.

Once that was complete, Michael looked me in the eye and said, "I need to share something with you that I think you need to know."

"Sounds serious," I said, as I tried to make light of it, hoping he really would open up if I played it casual.

"We've shared a lot about our prior lives and other things, but there's something else about my brother that I haven't told you. I need you to promise me that no matter what I tell you, it will stay between us," he had that look people get when you're telling someone a relative just died.

Okay, now I was concerned about what he was about to share, but replied, "Of course, almost everything we discuss needs to stay between us. I get that."

He crossed his arms and began, "I told you that my brother was killed during a traffic stop, but I didn't tell you that the officer who caused his death is also dead."

"No loss there, I'm sure," understanding exactly where he was coming from.

"There's a little more to the story," he added, his head dropping and mouth drooping. Then, "I thought I was ready to talk about this, but I guess I'm not. Can we restart this chat some other time?"

I wanted to shake him and ask, what did you do? What the hell did you do? Instead, I offered, "Of course, whenever you're ready," making sure I sounded as relaxed as I could.

He didn't seem to be looking for anything other than understanding and patience right now, so I chose not to add anything nor discuss what Norie and I had worked on.

My own revelation could wait for some other time too.

Chapter Ten – Back in Halifax

We enjoyed the good times, weathered the not-so-good, and after our encounter with the pirates, we finally arrived at the port of Halifax. I was extremely impressed with Tony's sailing skills and that of his crew. They worked together like a well-oiled machine and were fun to watch, they had clearly been together for a long time. Rather than simply look on in admiration, I had to remind myself they were all probably involved in whatever Tony was really doing.

The Halifax harbor had not changed much since my last visit here, except for one or two more waterfront condo buildings. Michael and I watched as the crew began to drop the sails, Tony at the helm directing the oft-repeated dance. The powerful diesel motor roared to life as we moved slowly toward a slip right at the edge of downtown. It was not so much a boat slip as it was a large jetty out into the harbor. Halifax is one of the largest and deepest ice-free natural harbors in the world, so it attracted cruise ships to tiny day sailers, and everything in between. It is certainly not the largest waterfront in the world, even in North America, but it has a great character all its own with shops and restaurants running from end to end along the boardwalk. Michael and I watched as Tony skilfully manoeuvred the massive boat, ever-so-gently cozying it up against the dock. This was about the only spot the *Maasai* could fit, except of course the Canadian Navy docks, where there were a few of their corvettes tied up.

I was a bit of a Navy buff, and I knew the Canadian Navy corvettes were just about the same size as the *Maasai*. They were fast little craft whose numbers during the war elevated the Canadian

Navy to the status of third largest in the world. I loved Naval history; it has always fascinated me.

Curious onlookers began to gather as the crew locked in the lines and secured the massive craft against the gentle movement of the tides.

Tony came up top and said, "I always treat the crew to a nice dinner after this sail. Let's change and head out. I assume you're both hungry."

Michael replied for us both, "We're always hungry after a day like that."

Soon we were all walking down the almost three-kilometre-long boardwalk, chatting about all kinds of things. Seagulls squawked overhead as mothers pushed prams, and kids shot past on bikes and scooters, shrieking as they struggled to stay upright. There was a real mix of shops and restaurants, each eatery with its own strong and alluring smell and Tony seemed to have a comment on each one that we passed.

"The food at The Bicycle Thief is just superb, the oysters at Shuck are the best down here." He pointed up a street and said, "There's my favorite Irish pub, The Triangle, great folks, great music, and great food and drink." He kept up the running commentary until we turned a corner next to a large outdoor patio set back about eight feet from the edge of the water. As I read the sign, Pickford & Black, a gentlemen came out of the doors smiling in deference, his hand already reaching out to grasp Tony's.

"Ah Mr. Farnsworth, it's a real pleasure to see you again," the man said with the demeanor of an over-eager store clerk.

Tony smiled like he was greeting an old friend, "It's great to be back Georges," as he shook the man's hand. Georges led our group through the restaurant and around a corner to a private room with a perfect view of the water. You could even see the 246-foot-high mast of the *Maasai* out the side window, wavering gently from side to side. I figured that was why Tony probably liked this spot for these dinners, keep an eye on his baby.

Tony looked around the table and said, "If anyone doesn't like raw or cooked fish, let me know now and we can tell the chef. Otherwise, they will simply begin bringing us the food."

Everyone agreed, and when our server came, Tony ordered, "Four bottles of Tidal Bay from Grand Pre Vineyards, please." As we waited for the wine and the glasses, Tony explained that Tidal Bay is a wine unique to Nova Scotia. The server placed one glass on the table in front of Tony while a second person held the remaining glasses. She expertly eased the cork out of the bottle and poured an ounce or two into Tony's glass. He swirled it, held it up to the light, and then inhaled deeply from the mouth of the glass. Finally, he took a tiny sip, swished it in his mouth and then broke into a smile.

"That's perfect, please pour for everyone."

In no time we each had a glass and were hoisting them in the air where Tony slowly moved his glass around to touch each one of ours as he toasted, "Thanks again for all your hard work and another wonderful sail, and a special thanks to our new friends, Megan and Michael."

I replied, "It's been a real pleasure working with all of you," although it had already been far more work than pleasure. I too could play his game of fake.

We sipped our wine as the food began to arrive. Fresh shucked oysters were followed by the best Sushi I have ever tasted. Once that was done, the servers brought two large serving plates loaded with fish and veggies. We dug in and ate like royalty. When we were all done, our server brought a bottle of grappa and a bottle of Canadian Ice Wine along with a tray full of Crème Brulé and Tiramisu. We sat like one big family as Tony regaled us with stories while we drank our drinks and leisurely nibbled at the desserts.

Darkness began to slowly descend on the harbor as we stepped out of the restaurant. We all walked back toward the *Maasai* to settle in for the night and it seemed the longer we were here the more Tony seemed like a native Haligonian and not a brit. There were others along the walk who seemed to know him just as well as the fellow at the restaurant. As we got to the boarding stairs, the crew led the way and Tony suggested me and Michael join him upstairs for a nightcap.

It was a warm, typically humid, evening in Halifax and even on the water we didn't need jackets or anything. Tony suggested a bottle of Volnay and we both readily agreed. Thanks to Jonathon and Luke, I had learned a great deal about wines and, knowing Tony's status, I was certain this would be no fifty-dollar bottle. Tony disappeared briefly and then returned, carrying three glasses and the wine.

He set down the glasses, pulled a corkscrew from his pocket like a Sommelier announcing, "This is one of my most favorite wines," as he skillfully extracted the cork.

Even as I began to say the words, I felt a bit pretentious," Yes, I have heard the Dominique Laurent Clos des Chenes is a wonderful wine."

Tony replied, "I'm glad you are someone who appreciates such a bottle."

Michael chimed in, "I just hope it's not wasted on my palate which is clearly nowhere near as educated as yours." There it was again, Michael being so skilled at relating to people, disarming them with his wit.

Tony smiled back, "Education means little, wine is about appreciation, savoring everything the winemaker has put into it," as he poured into each glass. I knew there were more expensive vintages and wineries producing Volnay, some up to $7,000 per bottle. This one was much more reasonable at around $1,000, if you consider a thousand dollars a *reasonable* price for a single bottle of wine. We let it breathe for a few minutes and watched as Tony began to gently swirl his glass, tipping it sideways and holding it up to the light. We mimicked Tony and brought our glasses to our lips at the same time, each of us taking a small sip after inhaling the bouquet of such a special bottle.

I wondered if this was just Tony or was he putting on a show for us. As we enjoyed our treat Tony began to talk about the next few days.

"Look, I know you have your pistols with you, but I think you need to stash them on the boat like I asked. As I said, just carrying one in this country is a felony and I don't have any get out of jail free cards here," he said, pursing his lips and shaking his head.

"I know, I know, we will get them hidden tonight," I answered. Did he think we were idiots or something? Michael is a Canadian and we both served in the military so were well aware of the laws here. Why was he so concerned about whether we were packing or not?

Tony continued, "We should leave the boat no later than 6:00 AM as we will be carrying the two cases with us. I don't want to take any chances, even with you two here, better to move before sunup."

Michael replied, "No worries, we will be ready to go whenever you need us. If it's oh-six hundred you want, it is oh-six hundred you'll get. Is there anything else we need to know?"

Tony replied looking more serious, "I can't stress how careful we need to be here. There is a great deal riding on this for me."

"We understand completely and will be on high alert," I answered quickly.

I was wary of Tony's escalating concern. After all, if everything was legitimate, and this visit was a secret, then what would we have to worry about?

We finished the bottle and retired to our berths to get a good night's sleep, hopefully. Although the boat had A/C, I preferred to sleep with my window open so was thankful there was a large porthole that opened in my room. I locked it open and crawled into the cushy bed.

My watch was on the charger across the room, so I had no idea what time it was when I was awakened by voices on the dock. When I recognized Tony's voice as one of them, I moved closer to the porthole so I could eavesdrop. They were standing close enough to the lone light on the dock that I knew I would be able to recognize those two guys if I saw them again. Tony glared at them, "Look, I don't care what you think you have on me, we are not changing the plan," as he poked his finger into one guy's chest. One of the other two put his hand on Tony's shoulder replying condescendingly, "It doesn't really matter what you think now does it, Sir Tony," clearly mocking the title.

The other said, "You will do what we want, one way or another." I could hear the menacing tone of the man's voice and see the disdain on his face. The conversation continued as they began walking away from the boat, but I couldn't make out anything else.

I slept fitfully as I considered what I had seen and heard, wondering whose footsteps I had heard on the deck above as Tony was out on the dock. I rolled the conversation and the look of those guys in my head over and over which did nothing to help me sleep.

Chapter Eleven – Diamond Mining is a Tough Game

I knew I had to speak to Michael before morning, so I sent him a text suggesting we go for a run at five AM. I then texted Tony, letting him know we would be back on the boat by five-thirty, after a short morning run. My tossing and turning made five in the morning seem way too early, but I was anxious to talk to Michael. I awoke and quickly dressed in the darkness and then went out to the dock to warm up a bit and wait. I glanced at my watch and noted it was 4:55 when Michael stepped off the gangplank from the boat. There was a slight chill in the air and the heavy fog that was typical of this hour shrouded the waterfront making it appear like one of those old school horror movies. We began a slow jog down the boardwalk, not speaking until we were well out of sight of the *Maasai*.

We stopped once out of sight of the boat and I turned to Michael, "I think we have a problem."

"What might that be?" he asked, his tone mimicking how a person might speak to a child.

I began slowly, "Remember how you said that we didn't really know this guy and you had some concerns? It appears you may have been right. I woke up last night and saw Tony on the dock talking to two guys and nobody looked too friendly. I overheard one of the men saying that Tony would do what they want, or else."

"Really, that sounds ominous. Were you able to catch anything else they discussed?" Michael asked.

"That's the problem, they were out of earshot when the conversation continued. I just wanted you to know there was something more up, so we need to watch ourselves, " I reiterated.

"Always," was his simple reply, along with a wry smile. There was something odd about his response, something I couldn't quite put my finger on. We got back to running so our morning tour would not send up any red flags. We went pretty hard to ensure we worked up a sweat so the ruse would be convincing in case we ran into anyone. We got back to the boat on time and changed quickly. Tony joined us at the dining table in the salon and had a breakfast of toast and a protein shake.

Tony looked up at us like a CEO talking to his direct reports, "We cannot make any mistakes on this transfer, so please be fully aware," his tone oozing arrogance and poor management skills.

I glared back at him, my face scrunched up, eyes narrowed, "You will have nothing but our best Tony, no need to worry."

He smiled back, "I stay wealthy because I do worry."

Yeah, yeah, I get it, I thought to myself, you're rich.

He pointed at the two backpacks on the seat across from the table and said, "Guard those with your lives." A couple of black tattered backpacks hardly looked worth a life, but we had no idea how many diamonds were in them, or if there was anything else inside. Michael and I took a bag each and the three of us moved toward the stairs.

Tony turned and said, "I hired someone else to help, he will walk with us." He saw the concerned look on my face and added, "He is an ex-RCMP officer, and also a lawyer, which enabled him to get a concealed carry permit easily. Better safe than sorry, I always say." I didn't care who this guy was, I was not a fan of last-minute changes.

As we descended the slippery steps to the deserted dock, I got a good glimpse of the man's face and was shocked when I recognized it was one of the guys from last night. My gut told me we should call the whole thing off, but I wanted to see how it played out. We needed to find out what was going on here and what Tony was really involved in. Michael led the way with Tony and his guy walking together, while I was bringing up the rear. Michael and I scanned everywhere around us, including the many balconies above the street. There was nothing but the eerie, fog-shrouded glow of the streetlights making the whole scene seem a little other-worldly. The condos and apartments lining our route were all dark, the occupants no doubt still snug in their beds, making me wish I was still curled up in mine. It was like the whole city was still asleep. I kept a close eye on the new guy just in case the plan they talked about was already in motion. I had been wracking my brain to make sense of what I had heard them discussing on the dock but made no progress. Michael led us around a corner into an alley and the man suddenly stepped away from us, pulling out a large calibre pistol from his jacket and aiming it at Tony's head.

"That's it, everybody against the wall and don't move a muscle," he barked.

It felt like we were in some low budget film noire detective movie for a moment, but that weapon was obviously no prop.

"Take it easy, take it easy," Tony quickly replied. "Look, I said there's no need to do this."

"Everyone get on your knees and cross your ankles, or I start shooting," he growled at us as I heard the click of a round in the chamber. Some *extra protection* this clown turned out to be I thought, berating myself for not acting right away. We all did as he asked. I saw no way out of this without endangering everyone.

"You two, remove those backpacks and toss them out in the middle of the alley. NOW," he added when we didn't move as quickly as he wished. He was smart enough to keep his distance, but I wondered how he was planning to get away. He grabbed both bags and then backed up towards the street keeping the gun trained on us. A black sedan screeched to a stop behind him, the door swung open, and he was gone. Tony pulled out his phone and called the police.

While we were waiting, he turned to us and said, "You need to just say we were robbed at gunpoint. Nothing else. I'll explain everything later."

"Neither of us can afford to get caught lying to the police here, Tony," I replied, staring straight at him.

"Don't worry, I'll take of everything, and both of you. Besides, you won't be lying. We *were* robbed at gunpoint," stating the obvious.

I glared at him with a look you would give to someone you're about to crush in a fight, "We are not going to jail for you, that was never part of the deal."

Tony pleaded with us, "Nobody is going to jail, but I need you to do as I ask, my life depends on it, maybe yours too."

I nodded my head at Michael, thinking about some of the things I had done since leaving active duty, contemplating what I might have to do here. At least I would have been indemnified for most of what I had done while operating, but that was not the case for things after that. From what Norie and I had done to Bobby, to some other stuff, there was a great deal for which I could be prosecuted. Those thoughts alone should have given me cause for concern, but they didn't. I supposed a normal person would have been scared to death about rotting in a prison somewhere, but I was as far away from normal as one could get.

The police arrived quickly and soon each of us was in a different squad car. I thought that a bit odd considering we were the victims here. It was even stranger when they suggested that we go down to the station to file a report. Again, not typical. They had all the information they needed, and I knew we were not offering any kind of description, but it didn't seem like we had a choice. We were only in the cars briefly as the police station was quite close to where we were. I was led to an interview room, a space reserved for criminals and not victims, where the officer began to ask about my background. What was I doing in Canada? How did I know Mr. Farnsworth?

He asked many other questions that indicated Tony may not be the legitimate businessman he portrayed himself to be. There also seemed to be a disturbing familiarity with good old Sir Tony.

I looked at the officer, "Do I need a lawyer here, or am I free to go? It was us who were the victims you know."

"Just stay out of trouble and watch who you associate with," he said in a very pleasant tone, as if we had just been guests in his home. After about an hour, the three of us were released.

As we stepped out of the station Tony turned to us and said, "My office is only three blocks from here, let's just walk. We can talk about this when we get there."

I scowled back, "We certainly will." I felt myself losing patience and that was never a good thing, especially for those at whom my anger might be directed. I was only doing this to help Michael, he really needed the money, but my patience and commitment were wearing thin.

The three of us walked the short distance in silence. Tony led us to the elevator and said, "I'll tell you everything once we are upstairs."

Everyone along our walk from the elevator had something to say to Tony.

"Good morning, Mr. Farnsworth," said a young, attractive blond with a glint in her eye and an obvious connection.

"Welcome back, Mr. Farnsworth," this time a brunette, also easy on the eyes.

"Great to see you again, Tony," said a man who looked like your basic middle management type.

Finally, Tony put his eye to an access panel, I heard his office door unlock, and he pointed over to a table surrounded by four chairs.

"Look guys, I know I have a lot of explaining to do. I'll tell you everything in due course," he said as we each settled into a chair.

"Suffice it to say I am in a bit of a financial jam at the moment," he was speaking more like a friend than an employer now, a tired old management ploy to try to gain acceptance.

"Such as," I said, ignoring his tone, my elbows on the table fingers interlocked and body leaning in.

His gaze dropped, his face sagging as he spoke, "Well, the gist of it is I had some significant investments go south on me and I have had to make some difficult decisions."

"I bet you did," Michael said, the cynical look on his face adding to the sarcastic tone of his voice.

A knock sounded on the door and Tony's demeanor suggested he knew who was on the other side. He walked over and opened it, letting the man who had robbed us step through.

As the door closed, he looked at us smiling, "I bet you're surprised to see me, aren't you?"

"Not really," I replied matter-of-factly. He kind of struck me a bit like that old Canadian kids show comedy actor, Dudley Do-Right, the goofy RCMP officer everyone loved.

I did my best to disguise the fact it was taking everything I had to not grab him and choke the life out of the little turd.

Tony looked at the man, "Just sit down and shut up. Are those the cases?" Tony said, pointing to the small duffle bag the man was carrying.

"What do you think, big shot," he scowled back at him.

"Great, be on your way then. I'll be in touch," Tony replied, back to sounding like a boss, or at least trying to sound like a boss.

"Make sure you are, or there will be hell to pay," the man replied, pointing his finger at Tony like a mock gun, clicking his thumb down to make sure there was no confusion.

Tony sat down at the table with us, folded his hands in front of him and, with a look of resignation, began to spill the story. A combination of risky investments, gambling debts, and some other more minor situations had pushed him to the edge of bankruptcy. If he did declare bankruptcy, his ex-wife would get full ownership of the diamond mines and business and he would do anything to prevent that happening.

"I know I wasn't completely honest with you, but I really needed your help. If you are willing to stay, I will double the amount I am paying you once this is all settled," he pleaded.

I leaned back in my chair, crossing my arms as I responded, "Or maybe we'll just go back to the police and tell them everything."

Tony shook his head no, "I'd advise against that. They know me quite well here, and if you admit to lying in your interviews, you will be the ones in jail not I."

I knew he had us, but it didn't mean I had to like it. "What else is going on?" A smile crept across his face, "It's quite simple really. Those two backpacks you were carrying contained millions in diamonds, blood diamonds actually. My insurance company will pay up quickly and I will still have the diamonds plus millions in cash."

"You, sonofabitch," I yelled at him. "I knew you were up to something more," I growled back, slamming my fist down hard on the table.

Michael glared at him," What's to stop of us from getting rid of you right now?"

Tony smiled smugly at Michael, "the video of you two apparently killing those pirates and my partners knowledge that you two were involved."

"You lousy prick," Michael spat back, "Almost a billion isn't enough cash for you?"

Tony very calmly explained, "Once everything gets settled, you two will accompany me back to the Caymans where I will safely salt away a boatload of cash after I pay you what I owe you. Now, good night," he said, dismissing us as if we were just crew.

I sensed he was hiding something else, that even this was not the whole story.

Later in the evening when we were alone on the top deck, I confronted Michael, "What the hell, I only did this to help bail you out and now we're in deep shit. Do you know something I don't?"

"Look, I'm sorry I got myself in trouble and involved you, but I really need this cash. I cannot lose my Aunt's restaurant." He had a look of desperation that I had not yet seen from him.

"I've heard enough," I said as I got up and walked down to my quarters, locking the door behind me. Now I felt that there were two people hiding things from me, something I certainly never expected from Michael.

I wondered again if I had trusted Michael too soon, trusted him too much. Now I would have that thought rolling around in my mind, causing me to question my judgement. The same judgement that had kept me alive in so many dangerous situations had perhaps failed me not once, but now twice.

I sure wish Sonny was here, I knew I could trust him with anything.

Chapter Twelve – Waiting

In the morning, as Michael and I took a long slow walk away from the *Maasai*, we commiserated with each other on our collective poor judgement. As mad as I was at Tony, I was also pretty pissed at Michael. He just stared straight ahead the whole time, "Well, that wasn't much fun, was it."

"I have to agree with you there. Obviously, there's much more going on here. Any thoughts?" I asked. I truly hoped that Michael might clarify a few things on this whole situation. I felt I needed to give him that chance.

"I really have no idea at the moment, could be just about anything. Debts and mistakes can make people do strange things," he shrugged.

"I suppose the question is how we want to find out the real story. You and I have both gotten information out of way tougher people than our new friend, Fat Tony," I said gripping my fist with my other hand.

Michael, being the voice of reason, replied, "I don't think we want to get too carried away. My worry is us somehow being implicated in whatever else he has going on. If he really does have video of us, that's a huge concern." I kicked at the stones that had made their way onto the waterfront path while I tried to focus my thoughts, watching them bouncing along the asphalt offering some distraction that I hoped would help. I had come to no other conclusions by the time we arrived back at the boat, and I suggested a run along the waterfront and out to Point Pleasant Park, an urban oasis at the edge of downtown Halifax with all kinds of trails.

Michael readily agreed. Soon we were running along the waterfront boardwalk stealing glances of the sea as it grazed the massive posts. The harbor was relatively calm and what little wind there was helped to cool us down, it was ideal running weather. I knew that Michael was as deep in his thoughts as I in mine and the rhythmic pounding of my shoes slowly carried me into that zone where everything became clearer. There were no words exchanged as I focused on my breathing and my cadence, willing myself into a state of calm. Michael seemed to be doing the same. After a few kilometres, we transitioned onto the softer gravelled paths that wind throughout the harborside park. I spotted a large, stone monument of some sort about a kilometre ahead and suggested a little sprint.

"On three, buddy, no sneaky head starts this time," I laughed.

Michael said of course, and began, "1 – 2 – 3, GO," and off we went. We were stride for stride for the first half of the distance, but I began to pull ahead slightly. When I did, I really put the hammer down. My head steady, as if on a wire, legs pumping like pistons, body upright and calm, I was flying and felt like Usain Bolt must have in the Olympics. Michael did close the gap, but I was still a full stride ahead as we reached the imaginary finish line at the large granite statue. As we stretched and cooled down at the war monument, my thoughts went to my Father and Grandad, both veterans of war.

Michael looked at me and asked, "What's going on in that head of yours now?"

"Just family stuff. My Father was a Navy man. He saw some pretty terrible things in the war but came home relatively unaffected," I wished I could say the same for myself.

Michael replied, "Yeah, I think I knew that about you. Sounds like he was a pretty great guy. Was your Grandad a Navy man too," he asked.

"No, my Grandfather was a sniper in the Army. A real star too. They even did a big article on him in the newspaper called, *Old*

Soldiers Don't Just Fade Away. I always admired the fact that although he was a very proficient, highly decorated, sniper who was the go-to guy in his regiment, he didn't let what he had to do in the army affect him later in life."

"Sounds like a great man too," Michael said with a look of melancholy.

"He truly was, and one of the nicest men I have ever known. I try to emulate his attitude to help me get past all the things people like you and I have to do for the greater good," I felt like I was apologizing for doing my job again, I hated that feeling. Why should soldiers like us have to apologize for keeping the rest of the world safe from tyranny.

"I wish our vets today could come back and not suffer from PTSD or all the rest of the crap they get subjected to," Michael said. His tone made me think he was intimately familiar with that challenge.

I replied, "Yeah, that would sure be great. Or no war at all would be even better, but I don't think we'll ever see that day."

We sat on the bank, and I tried to ignore the dampness of the ground seeping through my clothes, chilling my skin, adding to the coldness I felt in my heart at the moment as I contemplated war.

I watched duck after duck dive beneath the water's surface in search of food. Each time one dove concentric rings of water spread larger and larger from that spot, and their heads would soon reappear in exactly the same location as if they were on a string. I could watch them for hours, but the chill was now working its way into my bones.

I looked over at Michael, "Let's get going."

We retraced our path back to the boat, no racing this time. I really enjoyed this waterfront and the way it isn't as crowded as so many others are. As I considered my own musings, I waited for any additional explanation from Michael, but none came.

We approached the boat and I said to Michael, "Let's relax, have a bite and see what we can figure out."

"Sounds like a plan," he answered, as we each grabbed a water from the outdoor fridge.

Chapter Thirteen – What's The Deal?

We spent the balance of the afternoon just hanging around on the boat. We used the well-equipped onboard gym mid afternoon, and then went up to the sun deck to sit and ponder. The staff were nowhere to be seen, likely all on a break for the afternoon, so we spoke freely. We quizzed each other on our thoughts and what else we thought Tony might be up to. Nothing really plausible came out of our discussion, but we did agree to build a solid backstory for ourselves and track everything in case Tony did go down. After what we had both been through in our lives, neither of us was about to let what should have been a simple escort job bring us down. I promised myself to seriously consider why I actually accepted this job in the first place. How had I been so easily influenced by Michael? Going along for the sake of going along was not something I had really done before, except maybe with that scumbag Bobby.

The shadows began to stretch out longer and longer, the sun beginning its daily descent, when Tony arrived back on the boat about a half hour after all the staff returned. Michael and I had come up with precious little, so we were anxious to see what we could get out of Tony. Tony stepped onto the deck, went straight to the fridge, and grabbed three cans of Keith's Pale Ale, a locally brewed favourite of which he seemed quite enamored.

"Well, have you both settled into the situation yet?" Tony enquired, as he took a big gulp of the ice-cold beer.

"I suppose we have, although reluctantly," I replied honestly.

Tony looked at us apologetically, "I'm sorry I had to put you in that position, but I really had no choice. I never thought I would find myself in this circumstance."

Michael said, "I suppose none of us can predict what will happen."

It felt like he took Tony's side a little too quickly, I knew I needed to push harder, "Look we are going along with what you've done so far, but we need the whole story or we're out."

Tony took a slow sip of his beer and looked at us, "I know you two are tough and all that sort of thing, but I'm desperate and you never want to corner a desperate man, do you?"

"We're a little more than just tough, Tony. I can't speak for Michael, but I have killed more people than I care to remember, in more ways than you could ever imagine. I will say this one last time, *we* are not the people you want to cross," I added, as I tilted my head and stared him down, hoping he was picking up on the calm rage that I felt.

Tony seemed a little exasperated when he answered, "Yes, I am well aware that one of you could easily kill me and the whole rest of the crew. You should both know that I have fully documented everything you have done so far, including your involvement in my insurance game. If anything at all happens to me, you will both go down too. Please don't be upset, I needed some insurance you would see this through to the end."

I looked over at him, unable to disguise my rage now as I felt my cheeks flush, "You had better make sure you know what you're doing, Sir Tony."

"Seeing as how you have covered your own ass quite well, why not let us in on the whole story?"

He answered with a sarcastic tone, "I suppose there's little that can happen now. There is indeed much more to this than simple insurance fraud." "Well, thanks for the tip," I replied, feigning surprise.

"Well, it's like this. Those *stolen* diamonds will be given new serial numbers and then sold as Canadian Fire & Ice diamonds," he said as if he was speaking about a simple, legitimate task.

"What's the point of that?" Michael asked.

"Thanks to my diamond mine and distribution business in Canada, those diamonds will increase ten times in value when I *convert* them. It's not all that difficult a task and I'm not really harming anyone," Tony explained.

"Tell yourself that all you want, but conflict diamonds carry a huge personal impact for the people in those countries," I chastised him. I knew whenever someone said something like that it typically means there is a lot more harm happening than meets the eye. People like him try to play down what really happens to assuage their own guilt.

Tony cautioned, "Everyone seems to think they have the high moral ground but, in today's world, there is no such thing. Everyone is out for themselves; high moral ground eroded away into nothingness long ago."

That was where I thought it ended.

I couldn't imagine there being any revelation to top what he had just told us. When it was time to turn in, I informed Tony that Michael and I were going to need a run in the morning and a little workout. He said he didn't need us until ten AM so that would not be a problem.

I again slept fitfully, tossing, and turning most of the night, unable to settle my mind and come to grips with this latest information. Luckily, I was trained to operate at 100% with little sleep anyway. I hoped Michael was in the same boat and, like me, couldn't wait until morning. I supposed we could have just snuck up on deck to talk, but it was best not to under the current circumstances. We needed to work through this to protect ourselves and it would be best to keep our deliberations private. Not only that, my newfound concerns with Michael and his true motivations would require me to be extra wary. I hated this feeling of not having complete trust in someone with whom I was working.

When morning finally arrived, Michael was waiting for me up on deck. We scrambled down the stairs and got moving. I knew there would be no calmness, no Zen-like zone on this run as we got up to speed. We were alone as we pounded along the path so we could talk freely while maintaining a good pace. I had so many concerns now, not only what Michael was holding back from me, but also this new situation with Tony. The SEAL motto, *the only easy day was yesterday*, echoed in my mind as I pondered what I had gotten myself into this time.

As we ran in the chilly, misty, morning air, I gathered my thoughts and turned to Michael, "This is nowhere near what we signed up for. I think I would rather cut ties with Tony and just get back to my boat."

I recalled Tony's talk about reporting us, but I figured it was more a hollow threat than substance. Fat Tony was no idiot, and I was sure he was accomplished at manipulating people.

I was expecting Michael to be on board, but he answered, "Look, we committed to him, and he even upped the dollars when the situation changed. I think we should see this through to the end."

I was floored by the comment, and Michael's desire to continue on with this. I stopped running and just stood there, waiting for him to come back to me. I wasn't sure if this was tied to whatever else Michael was hiding but, either way, it was a huge concern for me.

"Michael, I know you need the money, but this is a lot of risk to take on. I would much rather we get out while we can. I can give you however much money you need," I pleaded.

I knew I'd hit a nerve when he growled back, "I said I do not want your damn money. I want to earn this. Why is it such a big deal? We've both done worse under far more dangerous circumstances."

"That may be true but under those conditions we were not breaking the law," I said, quickly adding, "at least not *all* the time."

It was the combination of his tone, manner, and the words themselves that made me wonder even more what he was not telling me. The look of confusion on Michael's face told me there was something off, he didn't have his usual calm appearance. Of course, I had no business trying to act all high and mighty, thanks to my own past behaviour and lack of respect for all things legal. I had done things way outside the boundaries of the law with Norie, with Colin, all on my own. Maybe Tony was right, there is no moral high ground left to be occupied by anyone, certainly not by me.

Chapter Fourteen – At a Loss

We continued our run down the waterfront back towards the park as the sun began to peak out through the fog. I really wanted to enjoy the run, the day, just being here in this place, but my mind was not letting me. I kept recalling how many bad things I had gotten away with and the way I had involved my friends in some of those things. I wished I could turn back the clock and decline Tony's invitation, or maybe just wake up from this nightmare, but I knew neither was possible. I would have to do everything I could to protect the both of us and ensure we got back home. Whatever Michael was not telling me must be something serious. We had not known each other long, but I thought we had become quite close, although I was now questioning even that.

The friendly confines of Avalon, Huntington Beach, and Newport seemed a continent away at the moment, and not going to get any closer in the near future I feared. I took one more shot at convincing Michael, but I could tell there was no way to change his mind. If anything, he dug in even deeper and stuck to his resolve.

As we hit the gravel path, I looked at him and said, "You need to promise me that if anything worse comes to light, you will agree to leave with me." He stopped dead in his tracks and with a look of resignation he replied, "I'm sure we'll be fine, but yes, I can make you that promise. I want you to know my reasons first."

His eyes now dark and tormented as he continued, "You know how I said I had an unpaid loan?"

"Yes, of course I remember, that's why we're both here!"

"Well, there is a little more to the story than just a loan. I got mixed up with a couple of bookies and started to bet on football.

One loss led to another and another and soon I owed them a ton of cash. As you know, bookies are not all that eager to leave debts outstanding."

I looked at him sadly, "Michael, what the hell did you do. How much do you owe?"

He appeared defeated and demoralized as the explanation poured out of him. "It's more than just that. If I don't get it all paid by next month, they will take my restaurant. I already signed the note that would give them ownership if I don't pay up, so I can't leave this gig."

"I really wish you would have told me from the beginning, Michael, now we are both in danger. We will get you out of this one way or the other."

""I'm really sorry I wasn't up front with you about all of this, Megan."

I really wished that I had a better handle on the whole story. I felt like I was being manipulated not only by Sir Tony, if his title were even true, but also by my friend, Michael.

I was left in a quandary and for the first time in a very long time I was confused about my path forward. I wondered if I had again misjudged a man in my life. Why couldn't I learn from past mistakes?

Chapter Fifteen – What Now?

The night could not arrive quickly enough for me and when I finally closed my door, I thought I would be relieved. I was not. There were too many thoughts running around in my mind, crashing and colliding like bingo balls in a cage, each thought connecting to another. I laid in my bunk staring at the pattern on the ceiling above me, listening to the pitter patter of droplets of rain against the topside. I attempted to will myself to sleep. To help clear my mind, I even started counting the droplets of rain. I tried putting a musical rhythm to the drops, but nothing helped. I felt strange, odd, discombobulated, and that was when it hit me. I knew what I was feeling.

For the first time in forever, I felt alone, completely alone. No teammates, nobody that I could trust one hundred percent. Even Michael, whom I thought could be the one, could not be trusted completely at the moment. It was a terrible, confusing feeling that caused me to question my own judgement, my intelligence, even my training. I recalled the times when I thought I had been truly alone; when taken hostage, getting shot, almost losing a fight to the death, even the wars with the cartels. I knew I had never really been alone in any of those cases. I had my brothers in arms waiting for me and searching for me, or Colin working with me, or Norie having my back. There was always someone I could trust with my life. In all of those cases, I had been only temporarily alone.

This was a different feeling altogether.

I felt not only alone, but also a deep sense of loss, perhaps for what could have been. I now knew no matter what explanation or excuse Michael gave; he had broken our trust. I felt that our relationship would never progress past friendship, or if we would even be able to retain that. Friendship, like any relationship, requires trust. At the moment, I had no idea what to think or what to do next. I knew it was silly, but I hoped something might come to me in a dream while I slept. As I got closer to nodding off, I asked my Aunt for guidance, I spoke softly to my SEAL brothers hoping one might help, I begged for my Mother to tell me something, anything.

I awoke in a cold sweat, quickly realizing that none of them had spoken to me in my dreams. The only dream I had was of a cage-match when I was infiltrating the drug cartel. They pitted me against a powerful, dangerous looking man and I was told that only one of us would leave that room alive. My whole body tensed up as I recalled the fight, the details of the dream forever etched in my mind. The crashing of fists against body and bone as I delivered a blow to the man but received one right back. It was a rough fight, and I was scared for the first time I could recall, truly scared. I laid there with my eyes closed, bringing back the dream. It was astonishingly clear, and I began to remember every shot, every move, the intense pain. I circled the large man, allowing him to get closer but staying just out of reach of his massive fists. I was baiting him like Muhammad Ali used to do to unwitting competitors, luring him in close enough that I could deliver a debilitating blow, a kick to the inside of his knee.

A kick that I knew could collapse even the toughest opponent. That was always the great equalizer in fights against big guys – that weak, poorly designed, knee joint. It was just dangerous to allow your opponent to get that close, especially when they hit as hard as this guy did. I faked a left and when I saw him load up to strike back, putting most of his weight on one leg, I hit him with a powerful kick, right on target. He yelled and went down in a heap of pain, his knee completely separated, and I moved in to gain control. I think he was expecting a punch or another kick, but I spun quickly behind him and locked in a choke hold. As I held his neck tightly while he struggled, I was able to get my legs around him and lock my ankles together, sealing his death warrant. I squeezed and squeezed until long after he stopped squirming then I felt two people pull me off of him. My blood suddenly ran cold when I recalled spotting a face in the crowd, back in the shadows, a familiar face but one I could not quite make out.

I was jarred back to the present by a loud knocking on my door. I popped up and cracked open the door, it was Michael, wondering if I wanted to do something on our day off.

I wasn't up for it, responding, "You know what, Michael, I think I need a day to myself. I'm just going to rent a car and go for a drive. If I don't see Tony, let him know."

"Sure, I get it. No big deal, I'll just hang around," he replied.

I closed my door and, in that moment, decided where I was going. I was heading to the beach. I got dressed and, as I walked up the stairs, Tony greeted me.

"I heard you're going for a drive, anywhere special?" he asked me, trying a little too hard to seem only mildly interested.

"You've a problem with that?"

He shook his head. "No, no. Here's the keys to the company SUV. Go have fun." He tossed me the keys, told me where to find the car, and off I went. I found the parkade easily enough, and after a brief search, spotted the vehicle and hopped in. I was soon weaving my way through downtown and heading toward the highway as the GPS directed me.

I dialed my friend and former teammate, Sonny, really hoping he would answer. Finally, after the sixth ring, a gruff voice answered, "Whadya want?"

"Sonny, it's me, Megan. Are you at your cottage?"

"Sure am, about to go sit on the dock and drop a line in the water. Why, what's up?" he asked, in his usual folksy tone.

"I'm on my way to you now, I think I need your help," trying not to sound desperate, even though I very much was.

Without hesitation he answered, "Anything for you bud, when will you get here?"

"About two hours or so, I'm just leaving Halifax now."

"Sounds good, come on down to the dock when you get here. Me and Zeus are doing some fishing."

I was glad to hear he still had Zeus, our service dog when we were still SEALs. When Zeus got shot while serving, Sonny adopted him immediately. I used to bug the big lug constantly about how he loved that dog more than his wife, but we were all happy that Zeus had a home where he could live out his life happily. No more getting shot, no more getting blown up, just fetching sticks, and laying around in the sun. As I drove down the highway toward Antigonish, my head began to clear. I had been busy thinking through everything that had happened so far, trying to figure out what else was going on with Michael, and Tony for that matter. I knew I still did not have the complete story, wondered if I ever would.

Sonny and his wife had a cottage just outside Antigonish at a place called Cribbons Beach. From photos I had seen, it was a modest two-story, A-frame cabin that sat directly facing the Atlantic ocean. Like me, he had inherited it from a family member and that was where they spent every summer after active duty. Also like me, Sonny always liked resetting next to the ocean. Even though, as SEALs, the ocean often brought death and destruction, most of us still found it calming.

In what felt like no time I was bouncing down the rutted, gravel and dirt road towards Sonny's cottage, catching glimpses of the ocean appearing between the trees and houses. I spotted the weathered, dark blue cottage, as I crested a hill and pulled onto his parking pad out front.

I was so anxious to see Sonny I almost forgetting to put the car in park as I hopped out. The first thing that greeted me was that wonderful ocean smell, the freshness of the air working its way into my senses. I came around the corner of the house and spotted Sonny sitting on his dock, almost surrounded by the chilly Atlantic, his fishing rod slowly bouncing up and down in his hands. Zeus spotted me first and came at me in a full run. As he bounded towards me, I prayed he remembered me – an old friend who had pulled him from battle once and saved his life. When he was within about twenty feet, I got on one knee and watched him slow down as he approached. I know it sounds silly, but I believe I saw recognition, connection, in those large dark eyes. He leaped, his huge tongue slathering licks all over me as his massive paws struck against my shoulders, pushing me back onto the ground. I hugged him like a long-lost brother, which I suppose he was. He had saved my life more than once and many times he kept us all away from certain death, even when he could have been killed himself. I recalled the look I saw in his eyes when he got shot in battle as Sonny scooped him up and carried him away from the fighting, Zeus's head hanging over Sonny's arm, those dark eyes looking confused and sad. It sounds strange but it was every bit as gut-wrenching as seeing one of my SEAL brothers shot, perhaps even more so as Zeus wouldn't have the understanding that we did. The big guy wouldn't have understood the intense pain that we knew he was feeling.

I stood and noticed Sonny had not moved a muscle, the rod still gently bobbing in his hands.

He looked at me and said, "Get over here, I'm trying to catch us lunch."

As I stepped onto the dock he stood, gave me a big hug, and in his slow, Louisiana drawl said, "Ain't you a sight for sore eyes."

"You too, bud, you too." Sonny had always been as close to me as one of my own brothers. Our team had been through a lot together, but he and I had endured more than most. I was so glad to see him again. Here in the sunlight, and he without a shirt, I had forgotten how round he could appear. He was stronger than most any man I knew but, unlike Michael, for instance, his muscles were concealed by a cushier layer. Sonny was the SEAL brother I had always felt closest to, we chided and bugged each other as if he were one of my birth brothers.

He had a certain *je ne sais quoi* about him that told people he was more than just a tough-talkin', loud-mouthed, good old boy from Cajun country. I think that was what endeared him to me, the fact he was so completely unpretentious, oblivious to his own rural charm. He was just a guy from the bayou who loved to spend his summers in Canada, but I knew the true Cajun in him was always bubbling just beneath the surface.

As he always had, he stepped back, looked me up and down and said, "What's up buttercup?"

I always chuckled when he called me that, the name was so not me, but coming from Sonny it was a term of endearment. Just then his line jerked, and I watched as he cranked hard, spinning the line round the reel, water shooting off it as he fought with the fish.

"Oooh, It feels big, baby. Maybe a big, tasty salmon. Food for a week right there," he bragged.

"Just as long as it's something tasty, buddy," I loved all fish and straight out of the ocean was the best.

He yanked on his rod, then quickly cranked the reel repeatedly to take up the slack, digging in his heels as if he were battling a 500-pound tuna.

I couldn't help but laugh when he reached over and scooped out what looked like a two-pound Mackerel, three pounds at the most.

"Oh yeah, bud, that's a huge one all right, you're a regular Captain Ahab," I said as I slapped him on the back.

He smiled his huge grin at me, "Hey, it'll be a nice lunch for the two of us, unless I don't give you any."

"You're certain there's enough for two there?" I said, smiling right back.

He unhooked it and cleaned that thing in record time, I had forgotten he had the skills of a surgeon when it came to cleaning fish. Minutes later we were sitting around the grill as he prepared the fillets and heated up his well-used cast iron fry pan over the crackling wood fire.

"Where's Maggie?" I asked him, looking forward to seeing her again. She always used to joke that Sonny was my work-wife and she was glad I kept an eye on him whenever we were outside the wire. That's the SEAL term for when we were on missions and had left the safer confines of a camp to venture into the unknown. Calling it *outside the wire* made it seem much less foreboding than entering the death zone!

"Ah, she stayed home for a couple of weeks to take care of a new horse. You know her, they're all her four-legged babies," he said with a big grin.

"So, what's the deal. How can I help," he asked with an obvious look of concern.

"I do need your help, I just don't know how, yet. Let's have lunch and I'll fill you in," I didn't want to dump the whole story on him at once but definitely would keep nothing from him.

Chapter Sixteen – Sonny

After we finished a delicious lunch, we went back to the colorful wooden chairs on the dock that overlooked the bay. The sea was calmer than I had ever seen it, in stark contrast to the storm that was churning in my head as I considered what I was about to ask him.

"I'm helping a friend, who I am now concerned may not be who I thought he was, and I need to have someone I can trust with my life watching my back. Of course, you were my first choice," and he truly was just that.

He was agitated already as he asked, "It's that Michael guy, isn't it?" He quickly gathered himself, put his hand on my shoulder and continued, "I'm here for whatever you need, to do whatever you need, bud. Brothers forever. I hope that Canucklehead hasn't gotten you into a big mess."

I began to lay out what was happening, telling him what I knew about Michael and my concerns. When I mentioned Tony's name, Sonny's face paled, "What the hell are you doing with that guy? I'm just a part-timer here, but even I know he's bad news."

"What do you mean, what have you heard?" I asked, a little shocked that Sonny knew about Anthony Farnsworth.

"Nothing really solid, but I've seen his name in the news quite a few times. I did a little recon on the man. How much do you know?" he quizzed me.

"I know about the sailing and his companies, you know diamonds, and stuff. What else is going on?"

Sonny gave me a worried look, "So, you don't know about the overseas security company he started? Or the rumours that his company was involved in some military coups in other countries?"

Shocked, I answered sheepishly, "Well, I didn't get *all* the background on him."

"Well, sister, you're not hanging with the most reputable guy on the planet. I guess you should have dug deeper into him. Probably that Michael guy too!" I really wished he would get off this Michael-bashing, it sometimes felt like high-school jealousy to me.

"That's easy to say when you basically have access to any database you want because you still do work for SECNAV. I don't have that luxury," I had been on the outside for a while now, even though the Secretary of the Navy had turned to me more than once for off-the-books help.

Sonny grinned at me, "I can't help it if the Secretary of the whole damn Navy realizes what a genius I am and is willing to keep paying me without me ever having to get shot at again."

I had forgotten that Sonny, in spite of his folksy charm, rough edges, and generally foul language, was a computer wizard. Nobody on our team knew for quite a long while about his geek alter-ego, until his nerdiness saved the whole team the first time.

He had been somewhat of a child prodigy on computers but had always gravitated towards a good fistfight rather than a keyboard. He kept the geek in him hidden pretty well and when push came to shove, Sonny had always been the definition of a *door-kicker*, the first guy in and quite often the last guy standing. Although all of us were effective killing machines, when Sonny was around you felt even more bulletproof. More often than not it was Sonny who was there when the times seemed darkest, showing up to save the day, a ray of light, deadly light, but light, nevertheless. As we sat staring out at the water, I flashed back to one of those dangerous times.

I was strapped tightly into a chair and being interrogated in the most brutal manner. I was bruised and battered and had steeled my mind for what I knew was coming. We had been trained extensively on ways to resist and extend our lives without giving up any real information, but there was a finite time that anyone could withstand torture. Everyone has a breaking point, and I felt I was approaching mine. There was no part of my body that didn't hurt, blood pooling around my bare feet, arm broken, fingernails already gone. I looked up stoically as the man moved towards me, needle in hand, and then *bang*. His brains exploded out the front of his face, splattering all over me, as the large-calibre bullet ripped though him. He collapsed to the ground missing half of his head and Sonny's smiling face popped into view, "Hey buttercup, whatcha up to," he said as casually as if he were greeting someone at a bar.

"Not much," I smiled at him through bloodied teeth and cut lips, never so grateful to see a friendly face. That was just who Sonny was, a good ole boy at his core. He cut me loose, gave me one of his AR-15's and a pistol and we shot our way to freedom as he dragged me along beside him. We met up with the rest of the team before leaving that Godforsaken place, and I was happy to be free, once again courtesy of Sonny. There were far too many times to recall when Sonny had saved our collective butts, and I was concerned enough about my current situation to know that I needed his help again.

"After what you just told me, I need to know how available you are. Would Maggie be okay if you helped me out," knowing that spouses of SEALs spend a lot of time praying for us to retire.

His eyes welled up a bit as he turned to me and said, "About that, I didn't really tell you the whole story there. Maggie's been gone for almost two years now."

I laughingly replied, "You mean she got tired of taking care of your sorry ass, cleaning up after you, and finally left?"

My heart sank as he looked to me soberly. Damn my big mouth, I could clearly see that was not what happened.

"No, she passed. It was unexpected and quick, but she's with all her horses now, galloping around with the man upstairs." I noted his big, mean-looking eyes were still a little teary, so I knew he wasn't all the way over it.

That was Sonny though, he always tried to minimize the impact of events like that on him. I supposed that was a part of what made him such a great SEAL, others before self.

"My God, Sonny, I'm so very sorry to hear that." I was in shock, but even more stunned knowing that none of my brothers shared that with me. I felt sick to my stomach that nobody, including Sonny himself, had reached out during a time when one of my best buds needed me most.

"It was rough for a while, but I'm getting back to good now. Me and Zeus just hang here all summer long and talk about the good times. This dog is a great listener, you know," he said with a grin, as he reached down and playfully scratched Zeus's ears as the dog locked eyes with his owner, his friend. In a lot of ways those two had saved each other and it was obvious.

"I never knew, I never heard from anyone. I would have been there for you, Sonny," I said, a terrible feeling in the pit of my stomach.

"I know. Don't worry about it, Megs, what's done is done."

Sonny was the only person who called me Megs, or Buttercup for that matter. He could call me whatever he wanted after what we had been through together. I was not going to ask for his help after that revelation.

As he stared out at the bay, he pressed on, "What is it you need. How can I help you?"

"Are you sure, Sonny, are you positive you want to jump back into the fray?"

I was wary knowing that he would do anything for me, no matter the impact on himself. It was a lot. I already owed him so much more than I could ever repay in one lifetime.

He actually chuckled as he replied, "You think I'm concerned about some sailor? Besides, you know I love being back in the fray."

"There's a little more than that to the story. Like I said, Michael is with me and now I'm not sure if I can trust him one hundred percent either," I said almost apologetically.

"Aah, those damn Canadians. They come off all nice and friendly with sorry this and sorry that, but in the end, many of them are just like us."

"I've got your back if you need me, just tell me what you want me to do Megs," flipping right back to serious Sonny.

"That's the problem Sonny, I don't really know how you can help, yet. I just know you can help somehow. We only have today to flesh out a plan," I added, "so maybe we should get at it."

I felt bad about the news, but I also knew how Sonny operated best. He had always been able to face the worst, deal with it, and move on. I had always admired him for his ability to do that. I was saddened by the news of Maggie, but grateful that he was willing to be there for me, once again. We sat at the table in his cottage as we hashed through possibilities. I was certain Tony would not allow me to just show up with someone else unexpectedly, but perhaps we could create a plausible story that might allow it.

We started to brainstorm just like in the old days, as if we were sitting around a table in a safe house trying to decide how best to complete our mission. Ideas flowing back and forth, neither bad nor good in the moment, just ideas to be recorded and explored.

We were searching for the best idea, just like we had always done and knew that the best idea can grow from the tiniest seed of a possible solution or even the wackiest detail.

Chapter Seventeen – Back To *Maasai*

I was worried the plan we hatched at the cottage might be too transparent, so it was still a work in progress. Sonny and Zeus were going to return to Halifax with me but stay in the background until we finalized the way forward. I considered a chance meeting a possibility, but knew we had to get the lay of the land first. As we drove in separate cars back towards Halifax, we kept our phones connected and chatted almost the whole trip, continuing our reminiscing. Prior to leaving the cottage, Sonny had attempted a deep dive into Michael's background, even though we both figured that his involvement with the Canadian version of SEALs would make that challenging. We were right, he discovered little of value. At least I knew more about Tony though and that was a tremendous help.

Each time I looked in my rear-view mirror I chuckled at Zeus sitting in the passenger seat as if he were the co-pilot, his gaze appearing to be focused on the road directly ahead.

I couldn't resist, "Hey, Sonny, your girlfriend there is a real dog."

Sonny came right back, "At least I know I can trust her, better than most any other woman I've known. Present company excluded of course."

We arrived in Halifax early enough that we had time to get Sonny set up at a hotel close to the *Maasai* and do a little more brainstorming.

We still had made no headway towards creating a real plan and were starting to grab at straws, something, anything to get out of this.

"Sonny, I'm not exactly sure what the best approach is but I think we should start with you keeping surveillance on us for now. What do you think?"

"I can do that," he answered back quickly, "or I could just kick some ass and see what we can find out."

I smiled at him, "I figured that would be your first choice, but let's stay calm for a while. We can keep in contact via text. Right now, I need to get back to the boat and see if I can gather any more intel."

"Sounds good," Sonny replied, as he grabbed binoculars from his bag. "I'll keep a close eye on you from here, as well as Michael of course!"

I left Sonny and walked the short distance back to the boat. As I approached the bow, I looked up and saw Tony and Michael standing at the rail, both their faces scrunched up with what looked like concern. I sure wished I could hear what they were talking about. I wondered if I would ever learn the full truth about either of them. As though hearing my thoughts, Michael turned and looked down towards me, his face like a beacon in the full light of the sun. I halted, mid-step. His face. It was the face I had seen in my dream during that fight to the death! I recalled taking blow after blow as the people surrounding the small area looked on, their yelling and screaming as they urged on their favorite. My opponent was a large man and quite skilled, but thankfully not as skilled as I.

As the screaming ramped up, I started to exert my will on the behemoth. The room fell silent when I subdued him with a triangle chokehold and held on tightly.

I felt his death come more slowly than I expected. When it was finally over, I stood quickly and was ushered out of the room. In my dream, that was when I thought I saw Michael's face. Had he really been there? Or was this my subconscious playing tricks on me again? That seemed to be happening more often these days. I thought back to the many counselling sessions I had been through but nothing I could recall gave me any indication whether this was indeed real. I continued walking more slowly towards Michael. I had to know but I certainly could not come right out and ask him, or could I? I decided I needed to save that discussion for another time.

I climbed up the gangplank and handed the keys to Tony. "Thanks a lot for letting me use that vehicle," I said as I walked past him.

I was a little surprised at his response, "I hope you found what you were looking for." I wondered if that was why he lent me the vehicle, to keep tabs on me. It certainly had a trackable GPS and I wondered if it was also wired for sound. If it was, and he had heard Sonny and I talking, he gave no indication of it, but that did nothing to diminish my concern.

"I sure did, I just wanted to drop out and see an old friend of my Aunt's and dangle my feet in the water."

It made no sense to attempt to disguise where I had been, and I thought coming right out and telling him might put him at ease, keep him from digging any deeper.

He nodded and smiled, "Sounds like fun."

"Yes, it was, a good break for sure."

I glanced over at Michael, "What did you get up to while I was gone?"

I could tell by his look that he knew there was something going on in my head. I was sure that my thoughts were exposed at the moment, the fear of not knowing, the significance if he was there reflected in my eyes.

He responded with a veiled attempt to look disinterested, "Not too much really, just hung out and relaxed."

I knew there was more without even considering his tone or appearance. I glanced towards the hotel where Sonny was staying and looked towards the seventh-floor window of his room. I had Sonny in the corner room so he could keep a close eye on the boat and also see along the boardwalk. I was so grateful that I had him here to help me sort through everything that was happening. As I approached Tony and Michael on the sun deck for dinner they seemed to cut their conversation short when they spotted me. It was just like when you walk into a room, it falls silent, and you immediately know it was you they were talking about.

I knew they would never divulge the topic, so I asked, "Are we finished here? Will we be heading back to the Caymans soon?"

Tony responded with a vague, "Looks like we might have two or three more days. I'll know more tomorrow. Stay ready."

I recalled my counsellor and I had hashed through the many forms of PTSD and how each person's experience is unique. I wondered if *seeing* Michael in my dream was a manifestation of that. Was it my subconscious trying to warn me about him, warn me that my life was in danger just like in that fight? I knew I had to find a way to get Sonny closer.

Chapter Eighteen – Waiting, Just Waiting

Tony said nothing about what was planned for the next day. That evening I again found myself lying in my bunk, nowhere close to sleep. Out of desperation, I came up with Sonny pretending to be my cousin. We could add he was always called my cousin by my family but there was no familial connection, he was just someone my parents had a hand in raising when we were all growing up. That would be a plausible story and one which could not be traced so I felt good about it.

I would wait for the following day, find out Tony's plan, and then devise a way to accidentally bump into Sonny. I was still restless, so I grabbed a hoodie and went up on the top deck. I sat in one of the cushy chairs and took in the scenery before me. All the lights across the harbor and stars in the sky, unable to determine where sea ended and sky began, the two melding into one vista. I watched a large boat make its way into the harbor; the massive sails lit up with an otherworldly glow as it slipped through the darkness in silence looking like a mystical pirate ship. I wondered where they had been and where they were going, who was onboard. Now that I had figured a way to get Sonny involved and travelling with us, I felt calmer, safer, and a little less worried about whatever Tony really had planned. I couldn't be certain about anything really, so support was the best for which I could hope. Just then I heard voices from the salon below.

I recognized Tony and Michael talking and moved quietly towards the sound of their voices. I slipped behind a large sofa that gave me the best vantage point but allowed me to stay completely hidden should anyone come up here. At first, they seemed to be just speaking about general things, nothing of any real concern.

Then I heard Tony say, "Look, Mike, we need to get this all wrapped up quickly and get out of here. Can you keep her in line and out of my real business?" he asked. I was shocked to hear that my concerns about Michael appeared to be valid.

I almost laughed out loud when Michael answered, "Don't worry, I can get her to do whatever I need. She figures I'm her best buddy already."

That deceitful little prick, my heart sank, and I recalled the hurt of Bobby's betrayal as I processed Michael's response. I had placed my trust in him, but I was clearly right to hold some back. Rage began to boil up inside me, my fists cramping as they balled up tightly, trying to will me into hitting something, anything. I had to summon all my inner strength to stop myself from storming down there and taking them both out. The feeling of disloyalty was almost overwhelming, and I recalled I had not had a really good fight in a long time. I was due.

Tony answered back, "Must be that boyish charm of yours and those good looks keeping her distracted. You had better be certain as I don't want any more blood on my hands."

I tensed up as I thought the only blood on his hands would be his own, the bastard. I knew I could destroy Tony easily, but Michael was a wild card. One thing I knew for certain, I wanted to scour that boat as soon as I got the chance and toss any guns and weapons overboard. I certainly wouldn't need any weapons. If things did go South, I didn't want any equalizers around. I had not fully evaluated what danger the crew might pose either, so I knew I needed to do more research.

They finished up and I waited a half hour before sneaking back to my bunk. I sent Sonny a text and told him to be ready in the morning, letting him know that as soon as I knew the plan for the day I would get in touch. I was surprised when it was the sun streaming into my stateroom that awakened me, amazed that I had slept at all and more so that it was already well past eight. I felt relaxed, rested, and relatively stress free as I awoke. I did not know exactly what was going on but the knowledge that *something* was going on seemed to settle me. It was the opposite of what happens to most people and my shrink always said it was a healthy self-defence mechanism. I jokingly called it positive PTSD. Not exactly PC but accurate.

I lingered in the shower, letting the hot water wash over me as I took time to consider my life. In that moment I decided I needed to make a real effort to change, try to just enjoy where I was at.

I had attempted that before and had little reason to think I would succeed this time but accepted that trying was doing. I dressed and headed up to the table where there was already an assortment of rolls, fruit, and a couple of pots of coffee. We said our good mornings and one of the crew asked if I wanted a protein shake. My radar was on full alert now, so I declined, just in case. You could hide just about anything in a protein shake.

I knew that I could no longer fully trust anyone on this floating tub of lies and deceit. I briefly considered cornering Michael, but decided overplaying my hand was not in my best interest. My worry now, knowing that these two were working together, was it might be impossible to get Sonny onto the boat. Just then Tony came up from below, followed a minute later by Michael. I swallowed my disgust and looked up smiling, "Morning, men, how are things going today?"

Michael answered, "Too early to tell."

I looked towards Tony asking, "So, what is our plan?"

Tony smiled down at me, "We'll know more a little later. I think we should all stay on the boat until I can confirm details."

"Sure," I replied, as the gears began grinding away in my head. Tony's demeanor seemed very calm, but I was now fully aware of how well he can disguise what he is really thinking. I wished that I could simply disappear, hop on a plane, and go back to my boat, but I had never been able to leave unfinished business.

I have been that way my whole life and knew I could never change so I have just learned to accept it.

It galled me that I had to just sit here, with Sonny in the dark, and wait to be told what we were doing. I hit the gym for a decent workout, even though there were nowhere near enough weights for me to be able to *really* train. I did pound the hell out of the boxing training dummy he had installed. According to the readout on the screen I was "punching like Ali." I didn't know whether it was Muhammad or Laila, but I was okay either way.

Chapter Nineteen – Time To Go

I finished my workout, showered again, and returned to the deck where Michael was having a coffee.

"Good workout?" he asked, distracted, and obviously not interested in an answer.

I grunted my reply and left it at that. I looked at Michael and was about to ask him what else happened with his brother when Tony arrived.

"All right guys, we'll be moving in about an hour. We'll be heading to my office again with more backpacks, so I need you two to be ready," he stated, as if he were giving orders to his crew. I knew I was nothing more than crew at the moment, but still not sure where Michael really sat.

I felt I had to make some of my feelings known and looked up at him disparagingly, "No funny stuff this time, right. I warn you the next time anyone points a weapon at me, they're dead and I won't care who it is."

Tony answered with a cavalier tone, "Careful what you wish for but, no, there will be no robbery or anything else. We just need to get the bags to my office."

I got the sense he was actually telling the truth this time, although there was nothing to back up my gut feel. I would still be fully prepared though and would read Sonny in on our route as soon as I got the chance. I would feel much better if Sonny was close by during the transport but not sure that could happen.

Tony said that we would leave the boat at ten and asked Michael and me to check the areas around the dock for anything suspicious. I texted Sonny the details but really hoped that there would be no reason for him to jump in, yet. I didn't want to show my hand too soon and lose the advantage of surprise. About twenty minutes prior to us leaving, Michael and I scouted the area all around the boat. The waterfront was busier than at six AM of course, but nothing looked suspicious or out of place, so we returned with about five minutes to spare. We were in the main salon below when Tony walked in with the backpacks.

"You two know where the office is so you'll take the two backpacks, and I will meet you there," obviously revealing only as much of the plan as he felt was needed.

I was concerned that Tony was having us do this separately, so I said, "No problem, just let me use the head before we go." I had to contact Sonny to give him the plan and get his feedback. I went to the tiny bathroom, locked the door behind me, and instantly sent the text message.

"Sonny, we are leaving the boat at ten. I need you to stay in the shadows but do not let Michael and me out of your sight," I sat, not very patiently, waiting for a reply.

Sonny thankfully answered back right away, "Don't worry Megs, I got your six." His words pushed the aloneness I had been feeling into the background and that on its own was greatly appreciated. I tucked my phone away, ran some water, and then returned to the deck.

I pulled the backpack on and noted it was heavier than the last one which caused me to wonder what was in them. I had no reason to believe Tony would be honest, but I asked anyway, "What's in these, not just diamonds I assume?"

Tony sneered back, "You asked about drugs, so I'll tell you the truth. You've heard of cocaine and probably know that a kilo of coke is worth about 1.2 million US. Well, this is new stuff and worth ten times that much. You need to get it all to my office and know that there is nowhere for you to hide if it does not arrive." He added, "The people I work with have a track record of killing anyone who gets in their way."

I said nothing as I considered that a person would die in jail if caught with whatever this was. I wished he had just stuck to his diamond scam and was mad at myself for not doing something sooner. I was nowhere near as mad at myself as I was at Michael for bringing me into this damn mess.

I pulled on the backpack and said coldly to Michael, "Let's get this over with, I am about done with all this crap."

"I know you are, and I really *am* sorry." Michael appeared genuinely apologetic when he replied, his face sorrowful.

As we walked down the gangplank I turned back with a disgusted look, "Yeah, sure you are."

I was so close to bringing everything out in the open, I had to struggle to maintain my composure. I had no idea what may happen on this transfer, but I felt much better knowing that Sonny was close as backup.

We took one of the routes I had planned out, walking along with all the other tourists and office workers flooding the waterfront. I was certain we were the only ones carrying bags filled with millions of dollars in drugs and it was not a good feeling. I really hoped, now that his diamonds were safely in hand, Tony had not set us both up to tie up his own loose ends. I still wanted to see what I could get from Michael about the brother situation too, but I still didn't feel the time was right, wondered if it ever would be.

We walked in silence towards Tony's office, constantly scanning all around us. I thought how it would be much better if criminals tried to highjack us rather than police. I was as ready as I had ever been in Afghanistan, Syria, even Russia, as we walked a brisk pace while trying to blend in. I was on a hair trigger and that would be very bad if anyone did approach us - bad for them anyway. Michael and I still had not said a word to each other as we entered Tony's building and Michael texted the number Tony had provided.

We emerged from the elevator, a door opened directly across from us, and we were greeted by a very official looking lady who waved us in. She led us down the hallway to Tony's office where a man, with a jacket bulge that indicated he had a weapon, took the two bags from us.

He unzipped each, took a cursory glance inside and then sent us on our way. Where was Tony I pondered, he said he was going to meet us here. Nothing seemed off so I hoped this was an innocent change of plan.

As we walked back towards the boat, I decided I could wait no longer, I had to confront Michael.

"Hey Michael, let's grab a coffee on the patio here," I said, trying my best to sound casual.

He replied, "Yeah, why not. I'm quite sure we're done for the day. I'll just text Tony and tell him what we're up to," as he began to type. I watched closely, hoping that was all he was saying. I waited until his message was sent, and the phone was back in his pocket. I scouted the area around us, and Sonny allowed me to spot him a short distance away.

I folded my hands on the table in front of me and leaned in, "Look Mike, I know there's something going on with you and Tony and I am giving you this one opportunity to come clean." For just a second, he seemed surprised that I had called him Mike, as Tony had, I had never called him that before. He had always been Michael. It seemed so odd to me to use the less formal version. His eyes widened as he locked them onto mine. Unable to hold what he was seeing inside, he looked down, his surprise quickly giving way to shame, or something close, as he answered, "God, I'm so sorry, Meg."

I spat out, "Just give me the goods, *friend!*"

A slow nod. A hard swallow. A dejected look. "First, please hear me out, Meg. You have to know I had no choice here."

"We always have choices, Michael." As I heard myself say the words it sounded as if I were scolding a child with a platitude.

There was a sadness growing inside me that I couldn't shake. I wanted to lash out but knew that would not produce the result I wanted. Truth.

Michael put his elbows on the table, wringing his hands. "Remember when I told you what happened to my brother?"

"Of course, who could forget something like that?"

"I didn't tell you the whole story. The cop who killed him is indeed dead, but I left out the fact that I am the one who did it," he said, seeming genuinely sorry. His eyes were darting everywhere except looking at me, obviously worried, making sure there was no one who could overhear him.

"Geez, you killed a cop?" I said as quietly as I could. Of course, it's not like I was any better considering the many people I had sent to the grave.

"Megan, he was my only brother, and he was both innocent and naïve. He did nothing to deserve being killed like that, and I had no faith the law would do anything about it. You know the list is long of black people who have died at the hands of the police. I could never have lived with myself if I had not avenged his senseless murder."

The whole time Michael spoke, he wrung his hands tightly, gripping himself, trying to stay calm.

I snapped, "Okay sure, you avenged your brother's death. I would have done the same. Just what the hell does any of that have to do with Tony?"

"Sir Tony," Michael spat out, "was the reason that it all happened. This diamond scam is not new to him, and neither are the drugs. My brother was not as fortunate or as well-equipped as you and me to extricate himself."

"If you want to get even with Tony, why all of this? And why the charade we are currently in?" I could feel myself getting increasingly upset as I pushed the feelings deep down so I could retain some semblance of objectivity. I tried not to imagine what I would do if someone killed one of my brothers and the hellfire I would unleash upon them.

"I knew I could just take him out, but there were other considerations," he said, as his eyes dropped again and he visibly slumped.

"Oh, so your debt story was real, was it?" I kept my hands folded together, my knuckles turning white, to help prevent me from reaching across the table and wringing the life out of him. Luckily, the old me was long gone or he would be laying on the ground writhing in pain, or worse.

All pretense evaporated as he continued, "It's very real, and the people I owe have the reach to get at me no matter where I am. Plus, I had to confirm that Tony was the guy before I put another dark stain on my soul." "Why couldn't you just tell me the truth from the start? I trusted you, Michael." Even though I knew Sonny was close, that feeling of being alone was creeping back into my thoughts. I forced myself to remember some of the things Sonny and I had been through and the fact we had emerged relatively unscathed from so many bad situations.

"Megan, I'm telling you everything now. I must have that money to get out from under all of this and get myself a clean start," he pleaded.

I locked eyes with him, "So, is this the end of it then? Is Tony the last bit of revenge you need to deliver?"

His countenance changed to one of apology, his eyes glazing as he replied, "I have no reason to expect you to believe me, but I swear to you, this is it, there is nothing else. I say that within the bond we share as warriors."

"Fine then, but this absolutely must end here," I answered with finality.

A smile of relief spread across his face "That is so great to hear Megan. I'm glad we'll be able to get past this. I have few, if any, friends like you."

"Hold on there, cowboy," I replied, "It's not that easy. You have shattered my trust, endangered my life, and forced me to do things I said I would never again do. We will have to see what's next for us. For now, I need to get myself out of here, and you are going to help me do that. You can have my share of the money. I don't want any of it." I was happy that I didn't need money that was *this* dirty.

"Megan," he started, but I cut him off immediately, "Don't bother Michael, just don't bother." I stood and walked away. "I'm going back to the boat." I didn't give him a chance to answer or an opportunity to come with me as I quickly disappeared into the throngs of tourists.

I had so many questions and so few answers. Why bother with this whole fake abduction and the rest of the BS just to get me on this trip? I wondered if I was being setup as the patsy here, or if there was even more to the story. I decided in the moment that I needed to protect me. I had to speak to Sonny sooner rather than later, so I was glad he appeared when he did. We walked as I laid out my new idea.

"I want to get out of here as quickly as possible," I stated.

It was totally expected when Sonny asked, as if offering a simple favor, "Do you want me to get rid of them? All of them?" It was as if he was asking if I wanted him to pick anything up at the grocery store for me.

"No, no. There's no need to go ballistic on these guys. I don't want either of us to get into this any deeper. If I just disappear, I think Michael will get all the money he wanted, and Tony will hopefully just let it go." It sounded reasonable when I said it, I just wasn't sure how much I meant it.

Sonny was uncharacteristically sombre as he replied, "Are you sure you're good with that? It seems like we might be leaving a brother behind." It was odd to hear Sonny speak about Michael that way, a man he clearly wasn't impressed by, but that was how operators like us thought. Personal feelings were always suppressed by team commitment. Disagreements were settled in the ring, or the bar, never on the battlefield.

"I don't know one way or the other right now, and I don't much care. I just know that I need to get a flight to the Caymans as soon as possible, get on my boat and get home. Are you and Zeus able to come with me?"

"I thought you'd never ask, Buttercup," he said with a big grin.

"Okay then, you book our tickets as soon as you can for a late-night departure to a jumping off point. I will sneak off the boat and meet you at the airport," it felt like a solid plan.

"Why don't we just go to my cottage and lay low there until everything settles?" Sonny asked, making real sense for a change.

I shook my head, "No way, I am sure that he had the GPS tracked so he knows exactly where I went. He might even have someone watching your place right now. By the way, if they blow up your cottage, I'll buy you a new one. I'm going to get back to the boat, you go to the hotel and get us those flights."

It felt good to have a plan, a possibility of getting away from all of this.

Chapter 20 – On The Run

I laid as patiently as I could in my bunk that night, fully dressed, anxious to get going as I waited for a text from Sonny. I hoped he'd be able to get us tickets out of here tonight, but there were no guarantees, there were never guarantees for people like us. One thing was certain, I knew that unless I wanted to ditch my boat forever, we had to get to Grand Cayman in a hurry.

The buzzing of my phone woke me, and I sat up right in my bunk, bumping my head, surprised that I had been able to doze off at all. There was a text message from Sonny, "I've got tickets for us to get out of here. Our plane leaves at 8:00 AM."

I answered simply, "Sounds good."

I read his message over and over again wondering if we would actually be able to leave. That would be ideal, I could let Michael know I was going for a run by myself and then head directly to the airport and get out of here. I set an alarm and tried to get back to sleep as I rolled the situation around in my head. The boat gently swayed from side to side and rocked me to sleep until I shot bolt upright again, when my watch started vibrating. It felt like I had slept for only minutes this time. I scrawled out a note for Michael that I was going for a run and breakfast by myself, hoping to delay them starting a search for me. I changed into my running gear, packed a small backpack, and tossed it down onto the dock.

In case someone did see me I certainly didn't want to be caught with my pack. I tiptoed quietly down the gangplank, slippery with the morning dew, as I scanned all around me.

I picked up the pack, slipped it onto my back and began to run towards the coffee shop where we planned to meet. I loved the mornings on the waterfront, any waterfront. I took in everything that was going on as I made my way, the rich smell of freshly brewed coffee suddenly overpowered by the stench of garbage, feral cats rooting through the trash seeking food scraps. I passed homeless people with their change cups out, wrinkled old men contrasted against younger women, who at some point in their lives were likely viewed as pretty. I wondered what their stories were as I ran past and for some reason felt a little ashamed of the wealth that Jonathon and Luke had helped me acquire so easily. I saw people living in tents, hats or buckets set out front with a note designed to tug on the heartstrings of naïve tourists willing to part with a few coins, or even bills if the spirit moved them. The ones already sitting outside their tents lived in an atmosphere of isolation, their eyes clouded and dark, the lack of hope palpable. You couldn't help but feel for these people surrounded by wealth, restaurants, and million dollars boats, yet unable to eat, their faces often sunken in due to living at near starvation levels.

As my feet pounded ahead, one after another in perfect cadence, I felt something was off. There was something more eating away at me. It seemed each time my heel thumped onto the sidewalk another question dropped into my head - had Michael actually killed a police officer?

How much more was there to know about Tony Farnsworth? Was I going to be able to remove myself from this mess cleanly and get back to living a life that did not involve killing? I couldn't recall ever being so consumed by confusion. I tried to convince myself I was running towards something and not away from something. After all, SEALs never ran away from danger. We were like moths drawn into the flames that could cause our own death, knowing the dangers but unwilling, unable, to resist. I never ran away from danger anywhere, none of us did. We were trained to face everything head on and fight our way free and that's what I was going to do.

I finally approached the red door, a tattered canvas awning sagging lazily above it, the designated café for my meeting with Sonny. My thoughts were no clearer, no conclusions had been drawn, and most concerning, still no obvious path forward. I grabbed the dirty door handle and pushed my way through, grabbing for a handful of disinfectant from the pump before the door had even closed. Sonny casually waved at me from a booth near the back, his face not at all hiding his concern. He had a small backpack sitting on the bench next to him. I tossed mine against the wall, on the seat opposite, and slid onto the bench across from him. The server set down a large, steaming coffee in front of me, and instantly, before I'd a chance to return Sonny's greeting, two large, darkly clad men squeezed into the booth, one beside each of us. I recognized the one as a deckhand and I could see Sonny loading up to do what he does best, the concern that had been on his face earlier slowly giving way to rage. The last thing we needed was a messy public display.

I raised my hand to stall him. "Hold on, let's hear them out." Of course, my other hand was ready to strike just in case.

The one next to Sonny looked at me with a quiet shrug. "Before you try anything stupid, take a look at the booth across the way, and the rest of the restaurant."

"You boys are playing with fire, you know," I said as I stared him down. His lack of concern told me he was more than just a deckhand. It also told me he had no idea of what Sonny and I were capable of doing to their little gang.

Sonny looked equally unconcerned. He slewed his eyes from one of our adversaries to the other, "You do realize I wouldn't even have to lift a finger? I could just sit back and watch her shred you guys to nothin', the both of you, and your pals sitting across the way."

The guy next to Sonny mustered up a look of disinterest and replied, "I'm sure she could try, and might even get through a couple of us. But, hey, there are lots of guns here. We're not here to hurt anybody. Tony just wants to have a little chat. Consider it an exit interview if you still choose to leave."

With a look of disdain, I replied, "Sure, let's consider it that. An exit interview under threat of death. You really have no idea who you're threatening do you?"

The one next to Sonny gave me a dark look, "Oh, we know exactly who we're threatening."

I worked hard to suppress a smile as I considered how in the dark, they really were.

Sure, they may have been able to get some background on us, and they could also judge by what they had seen so far; but they had seen very little of our true nature. They had no idea of the things I had done, situations Sonny and I had remedied, or just how much damage the two of us could inflict. Still, I was not about to once again risk innocent lives, I had done that before and still struggle with the result. I scanned the restaurant and noted parents with kids, a mom and her daughter, an older couple, and more potential collateral damage if we tried something.

I looked across the table, "All right, we'll go. Please don't start anything in here, let's just get back to the damn boat."

I watched as two men stood up across the way and went to the front door while people at two other tables also stood. Including the two at our table I counted a total of nine people. Hmm, perhaps they knew more about us than I thought. We stood after they did, grabbed our bags, and walked out the door like some sort of honor guard was escorting us. Based on what I saw, I knew that at least two of them had guns, which likely meant they all did. Better to assume the worst. I wished I could communicate my thoughts to Sonny. I felt a need to find out exactly what Tony was up to. I also had to learn the truth about Michael and what his involvement was.

I was still consumed by the worry that I had made another poor decision, that I had misread Michael.

It was the type of mistake I don't often make, at least not since Bobby. I had decided I cared about him a little too early. Had I done the same with Michael? Are my feelings confusing my ability to think logically? Am I more damaged than my therapist thought?

What was normal for me now, I wondered. Hell, did I even have a normal anymore?

Chapter 20 One – Is There A Truth?

We all arrived back at the boat in relative quiet. I spotted Michael on the upper deck with Tony. Michael had a confused look to him, but Tony's pursed lips and furrowed brow told a different story. There seemed to be no confusion at all on Tony's face, his hand gripping the rail tightly and body looking stiff. Some part of me wanted to believe that Michael was still fighting *for* us, trying to calm the situation, but that was seeming less and less likely. My gaze turned to Sonny, thankful for him being here and the added safety I felt with him nearby. The knowledge that we could have escaped at any moment on our walk back to the boat was comforting and gave me the confidence to go further with this to find out what was really going on. We ascended the gangplank two at a time, with everyone keeping what they thought was a safe distance. We were steered away from where Michael and Tony stood on deck, and escorted below to the salon, directed to sit, and told to wait for Tony. I could see Sonny assessing the situation the same as I was, noting where each person was located inside and outside, who was packing and who wasn't. The four men inside had weapons trained on us from far enough away that I knew we could not get to all of them without getting shot. I recalled how much I had always hated the feel of body armor in spite of the safety it provided, I longed to be wearing that protective shield now.

We sat in angry silence as we waited what felt like forever for Tony to finally grace us with his duplicitous presence.

Keeping people waiting, wondering what was going to happen, is an old tactic that was typically used during interrogations to provoke fear. We both just sat as we had seen every trick in the book as far as interrogations go. I steeled myself for what might come, contemplating the retribution I would inflict on these idiots. Tony slowly descended the stairs and swaggered into the room, sat across from us, and began to speak in calm, measured tones.

"I'm a little disappointed in you, Ms. Hernandez. I thought we had a deal and yet I find you and your little friend trying to leave me high and dry. How do you think that makes me feel?" he asked, feigning disappointment.

"I don't much care how you feel. How about you start explaining yourself before I lose my patience," I said in a threatening tone.

Tony laughed as he replied, "*You* lose *your* patience? That's the least of my worries, honey."

Honey? My blood boiled, rage working its way through my body, my fists tightening, muscles twitching. My eyes sharpened onto him more closely while he spoke. The slight twitch to his mouth, the drawn brow, betraying his true feelings. He knew just how dangerous Sonny and I could be, and he was concerned, wisely so but he seemed more concerned about someone or something else.

I felt a tiny sting on the side of my neck, and I reached to swat what I thought was a mosquito. I slapped at it and watched as a small dart fell to the ground beside me, the last thing I saw before everything went black.

I came to feeling as if I had been hit with a cannon, my head repeatedly dropped to my chest as I tried to lift it and focus. When I finally shook off some of the cobwebs I felt the shackles on my wrists, I was handcuffed and tied to the mast inside the salon. My head was pounding as if someone was tapping it with a hammer, bang, bang, bang. I knew that I'd been shot with the same kind of tranquilizer they use on wild animals, extremely powerful stuff.

It hurt to turn my head, but I was able to catch a glimpse of Sonny off to the side, trussed up like I was. At least I still had an ally I knew I could trust one hundred percent. We had taken bullets for each other more than once, I hoped we would not have to do so again. As my head cleared further, I was surprised they had left us alone down here for as long as they had.

I tilted my head towards Sonny, "We have to stay calm and relaxed. We need to find out their game before we make our move."

He couldn't hide the contempt in his voice as he said without even a hint of a smile, "Thanks for the tip, buttercup."

That told me he was good to go, we were good to go. I chuckled a bit when he called me that under these circumstances, but oddly it gave me confidence. I had no reason to believe that Tony would enlighten us with anything of value, or if we could trust what he said even if he did. We would have to seek other opportunities. Just then, the taller Slavic female crew member came down with some food.

"Eat up," she snapped. "This trip might take a while and we don't want you dead when we arrive. Although it doesn't really matter."

I steadied my gaze on hers, "Oh really. I'll tell you what. You tell us what's happening here, what's really going on, and we might let you live, when the time comes for us to make that decision."

She moved behind me and I felt her add a second cuff to one hand and then release a cuff from the other, allowing me a free hand with which to eat. I was tempted at that moment to disable her, but she ensured she kept a safe distance just out of the reach of my free hand. She did the same for Sonny and then plopped down on the seat across from us, reached back and pulled a pistol from the cabinet behind her. The way she held it, checked the magazine, and pumped the slide to load a bullet in the chamber, told me she knew her way around a sidearm. She walked towards me and, without warning, slapped me on the side of the head, the hard steel of the gun stinging, tearing my skin, and raising a painful bump immediately.

"You're in no position to threaten me bitch. We'll get there when we get there. For your information, it doesn't matter whether we turn you over dead or alive, the choice is yours," her demeanor a little too calm for my likes. She went on, "I've seen these people and if I were in your shoes, I'd pick dead."

I smiled up at her as I shook off the stars from the unexpected blow and felt the warmth of my own blood trickling slowly down and around my ear, "I never pick dead, honey, and I've been up against way worse than this lot."

Then she made the fatal mistake of getting too close to my free hand. I grabbed a handful of thick blond hair and yanked her in close, transferring the hold to my cuffed hand. I held her tightly and punched her over and over again, her face now a boney punching bag. I smashed her to the floor, and watched her head bounce off the wood. I was about to deliver a deadly blow when I heard a familiar click behind me. I knew it was a bullet dropping into the chamber and a trigger being cocked.

"Enough, or you die right here, right now," he yelled, so I let her go.

He dragged her away from me towards the stairs. Her face a bloody mess and legs wobbling as he half carried her up. I looked in Sonny's direction, "Sorry bud, I think my past may be coming back to haunt us again."

He laughed and with that so familiar Southern drawl replied, "No big deal, we've all got a past. We'll teach 'em a lesson soon."

Time seemed to stand still as we sat there in silence again, each of us thinking through various scenarios as if we were back in the forces. The clackety clack sound of the diesel engine firing up jerked me back to the present.

I could tell by the motion of the boat we were leaving the harbor and likely heading into open waters. A few minutes after we began to move, Tony came back into the salon.

His concern looked almost genuine as he began to speak, "I like you, Megan, I really do. I mean you saved my life once already, and now you're about to save it again."

I glared at him, "Difficult to do that when I'm all chained up like this."

"I wouldn't worry about that if I were you."

He gritted his teeth and said, "Well actually, all chained up was the deal I made." He turned on his heel without another word and walked back up the stairs, heading to the bridge, I assumed.

My blood ran cold at his comment. I had made more than enough enemies in my life but had gone to great lengths to keep my identity, and my past a secret. A few people and groups ran through my head, but no single person or group stood out from another. I wondered if it wasn't one of the government agencies I had done work for cleaning up their own loose ends. One thing I have learned is you can *never* trust government, any government, and people like me can easily become expendable to extend a political career. Worse yet, it might be one of the drug dealers I had harmed, they had already failed a few times. I resigned myself to wait, continue to assess the situation, and be ready for whatever came next. I kept thinking about the deal Tony said he had made. What deal? With whom?

I wondered how much time me and Sonny had to get ourselves out of *this* predicament. I tried to think tactically as well as strategically, but I couldn't ignore the wondering about who was actually behind all of this.

Chapter 20 Two – Puta!

I knew by the sunrises and sunsets that we had now been sailing for more than two days. I couldn't sense the direction thanks to blinds on windows, I couldn't see exactly where the sun was. I'd almost given up on trying to figure why they were keeping us alive when the sound of heavy boots struck down the stairs and we were faced with armed crew members who appeared more than a little stressed. I looked to Sonny with both alarm and apologies. He gave only a slight nod, his mouth strained, brow furrowed. The first guy said, "Okay, we're close. We are going to disconnect you from the masts. Please understand, one false move and you will both be shot immediately. Got it?"

This was no time for bravado so we both just nodded our heads in resignation. Even though we still had cuffs on, I knew if we could somehow close the gap, we could take them out. I also knew a move like that might get one or both of us shot. I couldn't bear the thought of Sonny dying because of me. Michael's wry grin crossed inexplicably before my eyes. Why his face now? It seemed like much longer than only three days since I had seen him in Halifax, chatting with Tony on deck. What had he to do with all of this? Would he have me killed? Something in me still couldn't grasp that. Yet here I was. The uncertainty had my gut in knots when the sound of the winches brought me back to the moment. The sails were being dropped. Were we back in the Caymans already?

Wishful thinking. I recognized the grunt and Mexican accent before his footsteps sounded down the stairs. He stepped into view before me, greasy black hair and beady little eyes staring into mine.

He spat to the side with disgust, "Well Puta, it's great to see you again."

No doubt, for him at least. The Mochismo cartel seemed to be back, or one of the other cartels on which I had inflicted a great deal of damage. At some point they all blended into one, stringy black hair, ripped often-oily chinos, and well-worn dress shirts.

Tony showed his face from behind the guy, looked toward me and said, "I suppose you deserve to know. I am in more trouble than I let on. I owe these guys much more than I have, and when I was negotiating with them, one of them mentioned this fierce Hispanic woman. The more they spoke the more I was certain it was you. When I showed them a photo, they agreed that if I turn you over to them, all my debts would be forgiven."

I looked up at Tony, "You bastard," was all I got out before I watched the point of a large knife emerge from the front of his neck. He slumped, clutching at his throat, gurgling blood, nothing but garbled sounds escaping his dying lips. The man behind him casually stepped over him like he was a piece of trash and now stood glaring down at me.

"Well Chica, looks like we have a two for one here. El jefe will give me a big raise when I deliver you to him. You may even be the reason I am rewarded with a promotion."

"Perhaps I will even get to pull the trigger, after we learn more about you and who you work for, of course," he said through gritted, stained teeth. I was surprised they didn't come in guns blazing and just shoot us all without delay. Besides what I had done to them in the past, Michael and I had killed six more of their men when they tried to get me only a few weeks earlier. For the first time since I can recall, I did not feel like I had the upper hand. We were led up the stairs where I saw a familiar boat.

I could hear the powerful motors idling, hidden inside the dark blue hull, rumbling, as the exhaust bubbled out under the water. When I spotted the markings towards the bow, I knew it was Mochismo who had us, and they were probably the worst option of all the enemies I had made. They shut down the engines and transferred us onto the boat, shoving us over the edge. We both crashed hard onto its deck and just laid there. Michael flashed before my eyes again. Perhaps he was already as dead as Tony? A feeling of sadness ran through me. I felt a little odd, but I still wanted to know the truth about him. Had he really been at that fight of mine? Or was it my subconscious playing tricks on me? How involved in this whole thing was he? Did he feel the same for me as I, at least once, seemed to feel for him? I wiped those thoughts and got back to assessing our situation, the people on board, trying to determine exactly where they were taking us. I had an inkling it would be in international waters close to Mexico but couldn't be sure.

I heard the powerful engines restart and my anxiety ramped up again as we quickly started to bounce along the tops of the swells. Fortunately, they had been reckless enough to rustle us down into the cabin and leave us with only two armed men keeping guard.

I had counted a total of five on board and liked our odds, our lack of weapons notwithstanding. Me and Sonny could do a lot of damage without weapons, and I knew he was about to explode. After all, Sonny and I had escaped situations much more dire than this with much less at our disposal. These cartel boys figured they were tough, but they were pansies when stacked up against Afghani militants, Russian FSB, and many of the other ruthless groups we had dealt with in the past. They were in way over their heads and were too stupid to realize that the longer they kept us alive, the closer they were getting to their own demise.

Hands still cuffed behind my back, I adjusted my seating position and I felt something hard in my back pocket.

Chapter 20 Three – Payback

I maneuvered as slowly as I could, trying not to attract attention while getting my fingers inside that pocket. I felt the outside first, tracing the object with my finger, my heart jumped when I recognized what was there. My confidence boosted immediately. I struggled more each time their eyes were away from me, my fingers working their way further into the pocket. We hit a bumpy patch and as we bounced around in the cabin, I was finally able to get deep into my pocket. With two fingers I grasped that lovely, metal object. It was my handcuff key! One tiny little key that I knew would mean so much to everyone here. Sonny and I would be alive, and all these creeps would soon be dead.

Who had put it there? I racked my brain but could not remember anyone being close enough to slip it into my pocket. Had I stashed it there? I really didn't care to come up with answers right now as that was the least of my worries. I had the key in my hand, and I had to find a way to get my cuffs unhooked, without being discovered. Then I would need to get the key to Sonny, which posed another problem. He was far enough away that I couldn't just pass it over and if I made a move, it could get one, if not both of us shot. I remembered my bathroom break ruse when we took out the other group and figured I would try again.

When I felt the waters get a little rougher, I looked up at the one closest to me, "I need to use the bathroom."

His questioning look told me he knew absolutely no English, which I found strange. All the cartel goons knew English quite well, as I recall.

I glared at him, "Necesito usar el bano. Ahora," adding a little urgency to my request. I locked my hands tightly together so he would believe I was still cuffed in case he jerked one arm.

As I hoped, he only grabbed me by one arm and stood me up rather than doing the smart thing and taking control of both arms from behind. I was thrilled when the boat pitched just as I was standing, and I was able to drop the key next to Sonny. I watched as he put his leg over it to hide it. I knew he too would be free in a few moments. I held my hands together tightly as the goon turned me backwards and pushed me towards the head. I can't believe another one of these bozos was stupid enough to fall for the I have to go the bathroom ruse. I needed to give Sonny time to get out of his own cuffs, so I looked down towards my belt and pants with a questioning stare. I felt disgusted by the henchman's lecherous leering as he undid my belt, the snap on my pants, and lowered my zipper. I felt violated as he pushed everything down to the floor and just stared at me, nodding his head in lecherous approval.

I knew right then exactly what I was going to do to this pig when I did make my move. He closed the door as I sat on the small marine toilet, surprised that I actually did go.

I waited a minute more and then yelled out, "Finalizada," indicating I was all done.

I heard someone outside the door, and I hoped that Sonny was as ready as I was. I took a stance and prepared to punch. The door swung open, and I delivered a vicious blow to the throat of the disgusting pig. He dropped his weapon, both hands clutching at his neck, struggling to breathe as I pounced on him. I crashed my forearm down onto his face as I watched Sonny disable his guy. No shots fired and no noise to speak of.

Sonny glared over at me and quietly said, "Let's finish these bastards off and make a plan."

I briefly considered a little extra revenge on my guy, but knew discretion was much more important. I spun him over, grabbed his head, and snapped his neck with a quick twist. Sonny did the same to his guy and we both stood grinning into ear to ear.

I whispered to Sonny as he picked up the pistol, "Shooting is a last resort, we are going to need this boat to get us out of here. Let's wait until they send someone else down to check on things. Only three guys left."

Sonny smiled, "I'll get next to the stairs and wait for them to go to you."

We dragged the bodies out of sight of the stairs. I returned to where I had been sitting, holding my hands behind me so it would appear I was still cuffed. I was surprised at how long it took them to send a man. Finally, I watched as two men started coming down the stairs, noting that neither had any kind of weapon at the ready.

I had to stop a smile creeping across my face as I thought how clueless these criminals are. Our plan was to let the first guy get close to me and then Sonny could take out the other one. They did just as we expected and, after four quick blows, they were both out cold. We handcuffed them together using an old SEAL trick, hands to feet and feet to hands. They were going nowhere trussed up together like that, we even found some duct tape to keep them quiet. We moved slowly up the stairs, me leading the way. I poked my head out of the hatch and knew we were travelling at a decent speed when I felt saltwater spray whipping against my face.

I smiled when I saw both his hands on the wheel and no weapon in sight. "Shut down the throttles, now," I yelled out, startling him. His eyes grew wider when he saw Sonny had trained a pistol at his head. He was wise enough to just shut it down, I searched him and tossed the pistol I found into the ocean. Sonny directed him to sit in the cockpit.

"You speak English?" I asked.

He wrinkled his face when he answered, "Of course I speak English, Puta."

I smiled at him as if we were best friends, "You should watch your mouth as my pal here wants to shoot all three of you. I, on the other hand, would prefer to beat the life out of you with my bare hands. We have a few questions you should really think about answering honestly. Who do you work for?"

He spat on the floor in front of me, "I work for myself."

I shook my head no, "We all know that isn't true, I'll give you one more chance. Who do you work for," I asked steadily.

"None of your business," he replied and as the last word left his lips, I hit him with a hard shot right to the head. He stood, spat out a tooth and yelled, "You bitch," as he took a swing that missed wildly.

I smiled over at Sonny, "Let him fight, no guns."

The man laughed as he came towards me. I hit him with two hard blows, one fist connecting with his jaw and the other to his eye, quickly erasing his ignorant grin. When he screamed, I knew I had probably shattered his eye socket and he staggered back, trying to get to a ready position. I knew the only thing he could possibly get ready for was to be hit again, so I asked, "Last chance, estupida," purposely using the female form of the Spanish word for asshole. He muttered something I couldn't make out and as he swung, I trapped his arm and spun quickly around behind him. I had no desire to carry this on further, I locked in a choke, forcing his own arm against his throat, and squeezed as hard as I could. After I felt him take his last breath, I tossed him over my hip and sent him splashing into the water below.

I looked over at Sonny, "I guess we'll just have to find out from one of the other two."

We both strode down the steps as if leaving a boxing ring in triumph. We sat across from dumb and dumber and just smiled as we watched them squirm. After a few minutes of *friendly persuasion*, we finally got one of the bozos to admit that it was indeed the Mochismo cartel that had put them up to this.

Those were the last words either of them heard on this earth as we sent them off to join their buddies in a fiery forever. As Sonny and I discussed where to go, we realized we had to figure out where we were first. Luckily, they had complete instrumentation on the boat including all the required charters and plotters with satellite GPS capability. As the boat drifted lazily with the current, we began to review all the maps and charts at hand to determine our best course of action.

As near as I could figure, they had been heading towards the Caymans for some reason, or maybe straight to Mexico. It was difficult to ascertain. I supposed there was the possibility they had been following us all along and had left people behind to keep an eye on our boats. I was well past the idea of abandoning my boat, this was personal for me, and I was not about to give up anything or just turn tail and run. It's not like I couldn't just buy another boat but there were principles to consider here.

I looked at Sonny, "What do you think? Should we go back there and see what awaits?"

He chuckled like he always did before a good fight, "You bet your ass we're going back there."

His answer was no surprise to me. I knew Sonny missed the battle and it seemed he was still yearning for a good fight, even after being out of field action for a few years.

He was like those crazy hockey players you see, big smiles on their faces as they're taking and giving punches. We plotted our route back to Georgetown not knowing what was waiting for us, both eager to find out and exact our revenge.

Chapter 20 Four – Big Bill

When we again reviewed all the charts they had against where we were it seemed more likely they had planned to return to Mexican coastal waters. Now that I knew it was the Mochismo cartel I was positive they wanted me back on their home turf. They preferred to dispense justice in their own backyard so they could display what they had done as a deterrent to anyone else who might try to harm them or their lucrative business. I knew keeping this craft would not be wise. We motored to the nearest marina we could find as every minute on this particular boat would be another minute tempting fate. We had already escaped a couple of dicey situations and I was worried our luck might finally run out. We then decided rather than trying to get our hands on another boat, it would be safer to head to Florida and grab a flight to the Caymans from there.

I looked over at Sonny, "I know it's crazy, but I still want to get my boat back. There are too many memories and things I treasure to leave it in the hands of anyone else or have it sold off as abandoned."

Sonny smiled at me as only he can, humor mixed with confusion as he responded, "I know, I know. Let's head for Jacksonville."

He continued, "That will be a less obvious airport in case they are still looking for us. You remember Billy, right? I can give him a call. I think he lives close to there. Maybe he can help out."

I replied, "According to the charts and fuel gauges, we have plenty to get us there. Thankfully, these crooks always outfit their boats with additional fuel tanks for those long drug runs."

We sat side by side, me holding the wheel firmly, as Sonny eased the throttles forward. I watched the gauge bouncing around between 90 mph and 95 mph as we skimmed along the tops of the swells, the ocean spray stinging our faces at that speed. I knew this particular boat could cruise along at over 150 mph easily, but I had no stomach for the danger of driving that fast nor the attention doing so would attract. We knew we had about three hours of this to go and as we got accustomed to the speed and the rough ride, we settled into it. In my head it was just another car ride across a rough road.

I looked over at Sonny and noticed a change in him, a different, almost faraway look so I asked, "What's up. What's going on inside that melon of yours?"

He made a half-hearted attempt to chuckle as he replied, "The whole thing just seems odd to me. You show up out of the blue and it's Batman and Robin all over again."

I wrinkled my brow as I looked over, "You mean Batwoman and Batman, don't you," trying to add some levity to the budding conversation, but he was clearly having none of it.

His tone became more insistent, almost challenging as he responded, "Look, I'm serious here. What the hell are we doing?"

"Last time I checked, we're trying to stay alive just like always," I answered a little more seriously.

I was caught completely flatfooted when he turned to me and said, "I've missed you buttercup, you were my best friend and..."

Before he could continue, the winds and swells changed drastically and I yelled out, "Throttle down, throttle down." Damn. We could capsize if we hit one of those large swells at the wrong angle with too much speed. The boat would be tossed about, powerless against the wind and seas. Sonny pulled back hard on the throttles, silencing the powerful engines, and the boat quickly slowed. After some creative driving, we settled things down to the point where we seemed to be out of danger.

I had no desire to hear him complete what he was going to say now that I had an inkling what it was. We were buddies for life, forever connected by our life and death jobs as SEALs. We had seen each other in all states of dress, including no clothes at all, and not once did I ever have a sexual thought about him. It was Sonny for gawd sakes! I suddenly felt strange, perhaps a little creeped-out, wondering if he had those types of thoughts about me back in those days. I had spent so much time being alone after Bobby and now it appeared I had two men interested in being more than friends. Sonny was a known commodity, at least more known than Michael was at the moment.

I wondered what my therapist would think of *this* little conundrum.

As we began to ramp our speed back up, I looked at Sonny and asked, begged really, "Let's table this topic until this is all over, okay? We need to focus and get to Jacksonville and then the Caymans."

He nodded and mumbled, "Sure." His look of disappointment did not go unnoticed.

We sat next to each other with barely a word spoken for a little over an hour as we watched the GPS and the plotter. I thought it would be best to stay away from commercial aircraft and that was when I remembered Billy was always talking about buying a plane.

"Where does Big Bill live in Florida?" I asked. "Is he close to Jacksonville?"

Sonny replied, "I think he's closer to Orlando, but I'm not positive. He said something about starting a charter business the last time I spoke to him."

The prospect of a safe exit, with someone we both trusted, was exciting and I asked Sonny, "Let's call him and see if he still has his plane."

He dialed and I watched his face light up as the phone was answered and Sonny said, "You old frogman, how the hell are you?" I couldn't hear the other side of the conversation but when Sonny hung up, he told me that Billy would pick us up at the Port Canaveral Marina. He said it was due East of Orlando, so we adjusted our course further South and dialed in the coordinates for it. Another hour later and we were idling through the no-wake zone at the marina, happy to see many open spots.

It was early in the day so most of those empty berths would not have the owner returning until end of day or maybe even the next day. That would give us at least twelve hours before this boat would be discovered. We pulled into a slip, tied off, and began walking up the main gangway towards the building. We didn't want to get anyone killed so we tossed the keys into the water, a small splash and then they descended to the dark depths.

"There he is," Sonny yelled. Billy spotted us about the same time and began to run towards us. As he did, I noticed everything I had forgotten about him.

Billy was your All-American guy who moved like a cross between a gorilla and a jaguar. He was still in obvious great shape. I smiled as woman after woman turned to watch as he loped past, his long blond locks flowing behind him, powerful well-tanned muscles on full display. At six-five, 235, he had been a great college football player. His impressive height and physique made him a great SEAL too. As far as relationships on the team went when I was a SEAL, Sonny was first and big Bill was not far behind although everyone was pretty much on par anyway after Sonny.

The closer he got, the more I noticed he truly was a physical specimen, the kind women want, and men want to be like. He had always accepted that concept with grace and a self-deprecating sense of humour that still seemed humble, unlike those who use that device to brag.

When he reached us, his strength and agility were clearly obvious when he grabbed Sonny first and easily picked him right off his feet as if they were two lovers who hadn't seen each other for years. It was about as homoerotic as those beach scenes in Top Gun, and I felt strangely out of place for a moment.

He dropped Sonny down and, in contrast, turned to me and extended his hand. As we shook hands, he pulled me in close for the official bro-hug, "Megs it's great to see you again. It's been a minute, hasn't it?"

He stood back like some sort of fashionista, looked me up and down and added, "I see you're keeping in fighting shape."

I smiled broadly replying, "You too big guy, you too," as I tapped him on his very thick, very muscular arm.

He turned as he said, "Let's get out of here, my SUV's right out front."

We followed him, hopped in, and I quickly noticed that, although the vehicle had likely only been shut off for less than ten minutes, it was already scorching hot inside. It was another hot, humid Florida day and sweat was forming on my brow. I hated

Florida, the weather reminded of some of the terrible countries we had been in.

"Geez man, get the AC going in here, would you," I admonished him.

He laughed back, "Damn tourists," but cranked on the AC. Soon, the big black SUV was pumping out chilly air from every vent that I could feel, and the temperature mercifully began to drop towards reasonable.

"So where do you two actually want to go?" he asked.

Sonny responded before I could, "Buttercup here got herself in a situation. We got out of it, but we need to get to the Caymans and retrieve her boat."

"Well," Bill replied, "you bought a boat, and I bought a plane. What type of boat did you get?"

I explained it was a catamaran and we exchanged pleasantries about our toys for almost the whole drive to his house. He shared that in addition to his pension, similar to my own situation, he had inherited quite a bit from a favorite Uncle. One of the things he got was an executive aircraft, a twin turboprop I had never heard of called a Piaggio Avanti. He had been flying it for six years and was quite proud that it was faster than some executive jets and sipped fuel in comparison.

"That baby can fly more than 2,700 nautical miles and do it at more than 450 miles per hour." It was more pride than bragging, and coming from Billy, it should be taken as boyish excitement and nothing more.

I nodded in acknowledgement and said, "Well, Grand Cayman is only around 650 miles from here. I know it's a big ask, but do you think you could take us?"

I wasn't at all surprised when he quickly answered, "I need to get in flying hours before the end of the month to keep my license current, so I can definitely take you there." No shock at all there. He was the kind of guy who would give you a kidney without hesitation.

"Sonny said you were in a *situation*. Do you need my help when you get there?" he asked, although it sounded more like a statement than a question, him assuming that we needed him.

I smiled at him as I answered, "Nah, I've already dragged Sonny into my mess and just about got us both killed."

Billy laughed back, "It's settled then. We leave tomorrow morning and I'll help you guys out. Brothers forever."

"Brothers forever," Sonny and I answered as one.

Bill pulled the SUV onto his driveway, and I was surprised by the appearance of the house. The homes all around his were much larger and ornate and his seemed to be the smallest one on the block, but I suppose that was in line with his personality. He led us to the front door and swung it open wide.

"Geez Bill, you don't lock your door around here?" I asked in a dumbfounded voice.

He smiled at me and said, "I don't need to with Scout keeping an eye on things."

As if telepathically summoned, a massive greyish black furry dog came bounding towards us. He looked shaggy and cuddly, sort of like one of those doodles you always see nowadays, only much larger. He seemed friendly till its hackles rose upon seeing me and Sonny.

He bared his teeth as he stood at our feet, staring us down as he obviously waited for a command. Billy snapped his fingers, said "hugs" and the dog scooted over to him, stood on its hind legs, and put his paws on Bill's shoulders, wagging his tail. As Bill rubbed the monster's ears the dog leaned into him for more.

Bill looked at us, "Bouviers are the best guard dogs you know, but still really playful, once they know it's safe."

I always liked big dogs and so did Sonny. Seconds later Sonny was on the ground wrestling with Scout like two children as Bill led me through the house. It was as nondescript on the inside as it was on the outside, in great contrast to the massive in-fills that surrounded his humble abode. At least right up until we stepped outside into the back yard.

My only words were, "Wow," as I took in the whole space. It was a massive yard that backed onto one of those man-made canals they love in Florida. Completely surrounded by towering palm trees and dense shrubbery, it was like being in the forest. The only evidence of neighbors were all the docks reaching out into the canal like long, wooden fingers. A powerful-looking, ocean-going fishing boat sat at the end of Billy's dock. Strewn along the small embankment alongside the dock was an assortment of colorful kayaks and paddleboards. He was obviously well-equipped to fully enjoy Florida.

Bill turned to me a little sheepishly, "I inherited all this from my Uncle, too. Don't have the heart to change any of it. Reminds me so much of him." Sonny finally rejoined us, along with Scout, and Bill led us to the tiki bar that looked out over the water. He grabbed three mugs out of a freezer and poured us beers from the taps. Turns out, Bill had taken up brewing beer as a hobby and had an impressive keg system. He regaled us with everything it took to create the dark ale of which we were partaking, and I did my best to look interested, it was the least I could do. Sonny's interest was very real though, so much so it looked like he was admiring one of the classic cars he loves so much as Billy described the entire system.

The day ended with the three of us sitting and watching the sunset from Billy's backyard, reminiscing about all the crap we had been through together as Bill kept a steady flow of ice-cold beer filling our mugs.

Chapter 20 Five – Georgetown CI

The stark brightness of morning seemed to arrive far too soon. We were thankfully greeted with the nutty smell of fresh brewed coffee, the mix of sweet and bitter making my mouth water, and a big breakfast. We carried everything outside and went straight back to the tiki bar to enjoy the cooler morning air.

As we ate, we hashed through a number of possibilities and Bill finally said, "We should probably leave around 1:00 or so, does that work for you?" "Whatever's best for you will work for us. I can't thank you enough for being willing to get us there and help out too," he really was one more brother to me, just like Sonny and all the guys still were.

He smiled that big toothy grin that took over his face, "It'll be like old times. I'll file the flight plan, then we can head to the airstrip. I need to do a thorough pre-flight check, so I'll need an extra hour."

When the time came to leave, Sonny and I tossed our packs into the back of Bill's SUV and then watched as Scout hopped into the front seat.

"Uh, we're bringing the dog," I asked.

"Scout goes everywhere with me, and he always rides shotgun. Besides, you never know if we might need him," he announced.

Took us less than thirty minutes to get to the airport, only five more to board and buckle in after Billy completed his pre-flight.

"This sure beats the heck out of flying commercial," I chuckled, but was completely serious.

Even riding in a military C 130 Hercules was better than flying commercial as far as I was concerned. I'd much rather bounce around in one of the web-strapped chairs attached to the sides of the huge craft rather than sit next to someone with whom I had nothing in common. I laughed again when I watched Bill putting a pack onto Scout's back before buckling him in, "Is that a parachute?"

"Gotta be safe. Doggies, too." He quickly added, "Don't worry though, this is one of the safest airplanes in the sky. It can fly on one engine easily and even missing half a wing, but let's hope it doesn't come to that."

I heard the engines powering up and watched out the window. I had never seen an aircraft where the props faced backward the way these did. After a five-minute warmup, Bill eased the throttles forward and we began to move. We bumped and bounced along the airstrip but soon felt the landing gear separate from the earth and then nothing but smooth power as we climbed. Higher and higher we rose into the perfectly blue sky, the canals looking like so many snakes winding through the neighborhoods, all leading out to the open ocean. Scout was panting, tongue hanging out, as he looked out his window, and back to Bill. The dog seemed super chill about flying, which told me he must have been in here many times.

Billy looked back at us, "Sit back and relax guys, we'll be there in a little more than an hour."

After what seemed the blink of an eye, we began our descent into the Grand Cayman airport roughly 70 minutes after we left Florida – as promised. I watched out the side-window as he deftly manoeuvred the aircraft and we landed without a bump, as easily as one drives a car into a parking spot. Executive jets were lined up like taxis waiting along the waterfront reminding me of the massive amounts of cash stashed on this little island, half legitimate, half ill-gotten.

We taxied towards a spot, following instructions from the tower, "Sierra Echo 5, please go to spot fourteen at the end of taxiway 24L."

"Roger Cayman Tower, Sierra Echo 5 out," he answered, sounding very pilot-like.

I hadn't noticed the tail letters on the aircraft when we boarded, "Really, Bill, Sierra Echo 5, as in SEAL Team 5? Why not just use the whole name?"

"Nah, that would have been too much, don't you think," as he shot me his trademark ear to ear grin. I smiled as I thought about the various names I had considered for my boat. Great minds I figured. We pulled in, shut down, and Bill went about his post-flight routine check. Within minutes we were walking towards a waiting van, Scout again riding shotgun beside Bill.

Instinctively we were all on high alert, which was what kept people like us alive. Not preparing for surprises was how you ended up dead. We worried about Tony's henchmen at my boat, plus whether or not the Mochismo boys knew what had happened yet. They wouldn't know my boat, but they would certainly know Tony's slip where the *Amphitrite* was floating.

I couldn't wait to get back there. We got the driver to drop us off a few blocks away from where she was moored, and we sat in the back corner of a restaurant and started planning.

"Okay, we need to get the lay of the land before anything else" – I began but was cut short by Bill.

"None of these people have seen me, I'll go evaluate the situation, with Scout of course," as he tapped his leg and Scout moved right in next to him, eagerly looking up at his partner as he stood at the ready.

"Okay, we'll hang here, but please be careful. They're all killers."

"Still the mother bear, Eh Megs," Billy added with a smile.

I flushed, watched the two of them stroll out like they were going for a simple walk, and then began to twist the coffee cup in my hands. I never did do well waiting for something to happen, that was just not me.

Sonny once again started up the conversation I did not want to have, "Look Megan, I really need to get this off my chest."

I fidgeted while he spoke, looking all around and doing my best to avoid eye contact.

"You've always been my best friend and these last few days have been great, not just because we got to fight together again, but that we got to *be* together again." I finally looked at him and the look on his face told me he was speaking straight from his heart. I held my cup in both hands as Sonny appeared to be about to reach across the table. Gawd, why did he have to say this crap?

He continued, "I've always said marrying my best friend would be the best. Why don't we try dating at least."

I felt terrible as I replied, "I don't want to take a chance. Losing you as a friend would kill me."

I continued, "If we cross that bridge, we would never be able to go back, and my track record isn't so great in this area. I really think I might just need to be alone Sonny, but maybe we can be alone together if you get what I mean?"

I watched a look of disappointment followed by resignation creep slowly across his face, "So that's it. You don't even want to try."

"I didn't say I didn't *want* to, I said it's a really bad idea and I will not risk our friendship," his puppy-dog eyes were more than a little distracting.

As he nodded in agreement, my thoughts returned to Michael. Was I ignoring what Sonny and I might be able to build for the possibility that Michael and I could get together? Is that what I even wanted? I started to think of that damn therapist who was supposed to be helping me, but all our conversations did was create doubt in my mind. Doubt about my own judgement, and I hated that fact. Put me in a life-or-death situation and I had always made the right call, always had the right plan, never a doubt. Why couldn't this stuff be like that?

Before we could say more Billy stepped through the front door with Scout. He said, "Well, we definitely have a few things to consider," he had a grave look on his face that was uncharacteristic for him.

"There are six guys who appear to be watching your boat. I was able to take a quick swim and got a look inside. There are three apparently dead bodies below who look like they might be your friend Tony's guys. The others all seem to be cartel. I spotted one who had an auto-pistol hanging under his jacket."

I tried to maintain a casual tone, "Well, there are three of us, so six of them should be no problem, right boys!"

Back when we were operating, the three of us had taken out much larger groups than this. Two on one should be a walk in the park, guns or not.

Sonny chimed in, "Okay then. Do we go at night or maybe better to surprise them during the day?"

I offered, "I think we should dress like tourists and stumble around the area like we're sightseeing. Big hats, sunglasses, whatever we need to keep them from recognizing me and Sonny."

I went on, "If they all have automatic pistols it could be a real challenge, I sure wish I had my sniper rifle here." I loved the confidence that rifle gave me and knew that I could make short work of all of them from 1,700 yards or more away.

We looked at each other with quiet nods. "Ah, we've been through much worse," Sonny said with his trademark laissez-faire attitude.

That broke the tension a little and we decided to go shopping for some gaudy tourist wear so we could fit in. We went downtown and had success at the first store while Scout sat patiently out front. We made our selections from the packed racks and stepped out of the changerooms at almost the same time.

I felt ridiculous with my white clam-digger pants, sport sandals, and a gawd-awful big hat. I was sure the boys, similarly attired in an only slightly more masculine look, felt the same. We each looked at the other two and then back to the mirror at ourselves.

"Geez, we really need to look like *this* to blend in," Bill pleaded.

"Let's head over there and get going. Does Scout need a disguise too?" I asked, trying lamely to add some humor to the conversation.

I was not surprised when Bill replied, "Actually he'll be our back up and stay on the perimeter. It'll be better if we do need him, that he catches them unaware."

I was also not surprised when Bill reached into his own pack and pulled out a dog-sized flack jacket. Bill smiled, "Only the best military, cutting edge, bulletproof vest for this guy." The jacket was disguised as one of those support dog vests. It was just like the one that Zeus wore when we were deployed, and I know that it saved his four-legged life more than once. Made complete sense to me, after all he was a key member of the team too.

The three of us left the shop, and as we stepped out onto the sidewalk, I spotted our reflection in the window. Good gawd, we do look just like these clowns. We were about a ten-minute walk from the boat slip, and we strategized as we walked down the palm-tree lined, cobblestone sidewalk. I noticed each of the people we passed, wondering if they knew how they looked. Did they even care?

Even with our disguises, it would only be a matter of time before the goons figured out who we were. There could also be more than six – we'd have to be prepared.

In our favor, the access to Tony's dock funneled down between large rocks and the water so there was at least fifty feet where anyone coming at us would be in no-man's land, or more accurately dead-man's land. As we approached the area, we took up a position at a picnic table that gave us a good angle to see the *Amphitrite*. I longed to be lounging on her sundeck, sipping a glass of wine, watching the sunset over the water in Avalon. We had work to do first however, and it was time to do this. We moved around the area as we kept up our surveillance and determined they had indeed been stupid enough to leave only six goons guarding my boat. That was bad news for them.

Then I heard an all too familiar sound behind us.

Chapter 20 Six – Captured

I had heard that sound so many times before, the metallic click of a pistol being cocked causing the hairs on my neck to stand up. I knew there was a bullet sitting in the chamber and most likely a shaky finger resting on the trigger. With a strong Spanish accent, he told us to put our hands on the table and we all did as he asked. I figured this was it, but before he could contact his compadres, I heard a loud thump followed by one brief sound from the goon as I watched the pistol skitter across the rocks.

I turned to see the man on the ground, the gun settling a few feet away and a hundred-plus pounds of Scout perched on top of him. I watched the formerly cute and cuddly Scout take a huge bite out of the man's throat, tearing away at the flesh like a wild animal. Billy raised his hand and Scout came to his side and sat. Sonny jumped up and dragged the very soon-to-be lifeless body under the table. And now there were five.

Bill scratched Scout's big floppy ears, "Good boy, buddy, good boy." He pointed at the water to the side of us and said, "Go wash your face." The dog obediently loped over to the water's edge, dipped his head into the murky sea and shook it violently back and forth. He ran back toward us, water droplets flying from his beard like a cloud around his face, looking more like the carton character Pigpen than a vicious animal.

He then sat next to Sonny, absolutely no evidence that he had just killed a man, and stared up adoringly at his master like he was a big lap dog.

"Wow." Sonny was clearly impressed by both the precision and stealth of the dog's lifesaving attack and so was I. Normal people would have a visceral reaction to what we had just witnessed, but we had seen so much worse. Hell, we had *done* so much worse, besides, we were all quite far from being considered as even close normal.

Now was not the time to reminisce, they would likely try to contact him soon or were already waiting for the man to check in, so we had to move quickly. Sonny tucked the man's pistol into the back of his pants, but we knew it would be used only as a last resort. We definitely did not want gunfire that could alert local authorities. We moved to a different table where we could still see the boat and were quite pleased with ourselves when we watched as two of the remaining five, we knew of, left the area.

Sonny was the first to ask, "I get it's lunchtime but why send two people to get food, doesn't that seem odd?"

"I've got an idea," Billy offered. "Why don't I send Scout running down the dock towards those two and I'll chase him? That will get the two of us close enough to take them out. You two can keep an eye out from the rocks for the third guy and the other two."

I looked at him, shaking my head no, "It sounds too dangerous Bill, I don't want you, or Scout, getting shot because of me."

He laughed it off, "Ah, we've all been shot before, no big deal. You saw what Scout did to that guy just now. I'll be a lot safer than those idiots."

Sonny patted me on the shoulder, "He's a big boy, let him take his shot."

Sonny and I moved carefully amongst the large rocks, selecting a spot where we could remain hidden but still have a decent view. It was tough not to laugh watching that giant dog bounce and hop down the dock, every now and then stopping to look back at Billy as if to say, come catch me. Billy chasing behind him calling, "Gucci, Gucci, get back here. Get back here." The two goons seemed to be buying the act. They were clearly not members of the Mensa Society! It was over in seconds as neither one even got their guns out of the holster.

As Scout bowled over the smaller guy and tore at his body with his massive paws, Billy delivered a surgical blow to the other guy's face. We watched as the one-punch knockout exploded into a giant splash of blood and the man collapsed to the ground in a heap. We both knew he had driven the man's nose up into his brain and death was almost instantaneous, Billy always had one hell of a power punch. He went to the other guy, twisted his neck almost all the way around then effortlessly tossed him into the water. He then dragged the first one over, did the same and then wiped his hands together in a *that's all done* gesture.

As I stood to go over there, I heard a muffled pop and simultaneously felt the pain of searing hot metal, moving at 1,200 feet per second, tear through my side. I didn't even need to look down, I knew this feeling too well. I had been shot and it hurt like hell, just like getting shot always hurts.

Sure, it was a job hazard, but Sonny was the only person I had ever met who didn't seem to mind it too much. He treated gunshot wounds like badges of honor, tattoos even. He often used them to impress women, at least before he got married. I watched Sonny throw a baseball-sized rock at the guy with perfect accuracy. It hit him square in the head, he dropped his gun, and Sonny closed ground quickly and launched himself at him.

As I held my side, I heard Sonny yell, "You shouldn't have shot my friend, it's the last thing you'll ever do."

As the intensifying pain registered, and blood oozed from my wound, I watched Sonny literally beat the man to death with his fists, and he clearly enjoyed it. That was the one thing that had always scared me about Sonny, he seemed to take pleasure in killing sometimes. It was fortunate that his PTSD was of the milder form so it wasn't like he would be triggered and harm innocent people or anything, but it was always in the back of your mind that he might snap.

Billy was already at my side when Sonny came back, "Good news Megs, It's a through and through, it seems like it hit nothing important. We just need to plug the holes and then keep a close eye on you. Don't worry, I have a field kit in my bag."

Field kits were issued to SEALs, and many other military personnel, in case of a battlefield wound. Bandages, tourniquets, gloves, scissors, blood coagulants, and other medical items including antibiotics. It was all about creating time so the medic could get to you.

I bit down as he poured the powdered coagulant onto the entry and exit wounds, the burning pain almost as bad as the wound itself, but the blood was already oozing much more slowly.

He then wrapped me with bandages, taped it all around me and said, "Good as new, just stay out of the water for a few days."

I sat back, glad it was me that got shot and not either of them. I tried to get up and Sonny put a hand on my shoulder and gently pushed me back down, "You just hide here and relax Buttercup, me and Mr. Universe here will take care of business."

I reluctantly stayed where I was and hoped those two guys who left were the only other ones. Sonny handed me the pistol, "Just in case," as he turned and walked away with Billy. I watched them go back up close to the start of the walkway and laughed when they held hands and began to walk with overly effeminate gestures. My first thought was what an insult to gay men. They were exaggerating everything, and it looked silly, but I supposed that was the point. I knew it was just one more tactic to fool the goons and I watched as the two men actually split as they walked toward Billy and Sonny. Stupid move on their part as now they were both exposed. As they passed one another, Bill and Sonny spun quickly.

Before guns could be drawn, a flurry of fists and kicks put both of the goons on the ground. I wanted to feel relief and see some sign telling me it was over, but I felt nothing of the sort. I began to wonder if there were others. Would this stop them from coming, or simply strengthen their resolve to get even? Was there ever going to be a way to rid myself of these cartels. I rued the day that I answered the call and went after those damn drug dealers. I wished I hadn't, but I was compelled to. I really had no choice. It seemed too often that I never had a choice.

The boys wandered back over and lifted me out of the rocks and the three of us walked towards my boat.

Billy spoke first, "Are you sure you have to keep this boat, Megs?"

"After all this I feel I absolutely must. Let's try and get it painted, get new sails and the like, and change the name to disguise it?" Better safe than sorry and it would be money well spent.

Sonny said, "Let's go check out the Marina boat shop and see what we can find."

We were greeted by a man with long, curly, dirty blond hair who looked half surfer, half heavy-duty mechanic, thanks to the disgusting state of his fingernails. I explained what I wanted done and I could see him doing the mental math, roughly adding everything up. He was pleased there was no negotiating after he told me the estimate and asked, "When do you need her done?"

I smiled and said, "At those prices, as soon as possible."

He chuckled, replied, "10-4," and spun around pointing to his drydock area, "Just bring her over there tomorrow morning."

We dropped off the boat early the next morning and then headed to town to get a couple of hotel rooms. We goofed off and just hung out for a couple of weeks while we waited for her to be refitted.

There really wasn't a lot to do so we found a dojo and worked out daily, when we weren't exploring with Scout. We went to the marina shop just as the finishing touches were being applied. Decals on the back with a new name and new registration numbers on the front in bright white that stood out against the shiny, dark green of the hull. No longer the *Amphitrite*, she was now simply called *Scout*, an homage to the amazing dog who had saved us and made the mission a success. We had been able to get new registration numbers as we applied for the boat to be a salvage recovery. That way there would be no way to trace its previous life and hopefully no way for the Mochismo cartel to track me down again. I supposed it was possible they were only after Fat Tony anyway and I was just the accidental prize, but I couldn't count on that.

We launched her the following day and moored it in with all the other catamarans. I was glad the marina was such a huge operation, so they had the manpower to get the job done quickly. The hundreds of boats in the marina would make it easy to hide.

We all boarded, and I directed the boys up to the sundeck. I went below and was shocked to see they had not raided my wine fridge and hadn't found the high-end wine cellar either.

For some reason that would have felt like I had been completely violated. I was excited to celebrate and share with my brothers in arms. I knew Billy enjoyed a good wine, but Sonny was a little more low country.

I looked at both, "How about we celebrate with a good bottle of wine?"

Billy broke into an ear-to-ear grin, "You know me, I'll never turn down a good wine. Not so sure about our somewhat uncultured Southern friend here though," joking in a good-natured manner, the way we often did.

Sonny squawked back, "Hey now pretty boy, let's not get nasty. But now that you mention it, I would prefer a nice cold beer if you have any."

Without answering I turned and went below, grabbed a bottle of wine, two glasses, and a Stella for Sonny.

"You know me too well," Sonny said, as I handed him the frosty bottle. I poured Billy and I a glass each and we all just sat there in silence, watching the sun descend slowly into the sapphire blue waters as if settling down into a feathery soft bed for the night. My gunshot wound was pretty much healed, and I was feeling good about the future as I sat there with two of the best friends a person could want. We got rigged up and ready to leave first thing in the AM to head back to Avalon, I couldn't get away from the Cayman Islands soon enough.

Then I remembered Michael...

Yes, Michael, always Michael, his absence so very noted and strongly felt.

Chapter 20 Seven – What Of Michael

The sail back to Catalina was relatively uneventful and here we were lounging at the slip again. I tried to remain present with Sonny and Billy, sipping our drinks, but I was still confused, worried even. Where *was* Michael? Had they eliminated him just like Tony? I had to find out how he was involved and how he had gotten involved and hoped he was still alive so I would have that opportunity.

"Hey. What's rolling around in that brain of yours now?" Sonny loudly demanded, startling me back to the here and now.

"Jeezus, I was just thinking, okay," I said, screwing up my face. "I can't stop wondering what the deal is with Michael, it's like he disappeared from the face of the earth. No calls, no texts, and no indication as to whose side he is actually on. I'm not certain whether that's good or bad."

Big Bill chimed in, "I'm sure he will let you know when the time is right. You're never wrong about people, it's like you have a sixth sense."

Sonny started in on me, "I never did trust that guy. I really don't understand how you can, he's not even one of us. As far as I'm concerned, he's not much of an upgrade from that Bobby creep."

I glared at Sonny, "That's enough. I've heard all I want to hear about him from you."

We slipped back into an uneasy silence, watching the sun slowly set while the gulls and other seabirds howled and squawked like a badly out of tune winged symphony.

I watched as one dove from high above, sliced through the surface of the water, and popped up seconds later, a fish flailing in its razor-sharp talons. As the fish struggled and flapped, trying to escape the powerful clutches of its captor, I considered how many times I had been just like that fish, fighting to escape, struggling to avoid death. As I wondered if I had already exceeded my own best before date, I saw the fish free itself from the grasp of the deadly raptor, plunging back into the waters to live another day. Like the fish, I was still alive, traumatized and shaken but alive. It was not through any testament to my own invulnerability though, it was more my will and determination to succeed, to win, to keep going. Just like that fish, I did whatever it took to keep living, although in my case that usually involved taking the lives of others.

It amazed me that people like me and Sonny can kill another human being, and only minutes later be enjoying ourselves as if nothing bad had happened, our clothing often still splattered with the enemies' blood. My therapist says that is the trait they watch for when evaluating people for jobs like ours. She has more than once called it *positive sociopathy*. She explained that true sociopaths completely lack empathy and remorse, and I had little of either, at least when looking at the crooks, war criminals, and others I have killed. I often argued with her that at least my sociopathic tendencies are only for the bad people in my life.

I couldn't speak for anyone else, but I knew exactly how Sonny thought. Sonny was just like me. Bill always seemed more of an unknown quantity in that area, much more difficult to read.

I wanted to dig a little deeper, "Hey Bill, me and Sonny are cut with the same thread. If we were criminals, we'd be called cold blooded murderers and I can't disagree with that. What about you? Do you have any regrets or feelings of any sort about the people we have to hurt or kill?"

Bill's body sagged and a grave look washed slowly over his face as he answered, "That's a good question, Megs." There was a darkness in his eyes, and I sensed that it came straight from his soul. "I know what you're saying about the remorse and empathy, and I think I do have those feelings sometimes. I mean, even though a bad guy is a bad guy I don't like taking someone out while his wife, or worse yet kids, watch. In war, sometimes we had no choice and John Q. Public just doesn't understand that, but our work must be done."

Sonny nodded, spoke quietly, "I'd like to see what those gun-hating politicians would do if people like us weren't around to do all their dirty work." Without taking a breath he continued, "They're all high and mighty spouting their hatred for guns, and people who own them, but they have no real idea what is done all over the world, even here at home, to protect their rainbows and roses lifestyle."

I looked from one to the other and added, "Yeah, sometimes it all seems a bit much. My therapist says that the sociopathy is self protection that people like us engage in to remain sane."

Sonny slowly nodded his head, "You sure seem to talk about this therapist a lot, maybe I need to get me one of those."

Billy and I laughed loudly as I replied, "I'm not sure that *anyone* could get into that little brain of yours Sonny, and if they did, they might regret it."

Sonny mustered up a mock look of hurt. "Sure, pick on the poor little guy from Louisiana. Nice, real nice."

"All right guys, it's getting late, and I need some sleep," I said, rising and stretching. "Stay up as long as you like but keep it quiet when you pack it in. You up for a run in the morning?"

I heard them both answer "sure" as I descended the stairs, anxious to get some sleep. I tossed and turned in my bunk, Michael taking over my thoughts once again. I knew there were no obvious answers, but I couldn't seem to stop making up possible scenarios about where he was and how he was involved. I tried not to, but I also began to explore my own thoughts and feelings about him. Was

I willing to take a chance on Michael? Was there something there to even take a chance on? How would Sonny feel if so soon after shutting him down I took up with Michael? I was already tired of this, so I downed one of the pills that my therapist prescribed to help me sleep. I think it was something that calmed your brain more than an actual sleeping pill, but it worked, and I drifted off.

As the warming rays of the morning sun caressed me awake, I realized I had slept a little longer than intended. I dressed quickly in my running gear and went up top, where the boys were already having a coffee.

Sonny barked at me, "Well, are we all going for a run or not?"

I decided I really wasn't in the mood for any crap from those two thanks to all the turmoil in my head. I glared at them both with a disgruntled look and answered, "Isn't that what we all agreed to do?"

Bill stood, held up his hands in surrender as he responded, "Okay, relax Megs. We were just jabbing you a bit."

I laughed and said, "You two lunkheads should be sharp enough to know not to poke this bear, especially first thing in the morning."

We all stood, did some warmup and light stretching for a few minutes, and then jogged down the ramp and out to the street. We picked up the pace quickly. It was already about 9:30 in the morning so there were quite a few people out and about. Either Sonny or Bill had a comment about almost everyone we passed. Whether it was kids, adults, or seniors, these guys always had something to say.

As we approached a mature woman sporting a top that barely concealed her, Sonny whispered "Geez, look at the rack on that one." I was not at all surprised that came from him, no class, so uncouth.

Billy looked at Sonny, "Let's watch the talk. How about a little respect? Besides, she's old enough to be your mother."

Sonny replied with a sly grin, "Respect? I'd respect the heck out of her if we were together, even for only one night. Megs is always telling me I have *mommy issues* anyway. Maybe she's right."

All I could muster up was a "Geez," as I sped up, I had heard all I wanted out of those two.

I knew both could easily run at that pace all day long, especially unburdened by a thirty-pound pack and a nine-pound rifle, so I went even faster. I looked out at the ocean as we ran past the ferry terminal, watching for harbor seals, orcas, or whatever sea life might show. As we rounded the corner, I saw the rough path that goes all the way up through the hills to the Wrigley mansion. The mansion could not be ignored when you were in Avalon as it sits on the highest piece of ground, its grandeur and majesty on display to be admired by all. Sometimes, when I sat on the sundeck of my boat, I imagined myself as a Wrigley, looking down upon all the common folk from my lofty perch as I was certain they did.

I looked back at Bill and Sonny and as I said, "Let's take this path boys, it'll be a good workout," I thought I spotted someone running behind us. I glanced back, a tall, dark-skinned, athletic figure and just as I tried to get a better look, he peeled off. I thought the face registered with me as he took off up the hill, but I wasn't certain.

I said nothing to them but kept running it over in my head. He was about the right height, and definitely the right build, from what I saw in my brief glimpse. I couldn't be sure though as it's not like Michael was the only black guy in Southern California, or even on

Catalina Island. I began to really pick up my pace as I wanted to get to the top of the hill first if that's even where he was headed.

I ramped up my speed and heard some whining from the guys as I put more distance between me and them. I was still pushing the pace as my legs drove hard, feet pounding on the gravel in perfect time as I powered up the hill. There was no *zone* to get into now, there was just my desire, my need, to get there. I didn't care that I couldn't see or hear the boys anymore, I just kept running as hard as I could. The path eventually levelled out just below the mansion grounds, greenery and flowers everywhere framing the rambling, white-walled estate. It was like I had run smack into the middle of a promo picture for the island. I stood there and scanned the paths and the hillside, trying to spot the man, but saw nothing. Just then Billy and Sonny crested the ridge, sweat pouring down their faces, shirts dripping with sweat.

Sonny yelled out, "What the hell. What was that about? You think you're that marathon guy Kip Keno or something, trying to break us on a hill climb?"

As I began to stretch out, I admitted, "I thought I saw something, someone."

Sonny looked over at me and in an aggressive tone asked, "Michael? Did you see Michael?"

"No, I don't think so. Maybe. I'm not sure. Let's just head back to the boat," confusion reigning in my mind once more.

Sonny pleaded, "Reasonable pace this time, right?"

I could tell from his demeanor that he wasn't too impressed, but I didn't know whether it was about Michael or the fact I had just run the hell out of them.

I wanted to explain I would have the same concern about either of them but knew it would fall on deaf ears, so I didn't even try. We ran in silence the whole way back as we wound our way through the streets, across the beach, and onto the cobblestones, dodging tourist after tourist.

As we approached the main town area, where Michael's restaurant was, I said, "You boys head back, I just need to check on something."

Sonny smiled sarcastically, "Don't you mean *someone*?"

I hated that he knew exactly where I was going, and I was still unsure why I needed to go or why I even cared what Sonny thought. They peeled off and I veered onto the pier, slowing down as I got closer to The Heavenly Pie.

I decided to just go in and ask about Michael. I mean, what's the worst that could happen?

Dante recognized me as soon as I stepped through the door. His heavily tattooed face, neck, and arms were not what told me he was one of the ex-cons that Michael always tried to help. He had told me himself that Michael had saved him, and after fifteen long years in prison, for manslaughter, he was never going back. He didn't complain about the lack of evidence against him, or even the fact that he really was innocent. I knew it was that he looked the part of someone who could easily kill another human being. He was Hispanic, like me, so that was already one strike against him, but it was the whole package that made him scary. He had massive arms, broad shoulders and virtually no skin left that was not adorned by a tattoo.

I broke into a huge smile as I stepped to the counter, "Dante, my friend, how are you doing?"

I was not at all surprised when his first words were, "I've got no idea where he is, he just told me to keep taking care of everything."

"I get it. I get it. When was the last time you spoke to him?" I enquired.

"It was a couple of weeks ago, I think. Can't be too sure, my brains a bit scrambled with handling everything around here," his demeanor displaying how tired he was.

"I'm sure you're doing an excellent job. Michael always says he would be lost without you," I answered, in an effort to be supportive.

"It's me who would be lost without him. In case I hear something, will you be at the marina?"

"Yeah, just hanging with a couple of buddies. Thanks Dante," doing my best to sound super chill. But chill was the polar opposite of what I was feeling inside.

"Sure thing," he yelled after me as I headed out the door.

Chapter 20 Eight – Back To The Beach

Billy left us after a long night of reverie and storytelling, so now it was just me and Sonny, and Zeus, of course. I was really anxious to see the gang and catch up with everyone. I was conflicted about bringing Sonny though, sometimes he was uncomfortable in a large group, especially if he didn't know everyone well. I still had not seen or heard anything from Michael and the wondering was driving me batty. I tried to convince myself the man I had seen was just a man, nobody special, certainly not Michael.

We had been on my boat in Avalon for more than a week since returning and I was quite happy that Sonny and Zeus were on board with me. I had missed them both, a crazy bugger, and a dog, go figure. I left my cabin and as I stepped onto the sun deck, I drank in that salty ocean smell and enjoyed the brilliant morning sun quickly warming my skin. Sonny was reclined on a sofa, whether he was awake or not disguised by sunglasses, his arms laying over his head. Zeus was curled up on a towel on the deck right below him. Laying on his back, his legs splayed out to the side and eyes shut, he too appeared to be enjoying the sun.

Their positions were so similar I laughed as I said, "Time to get up boys, you look like twins."

Sonny slowly slid his glasses down his nose and, looking over the top of them with a yawn, "Hey, we were just catchin' a few zzz's here Buttercup. Why'd you wake us?"

Zeus got to his feet and gingerly loped over to me and rubbed against my leg, his not-so-subtle hint to give him a scratch. I scratched at his ears and neck as he slowly moved forward, he always liked a good rub on his sides too. It was like a car moving slowly through a carwash only this was scratching. I suspected Zeus had soreness for the rest of his life from what he had gone through when he was a SEAL. I felt bad for him, but I had to remind myself he truly did love what he had been trained to do. Sonny had mentioned a few times how Zeus received veterinary care for free for life as long as he took him to the base. As long as Zeus wasn't too sick, I think Sonny enjoyed those visits for just a fleeting moment, he could again feel as if he was part of the teams. Sonny always talked about relaxing, fishing, and everything else but I knew he was still wound a little tight.

I grinned at Sonny, "We have a party to get to. You're going to like all these people and wait until you see where they live."

I considered the three of us, each somewhat broken by what we do, what we've done. At least Zeus's pains were only physical, I think. But who really knows? Sometimes I look into a dog's eyes and think how great it would be to know what they are thinking, IF they are thinking. Many of our scars are visible, but even more are kept hidden from the world in the depths of tortured minds. There had been far too many things that you simply could not un-see. It was a heavy price to pay for serving your country. Even Zeus had been impacted by war. I believe what many people say about dogs and how they can sense your mood, your feelings, and Zeus was very much like that.

That dog seemed more intuitive than Sonny was, or at least what Sonny let on. Having been in battle with us, and been shot himself, I felt Zeus had an even more accurate take on me and Sonny. We had experienced terrible things together and we could not have loved Zeus more even if he were human. As he laid around on the floor, I was always struck by what looked like sadness in his big brown eyes. It was like he remembered what we remembered, as if he were wrestling with the same demons as us. Perhaps he was.

Sonny sat upright and stretched his arms over his head as he groaned and then replied, "Can you take Zeus for a little walk while I hit the head? He hasn't gone to the bathroom yet either."

"Sure." I grabbed the treat pouch and Zeus followed me down to the dock. Zeus was so well-trained there was never a leash needed. As we walked down the dock towards the grass, I noted that he looked up at me every few seconds and I knew he was checking in for visual commands. He really was an amazing creature. I wasn't sure whether Sonny had adopted some of Zeus's mannerisms or it was the other way around, but they were eerily similar at times. A couple of minutes later Zeus bounded off to the bottom of the stairs and sat waiting patiently until Sonny reappeared.

Sonny looked over at me, "Let's get going then and get this over with," he grunted, then added, "We've been lazing around a bit too much, I think." He changed quickly and the three of us stepped off the dock and began to run along the cobbled street.

The sun was already warming everything, and people were scurrying about, most in shorts and flip-flops, enjoying the sun. We spoke little for the first couple of miles as we followed the road out past the ferry dock and into the hills again, Zeus ran between us, never wavering or stopping, not distracted by anything. As the three of us ran, I couldn't help but think, maybe this is how it's supposed to be, maybe this is what I have been seeking. A significant other I usually don't want to strangle, a dog, my own little family of sorts. The best married couples always say they are best friends, and I might be able to be convinced that a relationship with Sonny could work on that basis. But should I have to be *convinced*? Shouldn't that type of thing come naturally?

As if he were reading my thoughts, Sonny said, "What about you and me, Megs? Don't we have something more between us than just friendship?"

I was still confused about my whole situation and tried to deflect, answering, "Of course we do. Zeus is between us."

"Oh okay, it's going to be like that is it? Well, I'll leave the ball in your court, I've tried to talk about this a few times, so now it's up to you," it was just a simple statement delivered as casually as he could. He didn't seem put off or disappointed in any way, that was just the way that we had always worked. Straight talk always.

I was glad for that because, right now, I didn't have all the information I needed to make any decision. I was quite happy to just focus on running and let both of us retreat into our minds for the next few miles, and that was exactly what happened. It wasn't a strained silence or anything like that, we just both knew what the other required. After a good eight miles we were back at the boat, and it was time to get ready to leave.

Jonathon specifically said this little get together was a noon start which I knew meant he was already starting to grill up something for lunch. That was exactly what Jonathon always did, he really enjoyed having all his friends over and treating them. I remember how insulted he was when I tried to bring along a couple of bottles of wine. He wasn't nasty about it or all high and mighty, he just pulled me aside and politely said that there was no need for me to ever bring anything.

I figured we had just enough time to catch the ferry, but then saw the wind conditions and knew it was a perfect sailing day. There was a public dock not far from Jonathon's house so I texted him, told him our plan and asked if someone could pick us up. As expected, he readily agreed and in less than a half hour we were casting off lines and setting sail. The winds were in our favor, so it was a quick sail over to the mainland.

Soon, Sonny was hopping off and tying lines as Zeus stood watching from the bow, his big front paws resting on the edge, his back legs ready to pounce in case of trouble, as he watched the proceedings with an eagle-eye. Zeus scanned the area all around us, on high alert, and I knew he was looking for any threats. He had no idea the only threats here were sunburn and tequila!

I was glad that it was only Angela who came to pick us up. She ran up to me and hugged the breath out of me as she looked down at Zeus, "Who's this good-looking fella?"

"I'm Sonny," Sonny answered quickly.

I shook my head, "She's talking about Zeus, you bonehead."

I didn't want Sonny to be overwhelmed. Whenever he was, he tried too hard to be the life of the party, usually a little too boisterous for people who didn't know him as well as I did. I introduced them and wasn't surprised when Sonny said, "Well, are all you Californians this great looking?"

I admonished Sonny quickly, "Keep it in your pants big fella, she's married, and so will every other female be at this party."

"Yeah, whatever," he grunted, "maybe somebody can teach me how to surf."

I grinned at him, "Pretty sure that's an unattainable goal, but who knows?"

We chatted about Sonny and me on the short drive over to Jonathon and Angela's house. We parked the car, and as I always did, I envied their home, its location and grandeur disguising the homey feel once you were welcomed in.

I couldn't get to that sand soon enough as I practically ran through the house. Jonathon gave me a huge hug as I stepped onto the patio, followed by hugs from Luke and Kathy.

I introduced Sonny to the three of them and wished he could be a little more subtle about where he looked, where he stared actually. Kathy and Angela were both in tiny bikinis that showed off everything about them that challenged my own femininity. Long, tanned legs, smooth abs, and butts that were both curvy and solid. Topped off with perfect smiles and blond hair and you really did have the typical Southern California trophy wife. Fortunately, both Luke and Jonathon were supremely confident in themselves and didn't have a jealous bone in their bodies. I was always at odds with why I felt this way around them. They had never said or done anything to make me feel like this. I knew it was all in my head but there was nothing I could do to tame those doubts. Why did I sometimes feel I wasn't enough just as I am?

Jonathon put his arm on Sonny's shoulder as if they had been buddies for years, "They're awesome, aren't they? Sorry neither one has a sister for you."

Sonny smiled a little uncomfortably, "That's the story of my life bud." After that Sonny and those two guys were inseparable, standing at the large BBQ and sharing grilling secrets as if they were battle plans. I looked around at everyone as we sat there sipping margaritas, and I was so thankful they were all in my life.

I remembered the early days. It started with Kathy and Angela and then their husbands, Jonathon, and Luke, and grew from there. I recalled how bad I felt when I first assumed that Kathy and Angela were simply eye-candy, and then thinking their husbands would be bald, fat, rich guys.

I was way wrong on all counts. They were all accomplished professionals, and Jonathon and Luke had helped make me very wealthy with their investment guidance.

I grinned as I thought about the first time I met the sixties hippies, Arlo and Sage. I was impressed by their timeless love and ageless lust. In their late sixties now, you would think they were new-in-love teenagers the way they behaved with each other. It was so cute.

I felt no need to go around introducing Sonny as he was doing a fantastic job of that himself.

I saw Sage shake his hand and then put her hand onto his large, veiny bicep, "Well, you're a big boy, aren't you?" I chuckled as Arlo just smiled right along with Sonny adding, "I'm sure he spends hours in the gym to get that ripped honey."

I was so glad to be here, back with my people, my friends. Jonathon was in his happy place grilling up a storm as we all sat around drinking and snacking. Norie came out to the patio about a half hour later and raced straight towards me, nearly knocking me over as I stood to greet her.

"How have you been? Where have you been?" she asked emphatically.

"It's all good Norie, all good. How about you?" genuinely seeking an answer.

It was about ten minutes of small talk and catching up before she finally asked, "Well, is this your new boyfriend?"

"God no," I answered a little too quickly. I don't know why, it just felt weird to be asked that question about Sonny. I glanced over at him and was glad he seemed unaffected by my statement and the speed with which my answer was delivered.

We enjoyed our drinks as we soaked up the sun, the cool salty air keeping the temperature bearable. I turned to see two people coming through the doors, my heart nearly jumped out of my chest when I saw it was Michael, and Colin Sharpe. Michael strode through the doors as if he owned the place, oblivious to everyone around him. The quiet confidence and carefree disposition on full display. They were chatting as they emerged onto the patio and it was obvious, they knew each other. *What the hell* I thought. I rushed over to meet them. Now that I knew he was all right, my feelings morphed into anger, and I was unsure whether I was going to hug him or hit him as I got closer.

Before I could get to them, Michael held up his hands, "Hold on Megan, just hold on. Let me explain. None of it was my idea."

I felt the rage coursing through me, my body tensing as if getting ready for a fight. The closer I got, the more I wanted to kick his smiling Canadian ass all over this beach. I was seeing red as Colin stepped between us and hugged me, "Great to see you again, Megan. Glad you're safe and please give him a chance."

"What the hell, Colin, you're in on whatever *this* is?" I was super pissed at someone I thought I could trust with my life as I glared at him.

I turned to Michael and shoved him hard with both hands, "You bastard, I thought you were dead. What the hell happened? Where have you been?"

He stayed just out of reach, "Look, I'll tell you the whole story, but can we do it later, or tomorrow even? Let's try to relax and enjoy the day."

I scowled at both of them, "There had better be a great explanation for what you have put me through. What both of you have put me through, it appears."

Finally, my friend Colin spoke, "There is, Megan, and please understand it had to be this way."

I did my best to enjoy the rest of the day as I seethed, wondering what the deal was. Was this a Colin thing. Was it an FBI thing?

Colin had said more than once that working for the FBI can get messy sometimes, was this one of those times? Was it my turn to be in his mess?

The party could not end soon enough for me as I was distracted the whole time. My head was reeling with all the possible scenarios. We finally stood and walked around saying our goodbyes, and I asked Sonny to give me a minute. I walked over towards Michael and as calmly as I could stared him down, "You and me are going to have a chat tomorrow and you are going to tell me everything, everything!"

He looked at me sheepishly, "I will, I will, and I want you to know how sorry I am, Megan. Hopefully, I can clear everything up for you in the morning and we can get past this."

I turned on my heel without another word and left. Me, Sonny, and Zeus took an Uber back to my house, I really didn't feel like sleeping on the boat.

The driver didn't look particularly happy when he first saw the dog but when I told him Zeus had served, his demeanor changed completely. Sonny didn't say much at all as Zeus laid on the seat between us, his head resting on my lap as I scratched his ears.

I was furious with Michael, and I couldn't help but think what I needed was a reliable, honest, trustworthy dog, and not any kind of boyfriend or partner at all! There was something so calming about a dog, especially Zeus. He never seemed to demand much but gave a person everything they wanted, everything they needed. Especially this dog.

Chapter 20 Nine – Now What?

When we got to the house, Sonny wasted no time as he turned to me, "Well, looks like Michael is all right after all."

I pursed my lips answering, "He may not be after tomorrow! I am meeting Colin and Michael at the Red Barn for a seafood lunch. They must have something interesting to say if they feel a need to meet in a public place."

Sonny laughed, "Probably just self preservation. You *can* be a little scary sometimes, even to your friends."

I knew I wouldn't sleep hardly at all but had no intention of taking one of those damn pills. Nope, a nice bottle of red up on the roof deck to end the day was what I needed. It was another perfect evening, and I drank it in as we stepped onto my roof, the waning sun still offering some warmth. Sonny and I sat watching that giant orange ball descend slowly into the Pacific as we sipped on the wine. Zeus was standing on his hind legs, front paws dangling over the parapet, as if he were a human watching that same sunset. Just then, the dog turned around and stared right at me, his gaze locking onto mine, causing me to again wonder what goes on inside their heads? His eyes didn't have that sadness to them, it was more like he was just checking to make sure we were still there. We polished off that bottle and then worked on the second one as darkness began to creep in, the moon slowly assuming its nightly position over the harbor.

I looked over at Sonny, "You can sleep in as long as you like. I'll leave the car keys on the counter as I'll ride my bike over to the restaurant."

"Are you sure you don't want me to go with?"

"Nah, It's all good, Sonny. I promise I'll stay cool." I knew it was killing him being told I wanted to do this alone.

I told Colin I would be there at 11:30 and I want this all settled. The neighbors would not be thrilled to hear me start my Harley early in the morning, but I hardly ever did so, and I needed to clear my head first. The sun wasn't even up yet but I knew I needed a blast down the Pacific Coast Highway to get in the right frame of mind. Riding always seemed to relax me. I went out to the garage, got all my gear on, and rolled the bike outside.

There was a decline off to the right of my garage, so I pushed the bike a little further and hopped on without starting it. I could coast almost a block away, which was nowhere near far enough for my neighbors not to hear, but at least it wouldn't sound like machine gun fire in their ears when I started her up. At the bottom I flicked the starter button and the massive two-cylinder engine roared to life, that familiar syncopated vibrating sound *potato-potato-potato-potato* announcing the fact it is a Harley Davidson motorcycle. The entrance onto Highway 1 wasn't far away and I was glad to get there and begin to roll with the curves on my bike. It sometimes felt like skiing as you swayed gently side to side, the almost 1,000-pound motorcycle so steady and solid, almost a mind of its own in those curves.

I always found it so relaxing, just riding for the sake of riding. Right then I felt like I could ride the whole 620-mile length of the Pac Highway all the way up past San Francisco to its conclusion.

That wasn't in the cards today, I had more important things that must be handled. Still, I had a good two and a half hours before I had to be at the restaurant, so I headed South. In what felt like no time,

I was rumbling past Camp Pendleton, watching as a group of three helos took off in formation from the base. It was the largest Marine Corps installation on the West Coast, and I remembered part of my SEAL training being completed there. Sometimes I really missed the good old days. I was trying to clear my mind with this ride, but it wasn't helping. I turned into a small bodega right off the highway and sat staring out at the ocean. I finally got off my bike and went to a table.

I didn't even look up when the server arrived, "Would you like to start with a beverage?"

"Just a black coffee please," I answered, distracted, my gaze fixed on some indistinct spot far out in the ocean. I tried to figure out what I felt about Michael as I watched the gentle waves rolling slowly toward the shore. I decided I needed more facts before drawing any conclusions and I was sincerely hoping to get those facts this morning.

I finished the coffee, left a five on the table, and hopped back on my bike to head North to Newport where the restaurant is. I turned into the parking lot at precisely 11:25 and shut my bike off. I tossed my leathers over the seat, and set my helmet on the ground, as I checked the lot for Colin's car. My head was pounding, not from the helmet or the bike but, from the feelings I was having. I was so confused, first happy, then sad, then mad, I was all over the place.

As I walked towards the front door, I heard Colin yell from the patio on the side of the restaurant, "We're over here Megan."

I hopped the low fence and walked to the table where they were seated. There was nobody else on the patio, which I'm sure was part of their plan, and I sat across from Michael.

Before I could speak, and in very measured tones, Colin said, "Look, if you're going to be mad at anyone, you should be mad at me. This was my operation and nobody else's."

"Oh really?" I asked with an emphatic sarcasm that was reflected on my face.

Michael chipped in, "Just give us time to explain everything before deciding if you hate us or not."

"Sure, I suppose that's the least I can do. Or maybe I should just disappear for a few weeks with no calls, no texts, no communication of any sort? How would you feel about that?"

Chapter Thirty – For The Greater Good

The server came out with our meals, set our plates down and as if an afterthought, asked if we needed anything else. I was glad she was already walking away when I responded, "Just don't put anyone else on the patio."

Michael was first to speak, "Look, Megan, I am terribly sorry about all this, but I could not contact you in any way. It would have put you at risk while we rounded up the rest of the bad guys."

I virtually ignored Michael, and turned to Colin, "And what was your part in all of this?" I yelled, banging my fist on the table.

Colin looked genuinely apologetic, as he replied, "Meg, it came from way over my head, and you need to know I had no choice."

I dropped my head replying, "We always have choices though, don't we, Colin? Even people like us can say no."

Colin's eyes looked heavy as he answered, "No was not an option on this one."

I shifted my gaze to Michael, "What about you? You sticking to the *I had no choice* story too?"

Michael just nodded in agreement as Colin began to speak.

The next hour or so was consumed with a detailed explanation of the *mission*. Turns out, neither one of them had a choice.

Colin's superiors knew of Michael because he had done some small jobs for them, off the books. The kind where if the person got caught, there would be plausible deniability and they could throw him under the bus if they had to. It turned out the FBI had been interested in Fat Tony for a few years now and the whole diamond scam was only the tip of that iceberg.

Tony Farnsworth was involved in many other dark ventures including human trafficking and drugs, besides the diamond *business*. They had come up with a plan that would knock him out of commission, eliminate multiple criminal organizations, and there would be no record of the US government, or the FBI ever being involved. It had to look like an internal struggle as that was the way to set off a gang war of sorts. It was always much simpler to guide them into killing each other.

Once they had the bulk of their story on the table, I glared at Colin, "Why couldn't I be in the loop? Do you suddenly not trust me after everything we've been through?"

My focus shifted to Michael, recalling my life-or-death cage match, "So, it WAS you I saw at that fight? The one where I was forced to kill or be killed to entertain those criminal bastards."

Michael seemed ashamed as he replied, "Yeah, it was me. I watched you kill that guy and then leave with the bosses."

"Why, why were you there?" I barked at him.

Michael began, "I was checking into a lead about my brother's death, that's it. Nothing else, at least at that time."

Colin jumped in, "He wasn't involved in any of this yet. I really wanted to tell you everything Megan, but I couldn't. If I had, we would all be in jail by now, or worse."

I glared at him, "So the country I have been shot for, the country that I killed for, the country that turned me into a killing machine, didn't trust me? That's rich."

Colin shook his head no, "That's not it at all. There were extremely specific instructions to keep you out of the loop and play it the way we did. Believe it or not, there were people very high up doing their best to protect you."

I turned and faced Michael, "Well Michael, what have you got to say for yourself? Did this start before or after you and I first met? Or was you meeting me all part of the dirty little plan."

Michael measured his words carefully as he began, "Look, I honestly didn't know that the woman I saw at that fight was you. That being said, the plan was in play when I first delivered you pizza and we began to hang out."

My head was pounding again, and I could feel the rage welling up inside me once more, "So, was any of it real? You and me, the friendship, any of it?"

Michael pleaded, "Megan, can we talk about that stuff later?"

I scowled at Michael, "What's the matter, your new best buddy here, Colin Sharpe, can't hear everything?"

Colin waded in once more, "C'mon Megan, don't be like that. You know there are many factors at play, and my control over the mission was minimal."

"Wow," I replied, "Pretty much pleading the fifth, are you?"

Colin shook his head, stood to leave and as he passed me, placed his hand on my shoulder, "I'm sorry Megan, I'm really sorry."

I shrugged his hand away and said, "You and I can talk in a couple of weeks. I have a few things to settle with Mr. Personality here."

Once Colin was gone, I interlocked my fingers, placed my elbows on the table and leaned my chin onto my hands and waited, staring at Michael. I had nothing to say until I heard more, and this would be a defining moment. Finally, Michael spoke, "I need you to know I had no choice. They forced me to do jobs for them because of what happened with my brother."

"What's your brother got to do with the FBI apparently owning you?" I asked, now wondering how outlandish the real story might be.

"You remember I told you I was involved in the death of the cop who killed him, right?"

"Of course, who forgets something like that?"

Michael then crossed his own hands together in front of him and began, "Well, I made sure that there was no evidence of what I had done, but that didn't matter. The FBI was holding that over my head, they had fabricated *proof* that it was me. The bottom line was that if I didn't do what they asked, I'd likely rot in a jail or a place like Guantanamo Bay."

He continued, "Look, I'm not sorry for what I did. That bastard murdered my brother in cold blood, for no reason other than the fact he was black. I had to do something."

I shook my head, "So, now you are justifying a cold-blooded murder, worse yet, a revenge killing?" He now appeared strained, tired.

The life drained out of his face as he went on, "Megan, I know I'll pay for all my sins and I'm good with that. I couldn't just stand by and watch him go free as if he had done nothing wrong. There are always too many uninvolved bystanders."

I said nothing and Michael added, "So, where does this leave you and me."

I shrugged my shoulders as I stood to leave and left him with, "I don't know. I just don't know."

That was it. I had no idea what was next. For me or for Michael. I knew that I needed some boat time, lots of boat time. I needed to sort through this whole mess. It was like when a partner cheats, you need to determine if there is a chance that you can forgive and put it in the past. I'm not sure I have that capacity.

Chapter Thirty 1 – What About Us?

When I awoke the next morning, I went about the daily boat and life tasks on autopilot, I was detached and confused, my mind as cloudy as the day. Later in the afternoon the sun finally peaked out and I sat on the deck of my boat, surveying the bay, the boats, everything around me. Gulls flashing past and then circling high as they inspected the water for food. Then I saw a massive Albatross, with its wingspan of more than 3 metres soaring up high, scanning the ocean. They amazed me. Huge birds who can go years without touching land the same way I seem to be able to go years without being touched. I knew they mated for life, and I wondered if that wasn't my problem, after Bobby, nothing.

I went back to looking onshore and saw individuals and couples, always wondering what their stories were. Each time I created their situation in my head, I wondered what my story was going to be. I watched a middle-aged couple toss a ball up ahead for their golden retriever and immediately thought of Sonny and Zeus. That was the first decision I arrived at. I knew that Sonny and I were friends, brothers, for life but that was where it had to stay. As much as I loved him, and would take a bullet for him again, I knew it wasn't the kind of love that you marry. It was a love and connection forged in battle and had nothing to do with chemistry, physical, or otherwise. Sonny was now, and would always be, someone I would die for, and I knew we would always be there for each other, but that was it.

My head dropped and my spirits sagged a little when that concept settled fully with me. I think I always knew it, but I had just avoided the pain of such a decision. I remembered that jerk Bobby again and wondered if that experience was still somehow affecting me. Was that one more PTSD-type affliction that was coloring my judgement, blocking out real feelings? I decided it didn't matter, I just couldn't make myself feel that way about Sonny, like Arlo & Sage so obviously felt for each other. So, that was that I supposed. I believed I was now ready to think about Michael, so I called him up. I had no idea how this would go but I felt I owed it to him to at least talk about it and not simply disappear. I also owed it to myself, just in case.

I dialed and as the phone rang a third time, I thought about hanging up but then heard a click, "Hi Megan, I wasn't sure I'd hear from you again."

"Good old caller ID, nothing's a secret anymore, is it?" I asked. It was about all I could think of saying in the moment, my weak attempt at humor.

I was quite pleased when he replied, "How about I bring us over a pizza tonight? Pepperoni and mushroom?"

"Sounds good," I answered, "Around seven works for you?"

I thought he sounded happy when he answered, "That'll work perfect. I wanted to give Dante a few days off, so I have to get everything set up for tomorrow before I leave. See you in a few hours," and he hung up before I could respond.

As I waited for him on the boat I wondered if he had mentioned Dante for any particular reason other than to prove to me, they were tight and had no secrets. Clearly, Dante had told Michael I enquired about him. Whatever, it didn't matter to me anyway. I still had no idea what feelings I had, if I even had any feelings at this point. I do know that I still felt deceived, used, and wronged on so many levels, not a solid foundation for any kind of relationship.

I didn't like that I was so confused about all this crap and wished I had maybe taken a day to go visit my therapist and talk this through. There were no guarantees it would have helped but, you never know. She had actually helped me in a couple of areas, although she had no idea what was *really* going on with me. In her defense, I wasn't even certain that I knew what was really going on with me.

I had taken a late afternoon swim, so I hopped into the shower to get rid of the salt. I told myself that was the only reason, it wasn't like I was getting ready for a date. I stood in front of my mirror, fiddling with my hair and wondered what this actually was. I was still unsure. I knew I liked Michael and there was something there I didn't have with Sonny. I went up top after grabbing a bottle of wine, poured myself a glass, and drank in the whole scene around me. The smell of the salt air, the warmth of the sun, and the slight breeze all working in concert to put me in a calm state.

As I took my first sip, I spotted Michael coming up the dock and was taken back to when he delivered that first pizza. His casual swagger but commanding presence, attracting attention now, just like it had then. I had to admit, he was certainly a good-looking SOB. The sun hitting him the way it was only made him look even more ripped, more powerful, his broad shoulders casting a wide shadow behind him, sinewy muscles highlighted by the rays of light. Even with a pizza box in hand, he carried himself like royalty. That's when I finally clued in!

It wasn't his looks that made him attractive, it was how he made me feel when I walked next to him. When I was with Michael, I could allow myself to feel like I'm sure Kathy and Angela did when they were walking with their husbands. Sure, nobody would ever call me petite, but I felt more feminine when I was with him, like I was on a par with my two best girlfriends. I think my therapist would be pleased with me being this self-aware. I didn't bother going down to meet him, he knew the drill and I didn't want to look overly anxious. I wasn't about to be boorish though, so I stood before he got up top, poured him a glass of wine, and waited at the stairs. He stepped onto the deck and handed me the pizza and as I handed him the glass of wine he said, "I'm really glad you called."

"Yeah, we really needed to sit down for a while and get everything on the table," I replied honestly.

As we sat, he stared out at the Pacific still sparkling in the sun, "It's a great day to be alive, isn't it?"

I smiled at him and answered, "Yes, it is," deciding that I needed to give him all, or at least most, of the facts about me, "'Look Michael, before you say anything I need you to know a few things about me."

"This is going to be one of those get everything on the table talks, isn't it?" I do enjoy his candor and willingness to just cut to the chase.

"I can't tell you everything, but I will share with you the things I have done of which I am not proud. You should know, I have killed not only for my country, not only for my friends, but also for me." It was the first time I made such a statement out loud, and the full impact of my past actions resonated in my mind, reaching deep into my soul.

"I'm not super surprised about the first two, but the third concerns me a bit," he said, trying to make light of the weighty subject.

"Remember that Bobby guy you've heard about, my ex-boyfriend?"

He tilted his head in a more serious look and just said, "Yes."

"He was a bad guy and he even tried to slap me around. I wouldn't have done what I did for just that, but when he started abusing my friend after we split, that drove me over the edge. I beat him to death Michael, and I didn't just beat him, I made him suffer. I made him suffer a lot. Torture would be an accurate description for what I did to him. The worst part of it is I have no remorse about it, none whatsoever," I said, my shoulders hunched and my whole body seeming to shrink.

He leaned towards me with a look of sincerity, "Sometimes we have to do things, bad things."

He continued, "It's not like you were robbing a bank, you were protecting other women. Our weak court system can't be counted on to do that, so you took the reins."

I stared into his dark eyes as I continued, "Just because I had to do it doesn't mean it was the right thing to do."

Michael put his hand over top of mine, "It's okay, it's okay, I get it."

The talk stopped as we ate our pizza and sipped wine. We just sat there watching the nightly show as the sun eased slowly towards the horizon and slipped down to the water once more. The birds became quiet as they settled on shore and soon the sky was illuminated by the moon and stars. Thousands of stars. I got up to stretch and went to lean on the rail. I looked down at the ocean, the stars almost as bright reflected in the black water as they were in the sky.

Michael came up behind me and enveloped me in his warmth. I felt his whole body against mine, his arms now around me as I leaned my head back onto his chest and looked up before closing my eyes and just being. I felt like I had never felt before. That was when I knew. Most of the men who were this much larger than I, were usually jerks, steroid monkeys, or both. It suddenly felt like this was what was missing in my life. It wasn't the friendship and camaraderie of Sonny and Zeus I needed, I needed this! I turned around slowly and looked up at Michael's chiselled face, his square jaw, his thoughtful eyes, and I reached up to kiss him.

I was on my tip toes as our lips connected and I felt his big, strong hands softly caress my face as we kissed. Everything else, all the problems, the mission, the lies, all faded quickly into nothingness as I melted into the moment. He easily picked me up so that our faces were level and held me there, "Megan, I love you."

I wrapped my legs around his waist, taking some of my own weight off him. "I think I love you too Michael," was all I came up with as I was flooded with emotions, mostly good ones for a change.

Nothing else happened that night although we slept on the top deck sofa under the stars, and I slept more soundly than I had in quite a while. His arms wrapped around me, our legs intertwined like high schoolers, or maybe even like Arlo & Sage.

Nothing else seemed to matter.

Chapter Thirty 2 – Michael

I was awakened by the sun warming my face, the blanket tucked in tightly around my body and Michael nowhere in sight. I stood and scouted around the deck but didn't see him up here. Maybe he was in the galley below, preparing us breakfast I hoped, I padded down the steps quietly to surprise him. The first thing I noticed as I moved down the stairs was – nothing! No aroma of sizzling bacon, no coffee brewing, nothing. I couldn't imagine he would just leave, maybe he went over to a restaurant to grab something or perhaps he just went for a solo run?

I looked around for a note and picked up my phone but neither yielded anything. None of this made sense to me, he wouldn't just disappear after last night. My head started pounding as my mind raced. Who does that, just disappears after having a moment like that and staying together all night? Something was off, I could feel it in my bones.

I dressed quickly and headed down the main street to check out a couple of restaurants, just in case. As I walked past the only three that were open and didn't see him inside, I went towards The Heavenly Pie, figuring that must be where he went. When I got to the restaurant and grabbed for the door handle my grip slipped off when I yanked it.

Still locked. I checked the door around back and peeked in the windows but still empty. There was no evidence the restaurant was even about to open soon. No staff, nothing. I was at a real loss now and not sure where to turn, so I decided to head over to Michael's house. Although I still had not *officially* seen it, I had an idea where the house was as we had walked close to it a couple of times. I started walking that direction doing my best to appear to be just strolling through the hood as I scoped out house after house. I was ready to give up when I spotted a large picture hanging on the wall of a modest, white bungalow and saw that it was a woman in front of The Heavenly Pie. This had to be where Michael lived, and that woman must be his aunt. I went up and knocked on the door.

A lady opened the door, "Hello miss, what I can do for you?" she asked politely.

I looked from her face to the picture and back and it was indeed her. I pointed to the large painting and said, "You must be Michael's aunt?"

She responded with, "Who's Michael?" a puzzled look on her face.

I pointed back to the photo, "Michael, your nephew, the guy that runs the restaurant now."

"I'm sorry, but you're mistaken miss. I own and operate that restaurant with help from my two sons. There's no Michael at all," she had a calm, somewhat detached attitude already as if I was one of those door-to-door religious folks.

"Is Dante one of your sons?"

"No, he isn't," and she began to pull the door closed.

I was confused, anxious, upset, all at once, and I blurted out, "Never mind, ma'am. I'm sorry for all the confusion."

I walked directly back to The Heavenly Pie. When I got there, I could see it was still empty so I grabbed a coffee from Java The Hut and sat on a bench where I could keep an eye on everything without being too obvious. I sat and waited, my head spinning as I tried to comprehend what was happening. Finally, after two and a half lattes, there was some action. A man I had never seen before unlocked the front door and an equally unfamiliar guy followed him inside.

I gave it a few minutes before checking around back and the sides so I could see if they actually worked there or if something else was going on. I peered in the windows and saw the one guy making dough while the other was out front getting all the tables prepped for lunch. Clearly, they did work there so it was time to see what I could find out.

I cracked open the front door, stuck my head in, and yelled out, "Is anybody here? Dante, are you around?"

The fellow who had unlocked the door poked his head out from behind a wall and said, "We're not quite open yet and there's no Dante here."

"You mean he's not working today?"

He stared at me answering, "No, nobody named Dante works here."

Now I was getting pissed, "Where's Michael then?"

"Sorry, Ma'am, no Michael either."

"You mean he's not here or there is no Michael," as I held the door open with my foot.

"There is no Michael, just us two. We run the place for our aunt." He added, "We have to get ready for our lunch rush so, if you don't mind."

"Sorry to bother you," I said, and turned away. I needed to reason this out and figure out what was going on.

I returned to my boat, heading straight to the top deck to sit in the sun and think things through. I considered everything that had happened, including Colin's involvement. I carefully reviewed each time I had been with Michael and then it hit me. I had never actually seen him lock or unlock the shop. There was nothing solid to tell me that he really did own it, especially after my visit to the woman he claimed was his aunt. If that were the case then what was the whole money story all about, just something to make his story more believable? I had never seen him interact with staff either, except Dante, who was also now missing. Perhaps not exactly missing, more like never been there at all. Michael usually just showed up at my door with a pizza and I never once considered that he had intercepted my first pizza delivery and that was how all this started. Now I was thinking like myself again and not some starry-eyed, lonely person. I couldn't believe I had been so stupid. But wait a second, Colin admitted to his involvement. He showed up at the party with Michael and even provided an explanation for their plan. The whole situation was completely effed up.

Colin knows I would have helped him with anything, done anything that he needed, within reason of course. There was also the fact that I had just as much on Colin as he had on me. A real détente situation, or mutually assured destruction, since we had teamed up to get rid of the people who killed his wife. I mean, the FBI has certainly colored outside the lines every now and then, likely more than we know, but I was shocked and saddened that Colin might hurt me. I had to determine what the real deal was and who was manipulating whom. I went back, locked up the boat, grabbed my cash and cards, and rushed over to catch the next ferry back to the mainland.

As the large cat chugged across the bay over to Long Beach I went over all kinds of scenarios. I was confused, mad, and already thinking about retribution when the bump of the ferry against the dock brought me back to the present, still nothing settled in my mind. I had not been able to determine what the end game may have been, so it was even more important that I meet with Colin and see what more I could learn from him. I knew that face-to-face I could read him and know what was genuine and what was not. The Uber I had scheduled was waiting for me when I disembarked. I hopped in the back, gave him Colin's address and twenty minutes later I was banging on his front door. Colin had all kinds of cameras on his house so I knew he would see it was me causing the commotion.

Through the door I heard, "All right, all right, enough of the banging," as the door swung open.

I stood staring at Colin, wondering, hurt, but mostly suspicious at this point. He stepped aside, "C'mon in then. What the hell is such a big deal you have to get me out of bed on a Sunday morning?"

"You sonofabitch, you know what the deal is! Where's Michael?" my whole body immediately tense, on a hair trigger as if I were back in Afghanistan or some other godforsaken place. I hated feeling like this.

His smile seemed a little forced as he too-calmly replied, "Megan, I have no idea what you're talking about. Come in for a coffee and we can chat about this."

"Sure, let's do that, let's *chat*," was the only response I could muster, fearful I might take him out right here and now if he said the wrong thing. Jeezus, what was wrong with me? Colin and I had been the best of buds, I love him and loved his wife, we had even killed people together. I had to get control of these emotions. We stopped in the kitchen where he filled us both large cups of coffee and he led me out onto his deck.

I wondered if we were out on the deck so neighbors could see us, less likely for something really bad to happen when there were potential witnesses. I tried to gather myself, controlling my breathing as I stared blankly out at the Pacific. The ocean was not its usual calm self for this hour, the seas were a little rough, whitecaps crashing onto the shore one after another. My mind was in a similar state, thoughts, and ideas like waves, peaking, crashing, but then dwindling to nothing.

I turned on my chair towards him, asking quietly, "Do you want me to believe you have no idea where Michael is? Or Dante for that matter?"

I watched him very closely as he replied, "I have no idea. When did you last see them?" He was responding like any FBI agent would in a typical missing person case.

That raised a bit of a red flag for me as it was counter to what we both knew of this situation and Colin had never been a by-the-book type. His stoic facial expression, open body language, and controlled voice would have been coached into him hoping there was nothing I would be able to pick up on. Similarly, he would be unable to read me, so we were both at the same disadvantage in pursuing the truth.

I leaned forward, my forearms resting on my thighs and fingers interlocked, my eyes drilling into his, "I saw Michael just last night."

"And?" was the only word out of his mouth as he held my gaze.

"We had dinner and drinks and fell asleep up on the deck. Nothing happened." I had no idea why I decided to add that little tidbit. After his wife was killed Colin and I had kissed once or twice but it was more out of companionship and grief than anything else. Nothing ever progressed the way it had with Bobby or the way I thought it could with Michael. It should have been all old news. I relayed the rest of the story to him including what happened when I went to what I thought was Michael's house. I reiterated to Colin that the lady knew nothing of Michael, or Dante, for that matter.

Now I was glaring at Colin, "What is the deal here? What was really going on?" my voice getting louder, hands clasped tightly together as I tried to stay focussed.

"Look, I swear on Patti's grave that I have no idea what happened to those two. Yes, we had an agreement. Yes, Michael worked with me, but it ended when it ended."

He had never used that phrase around me since Patti's death almost two years ago now. I watched him very closely, measuring his response against his eyes, his brow, the fact his legs were peaceful in front of him. I believed I had to trust him and put my faith in our relationship that he was telling the truth. What choice did I have?

I sat back up in my chair, "All right then. How can you help me find out what the deal was here? Can you do some checking internally?"

"I will use whatever tools I can to dig into this, but I don't think the FBI has anything to do with him disappearing. I really don't."

"Just to keep you in the loop, I am going to talk to Sonny and have him dig into it as well. He has the resources to look a lot of places, maybe even more than the FBI."

Chapter Thirty 3 – Sonny

I was nowhere near confident enough to have this discussion over a phone or email or any other communication that could be monitored. I wished Sonny wasn't so far away and I wished I didn't have to ask for his help again, but I had no choice. I knew he could look into things just about anywhere thanks to his security clearance.

There was a chance I was being watched so I modified my appearance and went to a local store using cash for a pay-as-you-go cellphone, commonly called a burner. I had to communicate to Sonny that I needed him to come back out here but be coy about it just in case he was being watched. We had an old plan where, if one of us needed the other, we would send a text about the family dog dying. If you ever got that message, you were to acquire a burner phone and call the number from which the text was sent. Sometimes it might take a few hours and sometimes a couple of days, so I sent the text and dropped the phone in my pocket.

I went back to my house in Balboa and just hung out there for a while. I did some random cleaning and tidying up but that didn't distract me at all. I might as well have just set the phone on the table across from me and stared at it, willing it to ring. I was on the roof deck when the phone did finally ring, and I was pissed I had left it in the kitchen.

I tripped racing down the stairs but luckily caught myself before I crashed. I scrambled with the phone and answered with, "I need your help buddy."

Sonny answered with the expected, "Anything for you buttercup."

I reviewed with him everything that had happened and asked if he could use his access and sources to dig into this.

"You bet I can," giving me the answer I knew he would. He went on, "You know I never did trust that bugger, so I have some rather good photos of your pal Michael to use with facial recognition software I have. I also bagged a few samples I could use to gather DNA."

"You did what," I was close to yelling at him. I gathered myself and realized that although it was very intrusive, none of his business, and very annoying I was glad he trusted most people so little. I was unsure if any of this would help anyway but at least it was somewhere to start.

Before hanging up I added, "I'll check with SECNAV, I know I can trust him to be completely honest with me."

I knew that I could trust Thomas Harker, the Secretary of the Navy, with my life. He had always been there for me. When I was a newly minted SEAL and he was in his last rotation, we quickly formed a bond when I saved his life on a mission. He left the SEALs about a year later and, only four years after, was promoted to the position he has held since then.

Thomas Harker represented everything that was good about serving in any military, serving your country, and protecting vulnerable people. He elevated the Navy with his eloquence, general demeanor, and erudite speech, he truly led by example. In some ways, Thomas reminded me of my father, and I think he may have viewed me as the daughter he always wanted but never got. I knew I could trust him with my life and did not hesitate to get in touch.

Thanks to my having kept in contact with a number of people actively serving I was able to find out SECNAV was currently at the largest naval base on the West Coast, NB San Diego. I called his cell, my spirits buoyed when I heard his voice.

"Harker," always the same answer on the phone. No titles, no sir, no Mr. Secretary for him. I remembered in the field he always went by Harker too; I wasn't even sure he had a first name for the longest time.

"Thomas, it's me. Megan," I broke into a smile and relaxed, the same effect his voice always had on me. He was just that kind of guy, an odd quality in someone doing that job.

We had the typical three or four minutes of small talk then, "What can I do for you?" He was a real straight talker. It wasn't that he didn't enjoy pleasantries, he simply believed there was a time and place for them.

"Are you aware of anything that has been going on around me lately?"

I wasn't surprised when he quickly answered, "I know you were looking into that Farnsworth guy, and I know Sonny was helping you. Why do you ask?"

I knew I might be overstepping but asked anyway, "Were you or the Navy at all involved with this case or him over the last couple of months?"

I believed him when he answered, "Not at all, nothing to do with me or the Navy in any way. I was only made aware when Sonny began sniffing around databases involving Farnsworth's activities."

I needed to confirm, "So, you and the Navy were not involved in any of this? I really need to know Thomas, people are disappearing."

"Megan, you know that I would tell you if there was anything to tell. Sadly, there isn't." He finished off with, "I have to run into a meeting. Best of luck and stay in touch."

He hung up and was gone before I could even answer. I was confused as I sat wringing my hands together, my mind racing. I knew there was no way he would lie to me, even if what he might share was intended to be kept secret. The length of the call, and the way it ended, seemed to say there was something more going on though. I really hoped that Sonny would be able to get some clarification where I could not. There was nowhere I could look within the Navy after Thomas, he felt like my last hope. He ran a very tight ship, and it was close to impossible that someone would be going rogue anywhere in that organization without him being aware.

I put on my running gear and headed out the door, mindful of anything out of the ordinary around me. I settled into a rhythm once I hit the paved beach path, the warm salty air calming me as I ran, each footfall bringing me closer to *the zone*.

I was going at a strong pace when I felt someone fall in behind me. I took a quick glance back but as I did the man moved up next to me, our feet pounding the asphalt in lockstep as he turned and smiled.

"Morning," was all he said.

I just nodded back. I wasn't in the mood for talking nor was I in the mood for any company, so I picked up my pace even more.

I was rapidly approaching a sprinting pace, when he kept right up, I began to consider my options. I briefly thought of shoving him out onto the sand and taking off at full speed but realized that would be me overreacting. Besides, it's not like I had any worry at all with an unarmed man. I decided to simply slow down and stop.

He stopped when I did, I glared at him, "Look, I'm not interested in whatever it is you're selling, and I prefer to run alone."

He smiled at me as he responded, "I think you will want to hear what I have to say Megan."

I turned and was about to take him down when he collapsed onto the sand. He wasn't moving at all, and I was startled when I saw the blood oozing from his ear. I recognized instantly that he had been shot, likely with a small calibre sniper-rifle, I heard nothing so knew a sound suppressor was used, a pro. I took off at full speed, moving side to side as best I could and getting between houses as quickly as possible. I knew I needed cover, fast. I zigzagged through the streets with no intention of getting anywhere close to my house. Fortunately, I still stored my motorcycle at the condo garage I had used before. There was even a locker at the front of the half-sized stall where all my gear was stored.

Nobody anywhere knew about it, so I knew I was safe heading that direction. As I ran through the streets and alleys I tried to think about next steps. Where should I go? Even though I now had some reservations about Colin, I still believed him to be my safest option. I arrived at the underground garage, punched in my key code, and went inside watching the door close behind me. I opened my locker and started getting all my gear on. I chose my Hayabusa as it is the fastest production motorcycle there is, so I put on all my armored riding gear and the full-face helmet. The monster growled to life when I tapped the starter. I let it idle for a couple of minutes before hopping on. I gathered myself and guided my beast towards the automatic door. I didn't even wait for the door to open completely as I ducked down and moved up the ramp.

I saw no people or vehicles around, so I went directly to the freeway onramp. Most people feel too exposed on a motorcycle, but I knew this to be the safest way to get me where I needed to go. The bike is extremely powerful and yet still highly maneuverable. If I had to, I could put a lot of distance between me and someone driving a car or truck. This was no pleasure ride; I gripped the bars tightly as I moved from lane to lane moving just a bit faster than the flow of traffic. I saw nothing out of the ordinary behind me, so I watched for the second offramp past the one to Colin's house. It came up on me sooner than expected and I almost hit the ditch as I braked hard to be able to make the corner.

This offramp was about five miles from Colin's house. I rode paying close attention to lights and keeping to the speed limit. I thought about calling ahead but decided that would do nothing for me. If there was something going on phoning would only give them more time to prepare, I preferred to make this a drop in. I turned the corner onto the street before Colin's and parked my bike between two vehicles. I needed to see if there was anything strange before going over there. I had a perfect view of Colin's place between the two houses I had parked in front of. I was able to get a good look and spotted a strange car in the driveway that I knew did not belong to any of our friends. I decided now was the time to phone while I watched. When Colin answered I saw the blinds on two windows move so I knew there were at least two people there if not more. I supposed if whomever they were knew me, or if Colin was involved, they would know his to be a place I would go.

I hung up, grabbed my helmet, hopped on the bike, and took off. I sure wished Sonny was close enough that I could ride to him. I got to the number five freeway as quickly as I could and eased into the flow of traffic. Six lanes heading South packed with cars made me feel safe and allowed me to try to figure some things out. It's a little more than an hour and a half from the Los Angeles area down to San Diego but it seemed like only minutes had passed when I rolled past the airport offramp just North of the city. I had originally thought I might find safety at the Coronado Naval Base over on North Island, but I couldn't be certain.

My call with Thomas made me uncomfortable and I always had a solid sixth sense when I was in danger. I had survived this long following my gut, I had no intention of changing now. I decided to go to my friend Norie's vacation place at Imperial Beach. I trusted her just like I trusted Sonny. Imperial is a really cool spot at the South end of San Diego Bay, while NAB Coronado sits much farther North.

I had experienced so much during training there, learned a great deal about myself and always felt safer in that region. I motored down the five freeway, right past San Diego proper and watched for the highway 75 offramp to Imperial Beach. Now that I had something of a plan, I could not get there quickly enough. I pulled onto the driveway of her house, opened the garage door, and was pleased her car wasn't there. I would feel better speaking on the phone about this first. I pushed my bike into the garage, closed the door and went inside for a shower.

I always had a bag in my saddlebags containing some clothing, toiletries, basically everything a girl needs, including my two Berretta pistols. Thanks to Norie being the District Attorney for Los Angeles I had a valid concealed carry permit, and they didn't give those out to just anyone. I felt safer because occasions did surface where my fists and feet might not be enough. I had a long, hot shower, towelled off, put on shorts and a t-shirt, and headed out to wander the beach and pier.

I was thankful the whole area was packed with people, as usual. Hiding in plain sight was always best, even though I was certain that nobody knew I was here. I wandered out to the restaurant at the end of the pier, calling Norie as I did.

"Hey there Miss District Attorney," I was pleased she knew the voice immediately.

"Megan, where the hell are you," she blurted out, sounding like a college girl talking to her BFF.

"Funny thing. You know how you said I could always use your house at Imperial Beach. Well, that's where I am. I'm not sure if I'm in trouble, just trouble-adjacent, or trouble is following me around, but I need to lay low for a while. I hope it's okay?"

She answered eagerly, "Of course, it's okay sweetie. Whatever you need. Do you want me to come down there?"

"I think we should hold off. I may need you to check up on some things."

"Sure, no worries, Meg."

I was able to get a small table at the edge of the patio from where I could watch the sunset and think. I ordered some food and a beer and sat, staring out at the Pacific, wracking my brain trying to figure out what was happening. I spun down into rabbit-hole after rabbit-hole as I tried to find connections with everything going on, grasping at straw after straw but getting nowhere.

The sunset didn't even calm me, so I finished off another beer and then went back towards the house.

No answers, only more questions around all of it. Michael especially.

Chapter Thirty 4 – Michael, What Of Michael?

I took a pill and crawled into the big, cushy bed in the guest room and drifted off to sleep. I awoke rested and recharged before sunup. My body must have really needed it as I had a restful sleep somehow. I got out of bed and had a small coffee before heading out for a run. I ran North on a path along the water that led to the Coronado Cays Yacht Club. It was about six miles from where I started and that felt about right. I just needed to get out there and go. I kept up a strong pace, pleased that I was one of the few people out running at that hour. I enjoyed having the path almost to myself with few distractions to slow me down. I had intentionally not called Sonny yet as I wanted to settle and also give him a few days to see what he could uncover. I ran for the pure joy of running, my mind emptied of everything that had been going on, focussed on the goal. I got to the club, admired a few of the boats and then turned right around and headed back to Norie's. When I arrived back to the beach close to her house I cooled down with a walk past the pier and the few little stores. That was when I saw it!

I spotted a headline on the newspaper that stopped me dead in my tracks. Underneath a photo of Michael it said, "Fiery crash on the San Diego freeway claims the life of local resident." I felt like I had been kicked in the gut. My mind began spinning as I read the article.

He was on the 405 Southbound when the accident happened, and the body was burned beyond recognition. He was headed towards San Diego; did that mean he knew I was here or was that simply a coincidence? It said it was a single vehicle crash and he was the only occupant. I could feel sad later, right now I needed to find out what was happening. I had to get back to Norie's and do some research. I couldn't shake the feeling that this was one government agency or another covering their tracks, but why kill someone who had been so useful, so helpful? The Tony Farnsworth thing wasn't *that* big a deal, was it? I knew I had to speak to Sonny right away but did not want to do so anywhere close to Norie's house. I decided to go to the waterfront in San Diego, grab a new burner phone, and touch base with him.

My fingers struggled to hit the right keys as I dialed his number, I felt each ring with no answer as if another nail was being driven into me. I was about to hang up when a gruff voice finally answered, "Whadya want?"

"Sonny. It's me," I said, palms sweaty but a sense of relief spreading over me when I heard his voice. "Michael's dead."

"I know, I just found out. I had a watch on him. I don't think that crash was an accident," then the line went dead.

I dialed numerous times over the next hour and got no answer, no voicemail, nothing, just ringing and ringing. I finally gave up, no idea how many times I tried to call him. I was overwhelmed by that sense of alone-ness again, the lack of information scaring me.

I tossed the phone as far as I could into the ocean and went back to the house. I sat staring blankly at a painting on the wall, wondering, slowly being consumed by angst. What the heck was going on? Michael was dead and I had no idea what was up with Sonny.

I originally decided not to contact Norie until morning but then found myself dialing her cell not more than two hours after this all began. Ring after ring, I waited to hear her voice, getting more nervous with each additional ring. When it went to voice mail all I said was, "Call me," nothing else. I waited and waited. I was laying on the couch when I was startled by the ringing of my phone as it laid on my chest.

"Oh gawd, Norie, I'm so glad you're okay."

"What do you mean? I was out for dinner with some friends and didn't see the message until I got home. What's going on?" She continued, "I'm really sorry to hear about Michael. I'm coming down there as soon as I can get away."

I found it odd that she knew about Michael already but then decided it was all part of her job. I was really glad she was coming, although fairly certain she would not have any answers for me. Nevertheless, her support would be a huge help and having her to bounce ideas off of would be great.

"Stay at the B&B you're at until I get there." I wondered why the vague reference to her own house and realized she likely did that out of an abundance of caution. A clever idea considering what seemed to be happening around me at the moment.

I got back to the house and just sat, wondering what was really happening and if these events were connected. There were far too many situations for these to be coincidences. Sadness began creeping through my body, taking it over inch by inch as if I were being slowly submerged into a tank of darkness and despair. The pain and death of people I cared about was devastating, the fact I seemed unable to stop it overwhelming. I hated that feeling and the whole thing brought me back to the last funeral I had attended, for my Brother's wife. I went to the cabinet and grabbed a bottle of tequila, something I hadn't done in an exceptionally long time, unable to erase that day from my mind.

I recalled being consumed by my feelings of helplessness comingled with hopelessness as I watched my brother mourn his wife of more than fifty years. Some might say he appeared stoic, resolute even, but I knew that was not the case. He was buoyed by his faith, his unwavering love of her, and his steadfast belief she was truly now in a better place, a place with no pain, no suffering, only eternal light, and love. I envy him his beliefs, the best kind of envy though, more like admiration, and wish I had more of that myself. I wanted to support him, to really be present but instead I sat soaking in my own pool of sorrow, the loss so painful, so real, that feelings of my own mother's funeral, years earlier, returned. They bubbled to the surface like a pot of water that begins to gently roll with the odd isolated bubble but soon becomes a violent, boiling cauldron of water and steam that singes your very soul.

I remember doing my best to contain my own grief, trying to be supportive instead of a funeral spectacle, but when I caught sight of my brother, my efforts were rendered useless. Soon, I was just like that boiling pot of water, shaking and completely unable to stop. I've been there before but seem to be getting no better at stalling the relentless waves of emotion that quickly overwhelm me. I can't even look at other family members, my chest now so tight I feel I may pass out, my head pounding like it's being hit with a hammer, eyes already burning from the onslaught of tears.

How can I in one moment be a cold, merciless weapon of war, and then be like that? I considered that maybe that is the very reason, each job, each kill another black mark on my soul, unable to be erased, conquered, or forgiven. At odds with my job, I do believe in God, perhaps just not the traditional sacred Gods with their various religions often arguing about whose God is the real God. At this point in my life, I believe myself to be an agnostic. I definitely believe in God, a God, and wonder if he or she can ever truly forgive me for the things I have done.

Two of my pills, four or five shots and the combination thankfully turned my mind to mush, my body limp on the couch as I tried to numb the pain I was feeling. I thought I heard a ringing sound and through the fog of my brain noticed it was now dark outside. The only light in the house coming from the light on my phone as it rang, flashing onto the ceiling.

I fumbled to grab it, knocking it onto the floor as I tried to answer. I finally picked it up and was relieved to hear Norie's voice.

"I didn't want to scare you, I'm about fifteen minutes away."

I was ecstatic to hear that. All I could muster was a slurred, "Sounds good," as I did my best to sound composed instead of half-stoned.

I obviously passed out again as I was awakened by Norie gently shaking my shoulder, "It's me honey, it's Norie. C'mon, let's get you up and around."

She helped me to a seated position, and I spotted the time. I had been indisposed for more than *seven* hours. Sadly, I was no more rested and no less confused or worried than I had been. If anything, it was worse and now anger was creeping into the messy mix of feelings. I could smell the coffee brewing as Norie sat next to me on the couch. By the third cup, I was starting to come around as I explained what I knew, or what I thought I knew. She was here as a friend as there was little a District Attorney could help with in this situation, but she did have some information.

Norie looked at me, concerned, "I asked a good friend of mine at CHP if he had any information about Michael's crash." She folded her hands in front of her and with a grave look added, "There was brake fluid on the ground at the scene. He said it appeared the leak was not caused by the crash, and it looked like one or more of the brake lines may have been drilled."

I knew that was a method employed by contract killers, and government agents for that matter, to cause a vehicle to crash but make it less obvious the lines had been tampered with. It also allowed the target vehicle to travel thirty, forty, even fifty miles before anything happened. I stared at Norie, "Are there any theories on who could have done this?"

Letting out a big sigh, Norie said, "That's the thing Megan, I think we have a solid lead."

"Well, who is it?"

"Nothing is for sure yet, but it appears that the FBI may be involved. Or it could be Colin Sharpe acting alone. No way to be certain right now."

I felt like I had been throat-punched as her words registered in my still slightly foggy mind. Why would Colin want to kill Michael?

Norie had to take off early in the morning as she had a full day of meetings, so I was again left to my own devices.

Chapter Thirty 5 – Mission Ready

A loud knocking on the front door jarred me awake. I grabbed a pistol and went downstairs, first checking the garage and noting Norie was already gone. I peaked through the blinds and saw a four door, black sedan like so many agencies drive and only one man wearing a dark suit. Could be FBI, could be a contract killer, might be a well-dressed door-to-door salesman. I couldn't take a chance, so I yelled out, "Come on in," hoping to catch him unaware. I prepared as he opened the door. I grabbed his wrist, pulled him inside and quickly subdued him. No gun, no badge.

As I pressed his head down into the carpet he said, "Thomas Harker sent me."

I pushed harder, "Why didn't he call me then?"

"He said he had, multiple times. When he couldn't get through, he told me to come get you. He really needs to see you at Coronado, asap."

I was more focused on the fact I had ditched my phone so nobody could get a hold of me than wondering how he knew where I was. I let the man up, told him to sit on the couch and trained my Beretta on him. "One move and I'm pulling the trigger."

He remained calm, "Look, let me just show you my ID, it's in the breast pocket of my jacket."

"Open the jacket first and then pull the ID out. I'm still shooting first so be careful."

He pulled the black two-fold, standard issue ID wallet out of his jacket and tossed it into my lap. I kept the gun trained on him as I flipped it open. He was regular Navy and his ID indicated he was Thomas Harker's aide. I then told him to throw his phone over as

I knew he would have direct contact with Thomas if his card was legitimate.

I glared at him, "Tell Siri to dial your boss then."

"Hey Siri, dial Thomas Harker cell."

The phone rang twice, "Harker." He quickly added, "Did you pick up Ms. Hernandez yet?"

"Mr. Harker," I said in my most professional telemarketer voice, "Why exactly is this nice gentleman supposed to pick me up?"

"Megan, I can't explain right now, but I need you at Coronado as soon as possible. It's national security stuff."

I knew that when Thomas used that phrase it was indeed a profoundly serious issue, so I went, keeping both my pistols with me. Once we were in the car I told the guy, "Phone your boss and tell him that I want us waived straight through the gate. I have my pistols with me and I'm not coming in without them. It's non-negotiable."

He did as I asked, and I spent the entire drive trying to figure out what the heck was going on here. Why the emergency contact like this?

He drove at least 20 over the speed limit and we were rolling up on the Coronado gates in no time. We pulled right up to one of the outbuildings where we used to have strategy meetings when I was a SEAL. There was a gym, armory, and two smaller rooms all together, he led me to one of the rooms. Thomas opened the door grinning and extended his hand.

"It's great to see you Megan, although not the best circumstances. Let's go in here for a few minutes before we get with the others."

"Others," I asked, "Like whom."

"Let's just sit and let me explain before we meet with them. We have a grave issue, and the President has asked me directly to fix. He also told me to use only my most trusted people, whether inside the Navy or not."

"You know I'll help you however I can Thomas."

"I'll start with the part you may not like. We planted that story about Michael, he's fine and we'll be seeing him shortly."

"What?" I felt the rush of relief flow through me that was quickly followed by anger as I gripped the arms of the chair with white knuckles. Why the hell would you do that?"

"There are things which I cannot share but we had to do it that way. I needed people to think he was dead. People outside and inside my organization."

I scowled at him, "Why would someone in your organization care about some Canadian guy?"

"Canadian guy," he said with a look of surprise, "Michael's no more Canadian than I am."

"Thomas, what the heck is this all about? What is going on? Do you have Sonny here too?" I yelled, as I pounded the table.

"We do," he answered, almost apologetically. "Let's just head over to the other room and get started."

"Let's just do that."

Thomas led me out and through a second door. The first person I saw was Michael and right next to him was Sonny. I went to Sonny first and gave him a big hug and turned to Michael, "Michael, nice to see you're still alive," I said as coolly as I could. Thomas knew this was a tricky situation and said we should discuss what the President needs so we can all formulate a plan. I sat and listened as best as I could, half happy they were both okay, half totally pissed off, as Thomas laid things out. I just switched into autopilot, treating this like any other sales pitch one might have to endure when you can't simply walk away.

Everything that was said made complete sense as Thomas laid it out. They had no choice but to take out Tony Farnsworth and dismantle his organization. Everything had to be done this way because he believed there was a leak within his department, and he didn't want to take any chances with any of our lives. The trusted members of his team had made no headway uncovering the mole and that was a huge concern.

Thomas continued explaining the why's and how's of what had gone down, but I was still left confused about more than one facet of this operation, especially getting Michael involved. Everything he said made sense, when taken as a whole so my concern with Thomas slowly dissipated. I had no idea what would be next for Sonny or Michael, but Thomas's explanation and secrecy opened the door for more discussion with each of them.

I still really had no idea what was coming next but knew that I would be there for my country, be there for the Navy and ultimately, be there for Secretary Thomas Harker. I just hoped that all of them would be there for me too!

Other Books From C.C.Chamberlane

let them breathe

Megan Hernandez tackles the thorny issue of people of color dying while in the custody of the police. From the LAPD to the Minnesota PD, where Officer Derek Chauvin was employed when he murdered George Floyd, Megan fights for the truth.

Saving Ukraine

Megan, at the behest of her former boss, does her best to slow down the Russian onslaught in Ukraine. Mr. Putin didn't even see her coming, but then again, neither did anyone else.

The First Female Navy SEAL

Learn about the challenges Megan faced during training and the walls she scaled to become the First Female Navy SEAL. See the grueling training through her eyes, live through the pain and suffering she experienced as a woman in a very all-male world.

Samaela

The second book about Megan Hernandez, Samaela follows her fight against the drug cartels. When El Chapo was put away there was a great deal of upheaval and one of Megan's close friends was caught in the crossfire. Will she inflict vengeance?

Abbadon

Meet Megan Hernandez, the first female Navy SEAL. Megan uses her government trained skills to kill easily, and without mercy, as well as fight the good fight. This is the beginning of her backslide into lawlessness as she helps her friends.